Let Joy Arise

Let Joy Arise

Ashea S. Goldson

BRENT LIBRARIES

BR
KIL

Urban Books, LLC
97 N18th Street
Wyandanch, NY 11798

Let Joy Arise Copyright © 2012 Ashea S. Goldson

All rights reserved. No part of this book may be
reproduced in any form or by any means without
prior consent of the Publisher, except brief quotes
used in reviews.

ISBN 13: 978-1-62286-823-0
ISBN 10: 1-62286-823-4

First Mass Market Printing December 2015
First Trade Paperback Printing July 2012
Printed in the United States of America

10 9 8 7 6 5 4 3 2 1

This is a work of fiction. Any references or similarities to actual events, real people, living or dead, or to real locales are intended to give the novel a sense of reality. Any similarity in other names, characters, places, and incidents is entirely coincidental.

Distributed by Kensington Publishing Corp.
Submit Orders to:
Customer Service
400 Hahn Road
Westminster, MD 21157-4627
Phone: 1-800-733-3000
Fax: 1-800-659-2436

Let Joy Arise

by

Ashea S. Goldson

Dedication

This book is dedicated to Grandma Ruthell Sloan. Thank you for being the first person to introduce me to church. Thank you for those years of teaching Sunday school and leading the choir. You sowed a *God* seed in me, and *we* are now reaping the harvest. I love you, Grandma.

Acknowledgments

To my Lord and Savior Jesus Christ, without whom none of this kingdom writing or living would be possible: Thank you, thank you, thank you for the calling. A thousand times, thank you.

To my husband, children, and grandchildren, Donovan, Anais, Safiya, Jamal, Syriah, Jamian, and grandbaby number three (?): Thank you for giving me continual support, joy, and love.

To Mom: Thank you for being such an important part of my life, for being an encourager, a prayer warrior, a woman of wisdom, a mighty conqueror, and an awesome woman of God.

To Grandma: Thank you for being who you are in my life. This book is for you.

To the McClouds, Darryl, Tamicka, Lashydra, and Cameron, and my godchildren, Emmanuel, Hannah, and Faith: Thank you for making me smile on a daily basis. Thank you for being my family.

To my longtime friends Bernadette Page (sisters since fifth grade), Joy Jones-Garrett, Sherri Holmes-Knight, Hope Raymond, and Pastor Alfonso Jackson: Thanks for being consistent in your support of me from our youth until now.

To Shawneda Marks, the activist author and my writer-sister: Thank you for all your marketing help, but most of all thank you for being a good friend.

To Kendra Norman-Bellamy, bestselling author of at least a zillion books: Thank you for always including me in literary events and opportunities. Thanks also for being an all-around inspiration.

To Latoya Forrest-Heard: Sweet Latoya, thank you for always having a word of wisdom in due season. I can't wait to see your books in print.

To Cousin Thelma Davis: Thank you for caring enough to spread the word about my books throughout New York City.

To Bonnie Colbert and Joanne Redmund of LOJ: Thanks for always looking out for me on third Saturdays.

To the Faith Based Fiction Writers of Atlanta: Thank you for the literary sisterhood you represent.

To my editor, Joylynn Jossel: What would I do without your literary prowess? Thank you for seeing something special in my writing.

To my Urban Christian family: Thank you for carrying the torch for Christian fiction. God bless you in all your literary endeavors.

To my literary agent, Sha-Shana Crichton, of Crichton & Associates: Thank you for continuing to keep my literary and legal business in order.

To Tyora Moody: Thank you for doing what you do so well, using your creativity to bring literature together with technology. Congrats on your new release!

To Pastor Frank Salters of Word of Faith Light of Joy Church: Thank you for ministering the unadulterated Word with simplicity and transparency.

To Sister Merriam Salters and the LOJ Women's Ministry: Thank you not only for teaching but also for demonstrating the love of God.

To the Women of the Word Book Club (especially President Kimnesha Benns): Thank you for welcoming me into your circle.

To my Anointed Minds students: How I love you all! What would I do without your intelligent banter and amusing antics?

To all the Christian fiction authors, my fellow writers, bloggers, social media organizers, book clubs, reviewers, and radio hosts: Thank you for promoting, tweeting, hosting, or encouraging me in some way.

To all family, friends, and writer-sisters who have not specifically been named, to those in Atlanta, New York, North Carolina, and around the world: Thank you for being a positive influence in my life in one way or another. If you have ever gone the extra mile for me, know that I remember and I appreciate you.

To my readers and fans: We made it to another book. Thank you for choosing to buy my books, for supporting me, for offering a kind word. Thank you most of all for lifting up this kingdom writing ministry.

Prologue

Three years earlier . . .

Derek and I had danced, body to body, at the swankiest club on the Lower West Side of Manhattan until the early hours of the morning. He had thrown back Bacardi as if it were water the entire time. The lights were glaring and the music was jumping, but for some reason, I wanted to go home. It wasn't like me to leave any party early, but tonight I'd had enough. I looked over at my date, Derek, who was a fine brother, dressed in his sleek Armani linen suit, with his gold chains layered on his hairy chest, yet I could hardly see his chiseled features through the thick cloud of smoke.

I led him back to our table and began cozying up to him.

"It's getting lame in here," I whined.

Derek ignored me and kept bopping his head to the music.

"Get me out of here." I twirled his ebony locks around my finger with one hand and traced the skull tattoo on his arm with the other. "I'm ready to go."

Derek finished off his drink and licked his lips. "Soon."

I crossed my legs so that the slit of my spandex dress revealed the curve of my thighs.

"All right, Taylor. Let's go," Derek sneered before grabbing my arm with his rough hands.

The next thing I knew, we were making our way through the sweaty crowd, with fluorescent lights flashing in our faces. Before we hit the door, however, a few of the regulars caught us and asked us why we were leaving so early. I don't remember if we answered or not. I stopped to adjust my dress when we entered the lobby. It had been rising around my hips all night. Usually, that was a plus.

"You should really let me drive, since I think you're over your limit tonight," I said and snickered.

Derek brushed me off and continued walking through the building, with his hands in his pockets, confident. I followed him like a groupie as he navigated the way. Finally, Derek stumbled outside to the parking lot, rambling on and on about not going home to his wife.

Derek looked serious. "I was having a great time. I ain't going home to that woman, either."

He wanted to go back to his friend's place, the one he'd been staying with off and on for the past few months, for even more illicit partying. A few weeks ago I would've gone along with that, but it had been about two months already, and that was my limit for dating any man, especially a married one. He was already beginning to bore me, and to be honest, I was still tired from our date the night before.

"I need some rest before I go back to work," I said. Being a physical trainer and aerobics instructor was hard work.

He looked me straight in the eyes and called me everything but a child of God for not going along with his plans, but he was too drunk to stay focused on that for long.

"Come on and let me drive," I begged.

"That's not gonna happen. No woman is driving my truck," Derek said, shoving me to the other side of the Expedition.

"Not even me?" I giggled.

Derek scowled. "Not even you."

For some reason I didn't move. It was as if something was holding me back. Then he slipped his arm around me and said, "Come on, baby. Don't tell me you're afraid of riding with me just 'cause I've had a few drinks."

"No, I ain't afraid," I answered.

I climbed into the passenger seat, buckled myself in, which was a habit of mine, and hoped that I'd made the right decision to ride with him. He turned on the radio and took off down the crowded expressway, headed for the FDR Drive.

As he drove the car, I began digging in my purse to make sure I had my keys. My only desire was to go home and climb into my own bed. I had an enormous headache, and my sexy red stilettos were beginning to sting my toes. I dreaded the lecture I was going to get from my holier-than-thou twin sister when I got home, because deep down, I knew she was right. I was wasting my life, and Mama, God rest her soul, would be so disappointed.

The moment I looked up from my purse, I caught a glimpse of a truck coming straight at us. All I saw were round lights and a huge frame. I screamed, "Derek, look out!" but it was too late. The truck hit Derek's Expedition head-on, and I was sure it was all over for me. Even though Derek swerved a little at the last minute to avoid hitting the truck, the force of that truck was enough to split him in half, or so the coroner said later. His neck snapped like a twig, and he died instantly. As blood splattered across my face, I screamed again and again, but no one could hear me except me. My screams echoed in my own ears. I held on as we skidded, rocked, and crashed.

The burning smell took over my senses as I gasped through the smoke for air, coughing and wheezing. The way I rolled and tumbled in that car, hitting my head against the glass and twisting my bones, I just knew I was going to die. Sad part was I didn't even have enough good sense to repent right then and there.

I lay there for what seemed like forever, soaked in my own blood and listening to Bonnie Raitt's song in my head. *I can't make you love me if you don't.*

Later, patrollers said that we flipped over several times and that it was a miracle I was even alive. Being in and out of consciousness for days with a concussion, a fractured skull, and several broken bones was traumatic enough, but when I found out I was paralyzed from the waist down, I would rather have been dead.

Chapter One

I'd never been more satisfied living the life God gave me, working my fitness magic, secure in my own divaship, believing that after all I'd been through, things were finally looking up for me. Yet, just when things were about to really take off, misfortune ran up on me, snatched away my breath, and cut me to the core. It started chipping away at everything I'd been fighting and struggling to build in a moment's notice, and left me wondering why. Then I remembered a scripture Mama used to say whenever there was trouble, "Then my head will be exalted above the enemies who surround me; at his tabernacle will I sacrifice with shouts of joy." So even though the battle was on, I was prepared.

It was a peaceful spring morning at the Push It Fitness Center, the business I'd been grooming for over two years, since buying it from my former employer. The sun shone brightly through the glass windows, and I could see little white flowers blooming on the tree that stood in front of my eclectic Brooklyn building. *Good old Fort Greene,* I thought as a fire truck raced through the street with its blaring sirens. That was the neighborhood I'd handpicked for my fitness center. I wrapped my arms around myself at the thought that this was truly my own business. Owning this place was a dream come true for me, the only thing I'd ever wanted to do with my life, and I was just beginning to enjoy the fruits of my labor. I was feeling good about myself, feeling like a fitness queen, despite my physical limitations.

I gently cracked open the door, took a long breath of fresh air, or at least the early version of city smog, and felt content. "God is good," I said to myself. I used my wheelchair to roll over to the rowing machine, maneuvered myself onto it, and began moving my arms and upper torso back and forth, like I did every morning, as soon as I opened. Stopping only to sip on a strawberry smoothie my husband, Keith, had made before I left home, I worked my body almost as if I'd never had the accident. That was typical too. In fact, there was nothing unusual about this morning until I saw a brand-new Range Rover park in front of the building, and then I saw *her* come through the front door. She entered, then turned to lock her vehicle's doors with her remote control, as if she had forgotten to.

She had long, perfectly straight auburn-colored hair, long legs to match, and captivating bluish-green eyes. I immediately wondered if she was wearing contact lenses. Now, the fact that she was beautiful wasn't strange, either, because beautiful people came through here all the time, except that she came in wearing an immaculate ivory pantsuit and what looked like four-inch stilettos. Now, who wore stilettos to a gym? I stared into her flawless face as she came right up to me. Something about her seemed familiar.

"Hi," I said.

"Hello." She smirked as she approached the rowing machine. Suddenly I remembered where I'd seen those eyes before. I swallowed my spit. It was Derek's widow.

The memory of her visiting me in the hospital three years ago shook me, but I managed to catch hold of myself fast. Derek's wife looked so stunning that I almost didn't recognize her.

I didn't know what she had done to herself, but something was different. Maybe she had received insurance money and had used it to get some

kind of cosmetic surgery done or something.
I wasn't sure. All I knew was that she looked
different—younger, and more self-assured. Now,
I didn't have anything against anybody coming
up in the world, but a sista came in swinging an
oversized genuine Louis Vuitton purse, with a
brand-new Range Rover parked outside, and she
had me tripping. When I first saw her, she was
driving a used Toyota with a crack in the wind-
shield, and she was carrying a dollar-store tote.
What was going on here? What happened to
the tacky widow who stormed into my hospital
room, cursing and acting the fool almost three
years ago? Had she hit the lottery and been to
charm school or something?

The first thing I did was look over at my
wheelchair, knowing I couldn't even make a run
for it. So even though my heart was probably
beating a thousand beats per minute, I kept
working out on the rowing machine, moving like
I hardly noticed she was there. There was sweat
running down my brow as she walked up on me.
Never in a million years did I think I'd be here
with this Amazon of a woman towering over me,
dressed in Chanel, smelling of Ralph Lauren,
and probably ready to beat me down. Believe it
or not, I was ready to take my licks for what I'd
done. I guess some people would call it justice,

seeing as how I sho' 'nough took everything to the streets back in the day. When I was growing up, the streets of New York City were my training ground, but now that I couldn't fight anymore . . . well, that was another story altogether.

She leaned her shoulders forward, pursed her thick lips, and said, "Hello. I'm Elaina Dawson. D-a-w-s-o-n."

"May I help you?" I tried to sound calm as I looked her up and down. After all, maybe she didn't recognize me. Maybe she was on her way to work and just wanted to enroll in our gym membership.

"I'm the inspector from the New York City Department of Business Licensing," she said.

I leaned back and glared at her. "Are you serious?"

"As a heart attack," she said, grinning.

Neither of us blinked for a moment. It was as if we were both suspended in space and time.

Then she smiled a crooked smile. "I'm here to take a look around, to ensure that there are no violations that threaten public health or safety. The main items are ventilation, water, and layout."

"Okay." My heart beat faster.

"But there are other things I must check also." Elaina looked around the room.

My heart was practically in my mouth.

Elaina sustained the eye contact. "May I see your phone?"

"It's right over there," I said and pointed. As nervous as I was, I was surprised that my finger did not shake.

She checked to see that it was working and asked for the business telephone number.

My thoughts returned to her visit at the hospital right after my accident. She had come to accuse me of messing around with her husband, and to blame me for his death. Like I'd forced him to guzzle down glass after glass of rum and Coke and then get his stubborn self behind the wheel. That night I feared for my life because I'd heard the horror stories about drinking and driving. Not that horror stories meant much to me at that time, because I was a bad girl—invincible—and I was proud of it.

Back then, when Elaina stepped to me, she was only a rival and not a very good one. I had used her husband like I used all men, and I didn't care what she said or what she thought. I didn't even care what she did. Maybe that was because I had barely regained consciousness and was half dead at the time. But I sure cared now. Reason number one for this was that since I belonged to God, I didn't welcome drama like I used to. I had to watch the things I said and did, especially as they related to other people. Reason number two was that this lady most likely had a beef with me, and rightfully so. Worse yet, she stood on two good legs, and I had none to stand on. Reason number three was that she had a badge on, and the power to shut down my whole operation with the stroke of a pen. Now that was pressure.

"I noticed on your certificate of occupancy that you cannot have over five hundred people in this facility."

"Is that a problem?"

Elaina never looked up from her clipboard. "No, but if you had more than five hundred members, you would be required to have an external defibrillator."

I nodded. "Right. I remember that."

She let out a long breath, rolled her eyes upward, and walked away from me, headed straight for the back. I hopped off my machine and into my wheelchair, then rolled off behind her. There was no way I was going to let her roam around without me. Besides, I was still holding on to the possibility that she didn't recognize my face. I reminded myself that it was only a five-minute confrontation we had that day in the hospital, and that everyone didn't have perfect memories. Three years ago, when I first saw her, I was bandaged and swollen, and she had eyes blurred with tears. Maybe, just maybe, she hadn't paid so much attention to the details.

For all I knew, today I could be just a routine stop on her list of businesses to visit. To her, I could be just another client, and maybe she'd be out of my business, and my life, within minutes. But when she turned around and I was able to search her eyes, I saw that same venomous look I'd seen the last time. Maybe it was even worse, because at least the last time the look was mixed with grief, horror, and shame. But this time I knew there was no shame in this woman's game.

I felt awkwardly light-headed as she bounced through the gym, with her hip-length weave, carefully examining everything. She took her well-manicured fingers and wiped them across every surface, exposing dust, and tested every machine. Her long legs hustled across the tiled floor with haste. I wondered if she knew my eyes were on her the whole time, trying to figure her out as she moved. She started in the exercise room, checking the cushioned surfaces, the mirrored walls, and the impact-resistant walls. She even looked up to see that there was a twelve-foot ceiling.

"Over here is the warm-up and cool-down area, free weights are over there, circuit training over here, and the cardiovascular area is over there," I said, pointing to each section as I spoke.

She didn't look impressed with my knowledge or organization. She winced, proceeding to go through each room, including the restrooms, the shower, the locker rooms, and the indoor pool room. By the time she had finished checking the pool room, she had written so much on her little pad that I left her in there. Then she came out, asking to see my office.

She swung the door open before sauntering over to my desk. "Is this all?"

"Yep," I said.

Elaina scribbled on her pad. "May I see your certification in the study of the operation of AEDs and your certification in training of cardiopulmonary resuscitation?"

This woman was on a mission for sure. I pointed out both certificates to her, framed and hanging on the wall behind my desk. She examined them, and then she started writing again.

"Of course, you realize that there must be someone with this training on the premises at all times." Elaina looked up from her pad.

"Yes, I'm aware of that. All of my employees have the same training. I require it," I explained.

"Smart," she said as she walked out.

Apparently, nothing was off-limits, but I was too afraid to say a word. I looked at my watch and realized that Sharon, my aerobics instructor, was late again. I wished it wasn't so early that neither Jasmine, my personal assistant and number one employee, nor Jacque, my lifeguard, was scheduled to arrive yet. The timing was so unfair.

Finally, Elaina stopped in the middle of the weight room and put her hands on her shapely hips. "I'm done here," she said.

I knew it didn't look good, but still I felt hopeful. "Well, what do you think?"

Elaina smirked. "Personally, I think this place should be shut down."

"What?"

"I mean, the place is filthy. Of your only five customer stalls in the ladies' restroom, two toilets are out of order. Half of the machines aren't working to proper specifications. And that pool is suspect."

"Excuse me?" I put my finger up in the air, about to pull from the roots of my street background, but I stopped myself. "Proper specifications? Suspect?"

"One of your treadmills nearly killed me. It should be tagged if it's not in working order, and it should be recorded in your log." Elaina held up a pair of small running shoes.

I wondered when she had time to change into and out of those.

"I didn't know it wasn't working," I said.

"Ignorance is never an excuse." She shook her head. "Besides, there are so many hazards in the pool area, it's a recipe for disaster. Oh, you can just read the list." She handed me the paper.

"I . . . I mean, I'll work on fixing everything as soon as I can," I stammered.

"Still, it's very dangerous in here," Elaina said.

"How long do I have?"

"You have exactly two weeks to get it together. I'll be back. Good luck." She walked out the front door without even looking back.

Her Ralph Lauren perfume lingered long after she was gone.

For the first time in my entire thirty-two years, I felt small in comparison to this lady. It wasn't just the fact that she was tall and stood up high, while I sat down in a wheelchair; it was deeper than that. It was a lowliness of spirit I felt, remembering the life I used to live and the demons I used to befriend. The thought sent a chill up my spine. And then being alone with this woman, this stranger, this potential enemy, I felt threatened, ashamed, and helpless. *Lord, please give me strength.*

Shortly after she left, I rolled over to the phone to check out this lady's credentials, and as it turned out, her position as city business license inspector was legitimate. I still was not sure if she had it in for me, though. It wouldn't matter to her that I'd changed, and why should it?

My change couldn't bring back her dead husband or erase what I had done to her in the past.

I knew that my life had changed once again in the instant that Elaina Dawson walked through the front door of my establishment, declaring with her eyes that she was going to get me back for what I did to her if it was the last thing she did. Oh, she never actually said those words, but she huffed and puffed, and I heard them loud and clear, anyway, in her demeanor.

When Keith drove us home after picking me up, I told him what had happened with the inspection, but I didn't tell him *who* the inspector was. Even though Keith knew all about my accident, and about Derek being killed, I didn't want to remind him about the wild life I used to live. For once in my life, I was actually ashamed of it.

Keith and I had been married for only eight months, after a trying engagement period, when I made him wait to marry me because I couldn't walk down the aisle by myself. I didn't think it was a surprise to anyone that I was being stubborn, but it was a surprise to everyone that I was willing to risk losing him. He had come to my apartment one day and had given me an ultimatum: either I married him immediately or he was going to accept a job offer out of town. Apparently, he was tired of our illusive engagement, tired of waiting for me to get over my injury, and I didn't blame him. I was a big mess at the time, and my pride almost let me lose Keith. Thankfully, my wise identical twin sister, Alex, convinced me to let go and let God handle my walking situation. And she was right. Truth be told, she usually was right. Now, as I looked over at my handsome husband and soul mate, I was glad I had listened to her.

Keith raised his eyebrows. "So we've got two weeks on the violations, huh?"

"Right," I said, wiggling in my seat.

"That's not much time." Keith rubbed his chin as if he was deep in thought.

I sighed. "Not with our bank account, it isn't."

"We'll have to crunch," Keith said matter-of-factly.

"The business has never been in trouble like this before." I shook my head. "I don't know what we're going to do."

Keith kept one hand on the wheel and used the other to scratch his head. "Don't worry. We'll figure out something soon."

We arrived at home, and Keith parked the car. Home was a twelve-story co-op, a dark brick building from the forties era nestled among other buildings with a similar structure and blocks of renovated brownstones. This was Clinton Hills, the racially diverse neighborhood that was right over the Brooklyn Bridge, was home to many young urban professionals, who preferred Brooklyn to extra-pricey Manhattan, and was the neighborhood I happily moved into when I married Keith.

The first thing I did when I got home was to strip out of my gym clothes. Every time I saw myself naked, glimpsed the scar on my right leg, noting my leg's semi-uselessness, I was reminded of the accident. I rolled into the bathroom and used the bar to lift myself into the tub. I needed to feel the water against my skin. I needed to be purified. Thoughts came rushing back while I was under the shower. Thoughts of Derek and our last night together—drinks and dancing, skin-to-skin contact, moving bodies, flashing lights, then the sound of screeching tires and metal bending, and finally the smell of burning flesh. I remembered thinking my life was over as I was tossed upside down in the car. I blinked away the tears under the warm shower water, wishing it were as easy to wash away the memory. *Humph.*

When I came out, Keith was standing outside the shower stall, ready to hand me a warm towel. He always put it into the dryer for a few minutes before bringing it to me. He was that kind of man, and I loved him for it. I wrapped myself in the towel first, before I wrapped myself in his arms. The strength of his hands against the small of my back provided me with a false sense of balance, but when he let go, it was my walker that held me up, not my legs.

When I was fully dressed and ready for dinner, Keith escorted me into the kitchen and held my chair out for me. Sitting down was easier than getting up. I plopped my body down like dead weight, a less than graceful maneuver I'd learned right after I regained some feeling in my lower body.

The phone rang once, but when Keith answered it, no one said anything.

"That's weird. Just breathing," he said.

"Sounds like a crank call," I said, wondering if it was for me.

Keith matter-of-factly waved his hand and sat down at the table. "Probably."

I tried to keep my mind on my husband, but all during dinner Elaina's words kept running through my mind. *I'll be back.* Derek's words kept running through my mind also. *Come on, baby. Don't tell me you're afraid of riding with me just 'cause I've had a few drinks.* I remembered my answer. *No, I ain't afraid.*

That had been the turning point in my life, the day I got back into the car with that woman's husband for the promise of money and physical gratification. I was nothing more than a gold digger back then. Any good-looking guy with a nice car and a good paycheck who could wine me and dine me got my attention. I had risked everything for cheap thrills, and I had paid for it. The phone rang again.

"Don't answer it," I said.

Sin had taken my dignity along with my legs. Unfortunately, the widow was back to claim what was left of my life.

Chapter Two

The next morning I awoke to the buzz of my husband's electric razor and the sweet smell of his pine-scented aftershave lotion. A beautiful May breeze blew through the window and onto my warm skin. I knew it was time to get up and hurry myself down to the gym, but after yesterday's experience, I wasn't sure I wanted to get up at all. I wasn't looking forward to the possibility of Elaina Dawson coming back. I peeped over at my husband, who was now standing over me in only the Tweety Bird boxers I'd bought him for Valentine's Day, with his bare chest revealed. Any other time the sight of his perfectly sculpted body would've stirred something in me, but I was too weary to lust. Instead, I slipped back underneath my satin sheets, trying to pretend that everything was all right as my husband dressed for work.

My husband and I had met at the hospital right after my accident, and against all odds, he had nursed me back to health with his anointed physical therapy. I deemed Keith Bryant the best physical therapist in the city. Keith, the most brilliant and physically attractive man I had ever met, stood tall and was dark like chocolate and strong. But believe it or not, we didn't become friends overnight; I gave him a hard time for a long time.

When I reached my wit's end in trying to raise funds to buy Push It before my former employer sold it to the highest bidder, Keith gave me the necessary down payment, cosigned the business loan for me, without me ever negotiating anything, and afterward asked for my hand in marriage. He became my official Prince Charming at a time when I really didn't believe in fairy tales. Since he had secretly wished he owned his own gym since he was a teenager, he credited me with being ambitious enough to reawaken the dream in him. I credited him for being genuine enough to show me what raw faith was. Either way, I rejoiced in the fact that we were a team, business partners of the Push It Fitness Center.

As I peeped over the covers at him, though, I just didn't know if this magic could help us with our current business issue.

Keith leaned over to maneuver the radio control buttons on our alarm clock. "You want to hear some music, babe?"

"Sure," I said, knowing full well that as much as I enjoyed them, no Kirk Franklin or Yolanda Adams could help me now.

I had a bad habit of waking up and wanting to discuss whatever was on my mind from the night before. "It's funny how we thought the down payment and the loan for the purchase of the business would be enough."

"Yeah," Keith said, without any eye contact.

I shook my head. "How were we supposed to know there would be so many unexpected expenses after the deal went through?"

Keith sat down on the side of the bed to pull on his socks. "Right."

"All that equipment that needed to be replaced as soon as we took over. I mean, who knew?" I sighed. "All of the renovations that needed to be made."

"And a myriad of bad business decisions the last owner left us to deal with," Keith added. "Babe, let's talk about all of that later."

That was his way of cutting off the conversation.

Since Keith's savings had been depleted from purchasing the business in the first place and from doing the basic repairs that were needed, we were hardly financially stable. Now, with all the medical bills from my accident, on top of my less than desirable credit history, he probably had no clue as to how we were going to make any of the repairs on the inspector's list. As the man of the house, I knew he would never tell me that, though. Instead, Keith let the dial land on Tye Tribbet's "Victory," which was about as good as it could get at that moment.

"See, there's our song, babe," Keith spat out.

"Yeah." I bopped my head from side to side so I wouldn't alarm him about how upset I really was. The music sang in my ears, but not in my heart. My heart ached.

"We've got the vic-tor-y, got the vic-tor-y," Keith sang along, patting his hand to the beat.

"Keith . . ." I wanted to continue the conversation we'd started a few minutes ago, but I knew he was tuning me out. My husband was very good at that when he didn't want to deal with something.

Keith snapped his fingers periodically as he walked around the bedroom, getting dressed.

"Did you say something, Tay?"

The music wasn't up that loud, but it was almost as if he had headphones on.

"Never mind." It was no use trying to bring him back when he had escaped reality.

It was funny how we originally had big plans for our business, not fully understanding the true nature of our investment. We had already splurged on designer paint, fancy flooring, and African art, but when the money ran out, so did our vision.

The thought of even going down to the gym today concerned me, and I didn't scare easily. I didn't know what I would face when I got there. Would Elaina come by again? Was she waiting for the right moment to threaten me or worse? Was she just playing games with my life? I didn't know what to think. I didn't know about the mysterious phone calls. More importantly, though, I didn't know how we would make all the necessary changes, or how to begin. I wasn't sure how I was going to survive this attack, but deep inside, I did know this was spiritual warfare. So because of that, and despite how I felt, I knew I had to pray. I sprang up in bed with a quickness.

"Sleepyhead," Keith said, pulling on his blazer.

I sighed. "I want to pray."

"Cool." He sat down on the side of the bed. "Are you still upset about that inspection yesterday?"

"A little." That was an understatement.

"I promise everything will work out." Keith leaned over and kissed me on the forehead.

"God is faithful."

I knew it was sweet, but I hated when he did that. I wanted my kiss dead on the lips. Still, I looked into my husband's eyes and was grateful for his strength. "I love you, Keith."

"I love you too, but we've gotta hustle." Keith hit me with a pillow. Then he grabbed my hand, and we prayed together before Keith disappeared into the kitchen.

I pulled myself out of bed, used my wheelchair to roll myself into the bathroom, then took a quick shower. Showers were no longer a challenge since I had learned to balance myself with the handicapped bar to get in and to use the shower chair instead of standing.

In fact, everything in my home was set up for my convenience, courtesy of my husband.

He had hung hooks lower so that I could reach them from my chair, had positioned furniture so that I'd have more room to maneuver, and had bought a bed that had bed rails. There were other oddities around the house that made life easier for me to deal with. Two of the many things I loved about Keith were his big heart and his attention to detail.

I rolled in front of my vanity table and stopped to apply lotion to my skin. Then I dragged myself back into the bedroom to get dressed. I decided to wear my Nike sweat suit with my matching

Nike sneakers. I pinned up my braids and put a Nike cap on my head. Then I went into the kitchen, where I found Keith watching the news and eating a granola bar. There were two bowls of maple-flavored instant oatmeal, two low-fat peach yogurts, two slices of 100 percent whole wheat bread, eight strips of turkey bacon, and orange juice set out for us.

"Oh, you made another great breakfast." I took a seat in one of the chairs at the kitchen table. "Thanks."

"You're welcome," Keith said, smiling his biggest smile.

I was glad that Keith could throw down in the kitchen, because a sista was never into that cooking stuff, even though Mama made sure I knew how. Mama used to nag me about cooking, but my sister was the domesticated one, not me. I had better things to do with my time than spend it in a hot kitchen.

We finished our breakfast while gazing into each other's eyes, and then we were off to work. As usual, I leaned into his chest as we loaded my braces and walker into the elevator. Sometimes I used my wheelchair, and sometimes I didn't. It really depended on what kind of mood I was in.

I asked, "What's on the agenda for today?"

"We take everything one day at a time. Let's get through today by working on these violations, and then we'll see where we are and go from there," Keith said as he helped me into the car.

It didn't sound like much of a plan to me, but who was I to complain? I really didn't have any ideas, either. One day at a time didn't actually sound so bad.

While I was riding in the car, a million thoughts went through my mind, everything from how to get extra money for the business to where on the list to begin. Nothing in my physical training had prepared me for this. The only business training I had received consisted of a few workshops I took at the community college. Maybe, I thought, I should've gone to college like my sister. I wondered if that would've made me more prepared for what we were facing. Keith had been to college and had finished graduate school, though, and he didn't seem any more prepared for this catastrophe than I was. Maybe, I decided, this was not a college thing. Maybe it was a God thing. A sista needed a revelation.

I used to have what I'd called a simple life until now. Back in the day all I cared about was me, me and an extra serving of me. Sadly, I did so much damage to other people. I had folks praying for me day and night to get my life together, but I wouldn't listen. There was just too much fun to have, or at least that was what I thought, "wilding" out every night of the week. Mama would turn over in her grave if she knew half the stuff I compromised for the sake of not giving in to salvation. I must say I was Satan on wheels *on purpose*. No one could slow me down. Not until I was in that wreck, which changed everything, especially my mind. Not overnight, but over time.

By the time we pulled up in front of the gym, I felt nervous. I looked all around me and behind me. It was early, so it was still dark outside. Keith helped me to unlock the door, turn off the security system, and flip on all the lights.

"I love you, babe."

"Me too," I said.

Then he kissed me full on the mouth, jumped inside the car, and sped away.

As soon as he left, I locked the door behind me. I didn't feel so secure today, and it would be at least another fifteen minutes before my first employee, Jasmine, arrived. I went into my office, settling in behind my desk. I clicked on my computer and decided to Google Elaina Dawson. Sure enough, her name appeared right away. There were only two entries on her, though.

One was about how her husband died in a tragic car accident, leaving her and her son alone. I stared at the picture beside the article. Yep, Elaina Dawson was torn up back then. And the other entry merely listed her position as a city business license inspector, along with countless others on the city's payroll.

I searched and searched, but nothing explained her recent wealth. The city didn't pay that well. Maybe she had had a big insurance policy out on Derek. Maybe he had taken one out on himself. When I remembered his arrogance, it didn't seem likely. I didn't think that man had even considered the possibility of dying, and thus he couldn't have planned for it.

In the quiet of the building I began to hear things or imagine things. I wasn't sure which, but I knew I had definitely brought this on myself. Wow, a woman scorned was no joke, and that was the kind of mess I had gotten myself into.

Nobody could've ever accused me of being a good girl. That title always seemed to go to my nearly perfect twin sister. Now me, I was always known as the really rowdy one. "Too much to handle" Taylor was what folks used to call me, at least everyone except my parents. Come to think of it, I probably broke Mama's heart with all my escapades. I would've broken Dad's heart, too, if he had stayed around long enough. But that was another story altogether.

I didn't know why I was the way I was, except to say that God made me special. So even when I didn't know Him, He designed me, and unlike most, He had always loved me for *me*. Like during the summer of fifth grade, when I thought climbing onto the roof with our neighbor Brian Halloway was a good idea. We were up there throwing down spitballs and rocks at every passerby. And I mean God Almighty was watching out for me, making sure I didn't slide down off of that slanted roof and break my neck. Thank goodness none of the rocks we threw— they were really pebbles—ever actually hit anyone. Next thing I knew, Mama climbed up on a ladder, then dragged me down by my ear, whupping my tail at the same time. How she managed to do all of that and still balance her hefty body on a cheap wooden ladder I'll never know. That woman was something else.

I shook my head and smiled at the memory before returning my attention to the matter at hand.

By eight o'clock I unlocked the door for Jasmine. Jasmine was twenty-three years old and had pale, peach-colored skin, short, spiked sandy blond hair, and an attitude that said "The world is mine." I liked her because she reminded me of myself at her age. At five feet two inches tall and 120 pounds, on a petite frame, she was all mouth and muscle. She was my receptionist, aka my "do girl." She brought me lunch, made me coffee, took my calls, signed up new members, and occasionally filled in for my aerobics teacher. Of the three permanent employees that we had, she was my favorite.

Jasmine came in smacking gum. "Hi, boss lady."

I pulled her to the side. "Look, Jas, we had an inspection yesterday, and basically we failed."

Jasmine opened her mouth wide with amazement. "Oh, wow. Why didn't you say anything yesterday?"

"Well, I guess I was just a little bit shaken up then. The inspection came as a surprise and—"

"I understand." Jasmine squinted her ocean-green eyes. "So what's the plan?"

That was what I liked about her; she was always ready for action and, just like I used to be, was always down for anything. I smiled at her display of loyalty. "Keith and I are working on a plan to get this place into shape."

"I thought you would've done pretty good on the inspection," she said, looking around.

"Yeah, that's what I thought, but she found more violations than I was aware of." And that, unfortunately, was an understatement, one that I would later come to realize in its fullness.

Jasmine nodded her head. "I understand."

I grimaced. "Everything from the out-of-order toilets in the ladies' room to the treadmill that keeps accelerating. There's a lot we've got to get in order ASAP."

"No problem," Jasmine said.

"I have a list of stuff we've got to do." I looked at the paper I was holding and shook my head.

"You can count on me."

I smiled because I knew I could depend on her, and unfortunately, I knew I would have to.

I sneaked away into my office and fell back into my vinyl chair. I took a deep breath and looked down at the list of violations on my desk. I needed to make both phone calls and plans. I needed to prioritize, but mostly I had to get rid of the fear that gripped me. I wasn't used to being afraid. I was a confronter, a "face your problems and enemies head-on" kind of person. Facing my enemies didn't seem like such a good idea anymore. I constantly looked out the window, wondering if Elaina would return today. She hadn't said she would, but for obvious reasons, I didn't trust her. The two weeks she'd offered wasn't a long time. Unlike what I would have predicted, she hadn't threatened me with physical harm, nor had she asked me for anything unreasonable. In fact, the only thing she'd asked was that I get my business in order, but still there was a knot in my stomach that wouldn't go away. *Lord, you're my refuge.* I wasn't entirely certain about her intentions toward me, but in my heart, I just knew they couldn't be good.

"Boss, there is someone here to see you," Jasmine yelled.

Two weeks, huh? I clenched my teeth and braced myself for the worst.

Chapter Three

When I rolled out of my office, I was surprised to see that it was only the UPS deliveryman. I let out a sigh of relief and signed for my packages. This anxiety had to stop. I could no longer sit here and wait to be eaten alive by Inspector Elaina Dawson. So I decided to be proactive about this inspection disaster.

"Thank you, Mrs. Bryant," the UPS man said.

"You're welcome," I said, smiling a ridiculous smile because I had totally forgotten about my packages.

Jasmine had probably sensed the confusion by the way I wheeled myself out, as if I was on the defensive. "Are you all right, boss?"

"Yeah, I'm cool, Jas."

But I wasn't cool. I was under pressure, tremendous amounts of unnecessary pressure.

How did Elaina Dawson end up as the license inspector for my zone? Was it just a coincidence, or did she request it? The answers were unclear.

What was clear, however, was that sulking about it wasn't going to make it any better. I had to do something. And that was good, because I was a doer.

So I went into my office and wasted no time at all. I picked up the list of violations, looked at each item, and began to write them down on a separate sheet of paper. Then I started looking at the stack of bills on my desk: utilities, rent, payroll, office supplies, marketing, loan payments, and miscellaneous purchases. I began to regret subscribing to five fitness magazines all at once. One or two probably would've been sufficient. What was I thinking when I bought a new gourmet coffee machine? Who had time for gourmet coffee, anyway? There was nothing wrong with the old one. Finally, as I shuffled papers around so much that it made my head ache, I realized it was too late to second-guess myself. Knowing it was crazy to try to handle this without Keith, I stretched and yawned with mental exhaustion. Finally, I surrendered by putting my head down on the desk. I wasn't giving up, but I needed a break.

I jumped at the sound of a knock on the door. "Who is it?"

Jasmine stuck her head in.

I let out a deep breath. "Come in." I had to stop panicking at every sound.

Jasmine came in and sat down on one of my red vinyl chairs. "I'm sorry. I don't mean to bother you."

"No problem," I assured her. "What's up?"

Jasmine ran her hands through her spiked hair. "I have good news and bad."

"What's the good news? I need it," I said.

"Jacque is here, right on time, probably taking a dip in the pool as we speak and . . ." She giggled, while pretending to fan herself. Her face had turned a bright pink when she mentioned him. Jacque was a French exchange student, tall, dark haired, and handsome, who primarily played the role of lifeguard.

I interrupted her. "And the bad news?"

"Sharon just called and—"

"No, don't tell me," I said.

Jasmine put her hands up in mock surrender. "Sorry, but she called off today."

I rolled my eyes. "Again?"

Jasmine stopped chewing her gum for a moment. "You want me to take over her class?"

"The way Sharon has been calling in lately, you might be taking over her class permanently." I closed my eyes to calm down.

"She said she had an emergency with her son."

"There is always an emergency of some kind. Every other week, like clockwork," I muttered.

Jasmine twirled a lock of her hair between her fingers. "She did say that she'd be here tomorrow."

"How nice of her," I said with a hint of sarcasm.

"So what do you want me to do?"

I smiled because Jasmine was truly a godsend. "Just handle it for me, please."

"No problem." Jasmine tiptoed out and closed the door behind her.

I couldn't believe Sharon had done it again. I slammed my fist hard against the desk.

Didn't Sharon value her job? I didn't think so. The old me would have fired her on the spot, but I was trying to be patient and long-suffering. Funny thing was that since I'd become a born-again Christian, I'd been on that same good-girl track as my sister. Still, I thought, there was no way anyone who actually cared about his or her job would take off as much as Sharon did. Apparently, the fact that she was a middle-aged single mother made no difference in her decision making. I didn't understand her at all.

Sharon was a tall, slim, dynamic aerobics instructor who had come highly recommended by the industry. Unfortunately, even though her work was great, since she'd been working with us, she had not been reliable. Every other week there was some drama going on with Sharon, and she always had an excuse, as if missing work was never really her fault at all. I couldn't stand people who didn't take responsibility for their mess ups. In any case I was tired of Jasmine having to cover for her mistakes or for her absence. So I knew I had to talk to Keith about letting her go, since he was the one who had hired her.

I opened our ledger to check out our finances and see if there was enough money left over anywhere to handle these violations. I ran my finger up and down the columns, but as far as I could see, there was nothing left. Numbers didn't lie. I knew I could get Alex's husband, Joshua, the ex-banker, to look it over whenever he got a chance. I needed him to do his numbers magic and see if I had missed anything. I also knew I could ask Alex and Joshua for a small loan, but I didn't really want to do that. With the ministry and their kids, they already had enough on their plate. I closed the ledger and pushed myself away from the desk.

I began to pray. *Lord, please show me how to take care of these issues. You said that if I acknowledge you in everything, you'd direct my path. And so, Father, I'm asking you to lead and*

*guide me in the area of my business. In Jesus's
name, amen.*

I turned toward the window in my swivel chair
just in time to notice that a black, shiny Porsche
had pulled up and parked across the street. I
wasn't sure of the year, but I could tell it was
a fairly new model. The windows were darkly
tinted, so I couldn't tell if anyone was in there at
all. Yet there was something suspicious looking
about that car. There was no way a car that nice
was going to be parallel parked on an average
Brooklyn street. Maybe valet parked, but not
parallel parked. I swallowed hard as I waited for
someone to get out of the car. I watched closely
for twenty whole minutes while the car sat there,
yet no one got in or out. In fact, I did nothing but
breathe deeply and watch. Then, without warning, the car started up and took off down the
crowded street. Now that was strange, I thought.

I wondered if it was Elaina, but what would
she want? To intimidate me? To hurt me?

Maybe. Stalking was illegal, but I would have
to prove it was her first. The police weren't likely
to believe my instincts without a positive ID. My
nerves threatened to become frazzled as more
questions ran through my mind. If it was Elaina,
would she be back? And if so, for what? I didn't
know. What I did know was that a headache the

size of the Empire State Building was coming on fast. I took a bottled water from my mini refrigerator and swallowed down two aspirins as I continued to peek through the window blinds.

Ever since that woman Elaina Dawson had come into my life, I couldn't stop thinking about Derek's death and the accident on that fateful night. But maybe the accident hadn't been all bad for me, after all, because it had led me to my husband. I smiled as I looked at my desk, at a picture of Keith and me together.

The next thing I knew, my phone rang. First, I stared at it as if it were a weapon of mass destruction. Then I came to my senses and answered it. Thankfully, it was my sister.

I cleared my throat, then answered. "Hello."

"Are you okay? You sound a little sad." Alex could always read me.

"No, I was just sitting here thinking."

"About what?"

I sighed. "Life."

Alex chuckled. "That tells me a lot."

"It's funny how when I first got saved, I used to think I called all the shots."

Alex let out a big breath.

"But how could I have expected to manhandle God?" I shook my head, marveling at what a bona fide fool I used to be.

Alex burst out laughing.

"I honestly thought if I hollered out a couple of ultimatums, then God would be merciful enough to give me what I demanded." I sighed. "My thinking was way warped back then."

Alex continued to laugh.

"Okay, it wasn't that funny. I actually believed that once I accepted Christ, I could definitely have everything my way. Boy, did I have it all backward."

"Yeah, you did," Alex said in her wise older twin voice. "Do you remember me telling you that it wasn't about you?"

"Yeah, I remember, but obviously I didn't believe that. My kind of 'have it your way, Burger King' mentality was getting me nowhere—fast. I was dishing it out and coming up short."

"Humph. I know that's right," Alex responded.

At that time in my life I hadn't learned about faithfulness, deliverance, long-suffering, seasons, obedience, or the will of God. I had just thought He was my own personal genie to use at will. Needless to say, I got to know that God's ways were not my ways real quick and in a hurry.

"Okay, okay, enough. What's all this reflection about?" Alex added.

I hesitated before answering. "Just got a lot of pressure with the business, that's all."

"Uh-huh. And this is your twin you're talking to. Save that mess for someone who believes it. Not me."

I sighed before giving in to the truth. "Well, I ran into Elaina Dawson yesterday."

"Who?"

I cringed as I was forced to explain. "Derek's wife."

"Oh, dead Derek?"

"Yes, him." I whispered to make sure no one could overhear our conversation. I told her all about Elaina's surprise inspection and how much trouble Push It was in.

Alex remained quiet, and there seemed to be mystery in her silence.

"I saw her, and it wasn't very comfortable at all," I explained.

"Duh. I'll bet it wasn't," Alex mocked.

I paused. "So I've just been thinking about my life, choices I've made and stuff."

"Okay, but don't get so caught up in the past that you can't see your future. Let that stuff go," Alex said. "You're a different person now."

I hoped she couldn't detect that tears were streaming down my face, but somehow, I felt she did.

By the time I hung up the phone, I was ready to come out of isolation. I took one final glance out the window, and then I rolled out of my office, stopping by the front desk. I watched the clients work out on the various machines. One guy was running so hard on a treadmill, I thought he was going to go through the floor. A middle-aged lady was lifting sixty-pound weights like a champion, and a senior citizen was showing off her newly toned calves.

I felt inspired, so I decided to jump on my favorite piece of equipment since my injury, the rowing machine. I knew that a good workout would calm me. It always did. Whenever I pushed my body, it was like freeing my mind. Ever since middle school, when my track coach, Coach Glen, commented about my extra bulge and made me do five extra laps around the track, I'd never slacked on exercise. Food was optional, but not fitness.

Still, even as I moved my arms and my heart beat faster, I couldn't stop thinking about the inspection. Problems at work meant problems at home. The sooner I got rid of Elaina Dawson, I decided, the sooner my worries would be over.

Jasmine walked over to me. She was wearing lime spandex workout shorts and a matching top. "I just signed up another member, boss."

"Good, good. For a whole year or six months?"

"For the whole year. She seems pretty excited too." Jasmine did a little jump. "And another dude called a few minutes ago, looking for a physical trainer." Jasmine grinned. "He wants to start professional bodybuilding."

I high-fived her.

"We can do this." Jasmine broke into a dance and gave me a thumbs-up. "Business is looking up, huh?"

I peeped over Jasmine's shoulder and through the glass windows and barely caught a glimpse of the same car I'd seen earlier quickly pulling away again. "Yeah, it is, but with this insane inspector on our tails, I just pray we can stay open."

Chapter Four

When Keith came to pick me up that evening, I locked up everything, double-checked the back door, the windows, and then set the alarm. As usual, Jasmine and Jacque helped with the closing routine.

"See you guys tomorrow." Jasmine waved as she headed for the bus stop down the block.

"Good night," Jacque said with his heavy French accent as he jumped into his friend's little car.

"Okay, you two," I said, distracted.

"Good night," Keith said without even looking up. As he loaded me into the car, I couldn't help but stare at the fitness center. It was a dream come true that, thanks to Elaina Dawson, could soon come crashing down. Worse yet, I still didn't know what she wanted with me. Surely this was more than just a licensing issue. I had stolen her man, had toyed with him, and had disrespected her and her family. Even though it had been three years ago, if the memory was still fresh in my mind, I was sure it was still fresh in hers. How did it feel to be a widow, to have loved and lost to another woman, and then to have it all end so tragically? I couldn't even imagine something like that happening to me. The thought was horrible, and I didn't want to dwell on the kind of woman I used to be. I was a new creature. Old things had passed away.

As we pulled away into traffic, I couldn't help but look behind me. I guess it was obvious that I was nervous, because I got Keith's attention right away.

"What's wrong?"

I tried not to look distracted as I peered over my shoulder through the back window. "What do you mean?"

"You're a little quiet," Keith observed.

"So?"

Keith smiled. "You've always got a lot to say."

I wanted to sound offended, but I was sure it came out all wrong. "Are you trying to say I talk too much?"

"No, but you've got a lot to say, and I want to hear all of it. Now what's wrong?"

"Nothing. I just saw a strange-looking car outside today, and I'm just thinking, what if someone is following us? That's all."

"You've been watching too much late-night TV." Keith chuckled. "Why would anyone be following us?"

"I don't know. Maybe that inspector lady."

Keith kept his eyes on the road. "Okay, but why? Why would the inspector lady be following you?"

"I don't know." I hated lying to him, but I wasn't ready to disclose the inspector's identity. Maybe I was wrong about her, and this would all blow over after the license was renewed. Maybe, just maybe, she didn't want anything more than that. Maybe there was no need to bring up my past mistakes. Not that Keith had any doubt about who I *used* to be, but I certainly wasn't proud of it and I didn't want to rub it in his face.

"That isn't her job." Keith looked at me and shook his head. "You're paranoid."

"You're probably right," I admitted.

Keith's expression became serious. "Just don't be paranoid. God didn't give us a spirit of fear, remember?"

"I'm gonna stop it." I hit my fist into my hand, declaring that I was no longer going to be afraid. Yet my words didn't suppress the feeling that was rising up in me.

By the time we arrived at our apartment, I was ready to relax. I looked through the mail on my way to the bedroom. Then I slipped out of my fitted jogging pants and into shorts, while Keith went to take his shower early, like he always did. Within twenty minutes, Keith emerged from the bathroom, threw on his pajama pants, and we went back into our oversize living room.

Just as I got comfortable, putting my legs up on the couch, Keith took out the books for the business.

"Okay, let's get this over with," he said, practically burying his head in papers.

I could tell from his expression that since the inspection was bothering me, he knew he would have no peace until the issues were resolved.

He really didn't say much, except to grunt every now and then. Keith was never a talker, but he did know very well how to get his point across when he had to. I guess that was what I liked about him. I could go on and on, venting my frustrations, and Keith would hardly interrupt. Not at all like the men I dated before him, who were rude and arrogant, so full of themselves there was no room for me. Not with my Keith. He always left plenty of room for me. Besides that, he was the most beautiful man in Brooklyn, and better than fine, he was all mine.

Too bad we had come to a crossroads in our business relationship, though. There was no turning back, only forging ahead like warriors. The disappointing thing was that my husband didn't look like a warrior. In fact, he looked clueless. Although he was the college graduate, he was no business mastermind. Clearly, he was the brawn, while I was the brains and the beauty of this whole operation. I smiled to myself at that thought.

Within minutes, I saw him fling down the papers and reach for the TV remote. He flipped through the channels and eventually landed on a rerun of *Sanford and Son*. I started to laugh aloud, but I stopped myself, because the trouble we were in was no laughing matter.

Keith went to the kitchen and came back with a big bowl of fresh blueberries. He began pushing them into my mouth, one at a time.

"Thanks." I rolled my eyes without him seeing me. Didn't he know the stress I was under? Didn't he care that we might be closed down?

I decided to let it go for now, yet the quiet, uneventful evening I was hoping for was still shot. Even Keith didn't expect things to go down the way they did that evening. We were sitting in the living room, still watching television, when all of a sudden Keith's phone rang.

I sucked my teeth. "Aww, man. Not work."

"Sorry, babe. I've been expecting Dr. Shumar to call." Keith gave me a sad look. "I've gotta get this."

"Oh, go on." I playfully swung my fist at him as he got off the couch.

I watched his expression change from business to pleasure almost instantly. After a few seconds, he threw his head back in laughter and left the room. When he returned, the program was over and I was asleep on the couch. He leaned over and kissed me gently as I opened my eyes. That was a nice way to wake up.

Keith grinned. "Babe, you'll never guess who that was."

I shook my head. "Who was it?"

"My old buddy Paul, from college." Keith's dark eyes sparkled.

"I do remember you mentioned him once." I nodded my head.

"We lost touch over the past few years."

My curiosity kicked into high gear. "How did he get your number?"

"He's in town, and he ran into a mutual acquaintance of ours, and that's how he got it."

"Cool. So how is he?"

"Well, that's the thing." Keith reached for my hand. "He's having a hard time right now."

"Oh, I'm sorry to hear that." I cringed. The look on Keith's face made me nervous.

"Yeah, he's been laid off, lost his properties to foreclosure, and lost his wife to another man," Keith said.

"Whoa!"

It was a hard set of circumstances to come up against, so naturally my husband felt sorry for him. I sat next to him, listening as one thing led to another, and before I knew it, Keith explained to me that he had invited him over.

Before I could stop myself, I turned my head and sucked my teeth.

Keith sat down next to me and cradled me in his arms. "You're not upset that I told him to stop by, are you?"

Since Keith was always so attentive to my needs, I felt ashamed of myself for catching an attitude.

"No, not at all. I'm sorry for my attitude." Trying to reassure him, I kissed him on his soft lips. He hadn't put on his shirt yet, and I could feel the ripples in his bare chest.

Keith held my shoulders and looked into my eyes. "Are you sure you're okay?"

Whenever he held me close, I felt secure in his strength and wondered what I was afraid of in the first place. "I'm good."

Keith let me go and immediately began straightening up the living room while I watched. Watching him was an unexpected pleasure. He was tall and thick, not in an extra-bulky way, but in a broad-chested, firm, muscular-thighed kind of way. He could have been a bodybuilder, except that he spent more time working on others than he did working on himself. Still, he had the kind of looks that would make a church girl get up and shout "Have mercy."

Within a half hour his friend was standing in our doorway, dripping wet from the rain.

They threw their manly arms around each other before Keith invited him inside. "Babe, this is *the* Paul Meyers I've been telling you about. Paul, this is my wife, Taylor."

I rolled over and shook Paul's hand. "It's good to meet you, Paul."

"Same here, uh . . . Taylor." He looked shocked to see me in a wheelchair, but I was used to that reaction.

He seemed insignificant in comparison to my husband. How they had become friends, I would never know, but they seemed as different as night and day. He was short—at least according to my standards—about an inch taller than me, with a medium build and a potbelly. Keith towered over him with his six-foot-two-inch frame. He also had a raggedy beard and shifty dark eyes. He looked like he had been through a lot. His clothes were wrinkled, and he smelled of smoke. His hair was low cut, and he had a slightly receding hairline. Actually, he was balding. Even Keith in his house clothes looked neater in appearance than him. His voice was raspy too, like my father's, except that it was even less becoming on a young man. And he was loud and seemed to have a crude sense of humor, while my Keith was sensitive and soft-spoken.

Forget about why his wife ran away with another man. I wanted to know how she stayed married to him as long as she did.

For about half an hour, he sat on our couch, talking about his career in real estate and how the market had turned ugly, about how his ex-wife had taken him for everything he had, not that it could have been much, judging by the looks of him. It was obvious that this man had no shame, because he just kept running his mouth like a runaway freight train. Keith barely got a few words in about his career and about Push It. I wondered if Paul bored all his friends like this. If so, that would explain why he was here in New York, beating down Keith's door. He had probably run all his other friends away. I smirked to myself.

Finally, the conversation moved to the kitchen, where Keith and I proceeded to warm up leftovers.

"That sure was a good dinner," Paul said after we'd eaten. He looked over at me, chewing with his mouth slightly open. "Taylor, it's been a long time since I had a good home-cooked meal."

"Don't look at me. I didn't do it," I said. "I just do takeout."

Paul asked, "Keith, you're cooking now, bruh?"

Keith nodded. "Sometimes I do, yeah. That chicken you just ate was just something left over from what I cooked last night."

"Cool. Ain't nothing wrong with that, I guess." Paul hunched his shoulders before he started to pick his teeth.

"You're welcome to eat over here as much as you like." Keith cut his eyes toward me.

"In fact, where are you staying?"

"I was hoping I could crash with you for a while," Paul said.

I couldn't believe what I was hearing. Keith's pleading eyes met mine, and I knew it was over.

"Sure, you can stay here with us, in our guest room, until you get on your feet." Keith headed over to where I was planted.

Paul reached over to slap Keith's back. "Thanks, man."

"It's no problem. Right, Taylor?" Keith nudged me.

"No problem at all." *Holy Spirit, bind my tongue.*

"Maybe we might be able to get you some work down at the gym," Keith said.

I gave Keith a look, but he didn't even turn my way to notice it.

Now, that was going too far, if anyone had asked me. But guess what? Nobody asked me. Personally, I had more questions for Paul, but I found myself being sent off to change the guest-room linen instead. Ironically, that was the room reserved for any future child that Keith and I might have. And, yes, I did say *child*, and not children. That is, if someone could talk me into pushing out even one of those brats. Believe me, kids weren't my thing at all, and I knew it would take a whole lot of coaxing to get me to surrender to mutilating my body with childbirth. I smiled to myself, shaking my head. I had lost my ability to walk; I had not lost my mind.

When I went back into the living room, I heard Keith explaining to Paul about my accident, and I knew then that he'd asked how I ended up in a wheelchair.

"She's gorgeous, though," Paul said.

"Yeah, I've got a good one," Keith said as I wheeled myself into the room.

I must admit I didn't trust Paul from the moment I met him. His eyes were shifty, and his demeanor was slick, too slick. Even charming. "Never trust a man with charm," Mama used to say, and that woman was right about everything. There was something about this Paul that just didn't add up. I just couldn't put my finger on it. He was polite and friendly enough, but something about him being in my house just didn't feel right.

He seemed to be eyeing everything around the house, including me, not in a lustful way, but like he was sizing everything up. He kind of reminded me of my cousin Juney from around the way. Mama always said we'd better watch cousin Juney, 'cause he'd steal anything that wasn't nailed down. Meanwhile, my husband seemed to be having the time of his life with a partner to talk sports with and reminisce over the good old days back in college. Funny thing was, every time I'd get too close to them, they'd stop talking about those college years, almost as if they were hiding something. They probably thought I didn't notice, but I did. That left me curious about what went on that they obviously didn't want me to know about. Yeah, there was a lot I didn't trust about that Paul person. Something inside told me he was an unsavory character, but I just didn't have any proof.

"So, Taylor, I hear that you're the best when it comes to personal training." Paul squinted his beady little eyes.

I looked at him sideways. "I do my thing from time to time."

"You're modest. That's good. But you're gonna have to whip your boy over here into shape," he said, throwing a fake punch at Keith.

"Well, if you're talking about my *man,* he's already in great shape. He doesn't really need my help," I said.

"Your wife is sticking up for you, Keith. You're right. You've got a good one."

"Hey, I can hold my own," Keith said, playfully punching him back.

"Yeah, right." Paul laughed. "That's not how it used to be."

How it *used to be* must've sent chills of fear up my husband's spine, because he looked at Paul like he was horrified. There was more than a beat of silence. Then Paul burst into extreme laughter. I wasn't laughing, though. Neither was Keith. Something wasn't right with that situation. I sensed it in my spirit.

Later, when I came out of the shower, I thought of dressing in Keith's favorite candy apple–red Victoria's Secret negligee with the matching thong, but I decided against it. On the one hand,

I wanted Keith to hold me and shower me with his love, but on the other hand, I wanted him to listen to my concerns, so I slipped into my cotton pajama short set instead, wrapped myself up in my satin sheets, and waited for Keith to come to bed. By the time he finally came to bed, it was late and I was tired, but knowing the intensity of what we were facing, I sat up, anyway.

Keith came in laughing. "Paul is so funny."

"Yeah, he's hysterical," I smirked.

"I'm glad he's here from Chicago." Keith shook his head. "It's been a long time."

"How come you never talked much about him to me before? You barely mentioned him."

"Well, after college we lost touch, so . . ."

I kept the covers pulled up to my chin. "It's cool that you get to see your old friend again."

"It would be really cool if we gave him a job at Push It." Keith sat down on the side of the bed.

I pushed my head back. "A job?"

"Yeah, maybe he could help Jasmine behind the front desk or something. I don't know."

"Now, wait a minute, buddy." That was where I had to draw the line. I couldn't stay quiet on that one. In fact, it wasn't in my nature to stay quiet at all. Sometimes I would straight go off on my husband. I was still working on being delivered from that. "There is no way I'm gonna be stuck working with that dude all day. I know he's your homeboy and all, but I just don't think he's Push It material."

"Yeah, you're probably right." Keith stood up and started stripping out of his clothes.

"I'll have to help him find something else."

"That sounds like a better idea." I sighed because I knew I had just dodged a bullet.

"All right, but he can at least help out sometimes just to keep busy. Maybe once or twice a week."

"Maybe," I said.

Keith folded his clothes and placed them on the armchair. "Once or twice a week for a couple of hours can't hurt."

I twisted my lips. "Can't hurt *you* maybe."

"Taylor, don't be mean." Keith shook his head.

"I'm not," I whined.

Keith's voice was stern. "You are."

I didn't want to do it, but Keith very rarely asked favors of me, so I felt too guilty to say no. He was always doing things for me, even things he didn't necessarily want to do. "All right. I'll try it."

"Thanks, babe." Keith kissed me hard on the lips.

But I wasn't happy about what I'd agreed to. I didn't really want Paul hanging around at the gym, and I almost didn't want him in my home, either. In fact, I really didn't want anything at all to do with Mr. Paul Meyers, the slickster.

With his hand on the bedroom doorknob, Keith asked, "Don't we have a shipment of supplies being delivered tomorrow morning?"

I shook my head. "Actually, the shipment came early."

"Good. Paul can go down to the gym to help you with that."

I fell back onto my pillow. "Jasmine and I already handled that on our own."

"Well, maybe he can help with something else. I want him to feel useful. It's rough on a man with no job, no home, no wife, or anything."

"I know but . . ." I paused because I heard a rustling by the door.

Keith must've heard it too, because he quickly flung the door open, hitting Paul right in the face.

Humph. Eavesdropping, I thought to myself. I knew there was something sneaky about him.

"Sorry, man. I was just coming to thank you guys again and to say good night," Paul said.

Keith stood in the doorway. "No problem, man. Night."

"Good night," I said from under the covers.

Keith closed the door and looked back at me. "See what I mean? He's lonely."

"Lonely?" I sat up straight in bed. "Is that why you think he's lurking around outside our bedroom door?"

"He wasn't lurking around," Keith said, fluffing his pillow. "He just needs something to do."

I twisted my lips. "So I see."

Keith snuggled next to me and put his head on my shoulder. "If he can help out down at Push It, I'm sure it will help. Just till I can help him find something else."

"I don't know, Keith." I shook my head and sighed.

"Please," Keith whispered softly in my ear.

"All right. I'll give him a try." I bit my lip and closed my eyes, knowing in my spirit that Paul was trouble, and knowing I'd live to regret this.

Chapter Five

Against my better judgment, Paul ended up spending the next day with me down at the gym. He came to work wearing tight-fitting polyester basketball shorts and a Michael Jordan jersey. Like he could compare to Michael Jordan. Yeah, right. I introduced him to Jasmine and showed him around the gym, starting with the multipurpose room. Surprisingly, Paul marveled at the African art he saw hanging on the walls. I never would have imagined that he cared anything about culture.

"Nice place you have here," Paul said, yawning.

"Thanks," I said. "Make yourself at home."

Paul looked me in the eye. "What do you need me to do around here?"

"Can't think of anything right now." I scratched my head. "Just get in where you fit in."

As soon as I let him loose, he started to get in everyone's way, like I knew he would. He left candy wrappers on the exercise equipment, burped uncontrollably, and peeped over Jasmine's shoulder as she was working. Not only that, but he was a nuisance, starting up random conversations with the clientele and making crude jokes. One lady actually moved away from him when he came near her. Most people came to the gym to relax or blow off steam, not to be bothered by annoying strangers. So I came up with the idea to isolate Paul by sending him back to the pool room.

"Paul, I want you to be over the pool area for me. Jacque is our staff lifeguard, and he generally watches out for the patrons while they swim. But I've got a list of things for you to do and check for whenever you come down here that would really help me out a lot." I smiled at my brilliance.

"Okay," Paul said, scratching his raggedy beard.

"Are you okay with that?"

Paul smacked on a piece of gum. "Sure. Sounds great."

"Good." I nodded. "I'll just show you to the pool room."

Paul followed my lead, listening keenly, or at least pretending to listen, to my every word. The rectangular-shaped pool was located in the middle of the turquoise-blue room. The pool was white in color with green, and white lounge chairs and tables with little umbrellas surrounding it. There was an oversized mural of a tropical island on one of the walls, and huge artificial palm trees stood near the other three walls. There was also a swan-shaped fountain in the corner, a piece we had splurged on before the ink on the loan papers was dry. All in all, it would be my favorite room at the gym if I were still able to swim.

I introduced Paul to Jacque, explaining that Paul would be taking over the pool duties that were usually designated to me. I was glad that with Paul in charge, I wouldn't have to torture myself by going in the pool room all the time. I really didn't like going in there anymore, because since I used to be a great swimmer, it was a reminder of all the things I could no longer do. Sure, working out in the pool was occasionally a part of my therapy, but I was limited. I showed Paul all he needed to know and do, secure in the knowledge that even he couldn't mess that up.

Afterward, I set out to work on those violations one at a time. Two weeks was not a long time, and I needed to get started right away. I called in my equipment mechanic to look at the treadmill. He checked it out thoroughly, adjusted the settings, changed a part, and then handed me a bill. I gave him an IOU. Then I called in the plumber to fix the toilets in the ladies' room and maxed out my credit card with that one. I went around the whole place, dusting, polishing, and making sure that everything was in its place. That took care of the easy violations.

I spent the rest of the day in my office, sulking about the harder ones, like the flooring that needed replacing in two of the exercise rooms, the leak from the ceiling in one of the exercise rooms, the machines that weren't working up to their specifications, and the lighting in the pool area, which Elaina had claimed was too dim.

That evening, while Keith and Paul were out bowling, Alex stopped by with the kids. With three young kids, I'd say she was a walking school if you asked me.

"Aunty Tay Tay," Lilah squealed.

"Hey, babies," I said, hugging Lilah first, then giving Kiano a high five. Kiano, the child my sister and her husband had just adopted from Kenya, looked reluctant to speak at first, but he finally said hello. And last but not least, I took my youngest nephew, Joshua Jr., into my arms.

He was almost nine months old now and looked just like his father. Lilah, my sister's stepdaughter, was getting taller, and she looked like her father too.

"Wow! They're so big and beautiful," I said. "Motherhood really agrees with you."

In fact, Alex was glowing so much, and had gained so much weight, that at first glance I wondered if she was pregnant again.

"I don't know, girl," I said, patting Alex gently on her stomach. "Are you sure there isn't another one baking in that oven?"

"Girl, bite your tongue," she said.

We both threw our heads back and laughed at that one. The kids happily made themselves at home, covering my living-room floor with their toys and almost drowning out our conversation with their noise. Luckily, Alex and I had big mouths, so it didn't matter. We took our conversation from childhood to our marriages and back again as we sat on the couch.

I was grateful for this visit since I really didn't see enough of them anymore. Now that we attended different churches, it was difficult. Ever since Joshua and Alex had started their own church, the Faith and Freedom Christian Church, they had been so busy. I wanted to transfer my membership, but Keith insisted that we remain at Missionary. He had joined right after we got married, and had bonded with Pastor Martin right away. Almost everybody did. I could understand all of that, but I missed my sister. With three kids as her entourage, she didn't get out to the gym as much as she used to, and sometimes she was so worn out in the evenings, it was even a challenge to talk on the phone. Still, we had our moments. We snuck them in because we had no choice. We were twins, for goodness' sake, and we had to have that connection. Thank goodness our husbands understood that.

Alex rearranged the diapers in her baby bag. "You know we've got the women's conference coming up next month."

"Are you kidding me?" I smiled. "I can't wait."

"You can't wait? You know I need a break." Alex pointed at her three children and smiled. "Hey, why don't we all get together and do dinner or a movie soon?"

"Really? What about the kids?"

"We'll just have to pay Ms. Johnson to keep them." Alex shook her head. "I need a break."

"I don't know when we'll be able to go out, since we've got this new houseguest." I winced.

"Right. I almost forgot. Anyway, talk to Keith and see what he thinks."

I rolled my eyes up to the ceiling. "Keith doesn't have any time to think anymore."

"Maybe you two can ditch Paul for one night, or maybe you can just bring him with you."

"Nope. That would ruin everything."

"I don't know what to say about your issue, Taylor," Alex said, shaking her head.

"I don't know what it is, but I just don't like him," I said, filling her in on the little things that had put up a red flag as far as Paul was concerned.

"Well, there is no law against not liking somebody, especially if they're living with you and messing up your place."

"That's true, but it's deeper than that." I stood up and placed the baby in her lap. "I just can't explain it."

Alex looked serious. "I can see you're really bothered by this."

"I don't know. I just feel like Paul and Keith are hiding something from me. It's like they're talking about me behind my back."

"But they're not. Apparently, they're talking about you in your face." Alex chuckled.

I gave her the look.

Alex stopped laughing. "Okay, I'm sorry."

"They're doing it in bits and pieces, kind of code like, but every time I'm around, the two of them shut their mouths up real quick."

"Maybe it's nothing." Alex shook her hand.

I shook my head. "I doubt it."

"You're probably overreacting." Alex laughed. "You are Miss Drama."

"I'm not overreacting this time. There is something really shady about Mr. Paul Meyers, and I'm gonna find out what it is."

Later that evening, after Alex and the kids had gone, I started rummaging around the kitchen, trying to decide what Keith and I were going to eat for dinner. I wasn't good at the homemaking thing. Despite my mother's early attempts at teaching me to cook, take-out wings and salad were usually all I could handle. Tonight, however, as I went over to look in the refrigerator, I noticed that some of my fruit had spoiled. I had to make a mental note not to purchase so much fruit at once. As I was dumping the few spoiled apples and pears into the trash can, I realized that there was a bottle camouflaged by a plastic bag in our small trash can. When I bent down to take off the bag, I saw that it was a liquor bottle. I pulled it out to get a better look. It was an empty bottle of cognac, and since I knew that my husband never touched alcohol, I knew who it belonged to. It had to belong to Paul. Suddenly, I knew what I didn't like about Paul Meyers. It was his habits. This incriminating bottle was just proof of that.

I wondered whether or not I should mention what I'd found to Keith. The old me wouldn't have hesitated to bring it on, but the new me decided against it. Why would I start drama when, hopefully, Paul would be out on his own soon? Hopefully, the drinking was a onetime thing, maybe a part of his "back with his best friend" celebration the other night.

Day after day, right after putting in a few hours at the fitness center, Paul lay up on the couch, eating our food, paying no rent, and stinking up the apartment with his funk. He was a lousy houseguest. He didn't help around the house or look for a job. He just stayed at home, waiting for Keith to arrive. After the first two days they started going out for hours at a time and coming back home in the wee hours of the morning.

Usually, I lay in the bed, praying, while they were out together. At first, trying to be the understanding wife, I thought it was just harmless fellowship, an innocent chance to reclaim their childhood of long ago. That was how I felt the first couple of times they went out. After all, I was a grown woman, and I wasn't nearly as uptight as my sister and her husband were.

But after a couple of weeks of their going out at all times of the day and night, with neither an explanation nor any regard for my feelings, I was ready to go off. I wasn't used to that kind of garbage from my God-fearing husband. I mean, not that Keith was perfect or anything, but we went to church every Sunday, prayed daily, and sometimes we even went to midweek service. Since he was the one who led me to Christ, I guess you could say I considered him devout. Not sugarcoated or phony, but very serious about his beliefs. That was what I loved about him. He had always been a good man, and I didn't want Paul's foolishness to rub off on him. I trusted Keith not to get down like that, but still. After all, we'd been married for only eight months so far, and I couldn't wait until our houseguest was gone so we could get back to our normal lives.

Surprisingly, Elaina Dawson wasn't on my mind the day she came back to Push It. The two-week deadline had come fast. With all the drama going on at home, I had almost forgotten about my pending issues for a moment. Although we had almost expected our application to be turned down, we were finally able to get an increase on one of our lines of credit, just enough to make the necessary repairs to the fitness center. And just in time.

As soon as I saw her, I signaled Jasmine with my eyes that it was on. Elaina walked up to me, dressed in a tailored silk pantsuit. This time her long weaved hair was pinned up in a bun.

I guessed she had decided to play the conservative role.

I felt more confident this go-round because Jasmine was at the front desk, the illusive Sharon was teaching her advanced aerobics class for a change, Jacque was on duty as a lifeguard, and Paul was in the pool room, supposedly wiping down the lounge chairs. I was ready.

"Hello again, Mrs. Taylor Carter-Bryant," Elaina snapped.

"Hi," I said, faking a smile. It was hard to be happy when I knew this woman was out to ruin me. She had called me by a hyphenated last name, and yet I had never even mentioned my maiden name, Carter, to her. How could she possibly know my maiden name? Yes, she knew me. At least she knew the old me.

She strode through the gym like she owned the place, looking around and checking off her list of violations on her clipboard. Unlike the first time, though, she seemed agitated and distracted.

When we went into the pool room, the first thing I noticed that was out of place was Paul.

"Ms. Dawson, this is Mr. Paul Meyers. He helps us out around here from time to time," I said.

She looked over at Paul, who by that time was trying his best to look busy. "I see."

"Good to meet ya, darling," Paul said, tipping his head as if he were bowing.

"Yes," Elaina said.

Then I pointed to Jacque as he flexed his tanned, well-toned body in the chair. He grinned, because he thrived on getting attention from all the ladies. "That's our lifeguard."

Elaina didn't even blink. "Let's get on with it, shall we?"

I could tell that Paul had probably been lounging up until the moment he heard us coming, because he was caught walking around the pool with his hands in his pockets, wearing those ridiculous sunshades indoors. There was an odd look on his round face. *What a character,* I thought, frowning.

Elaina had a frown also. It occurred to me that maybe she didn't expect me to pass the inspection this time. Maybe she thought these violations would be the end of the Push It Fitness Center, or at least the end of me. Apparently, she didn't realize that I was a fighter. She didn't know how I'd fought to get the business from my former employer in the first place, and that I'd be more than willing to fight to keep it. And it was not that I didn't know what her determination was all about, but she'd almost fooled me with her professionalism the first time around.

Carter-Bryant indeed.

She had almost had me believing this inspection wasn't personal. Sure, it was her job as a license inspector, and that she had little control of, but I knew that as she walked around, hesitantly crossing things off her list, she was enjoying every moment of torturing me. This time I knew it for sure. Vengeance was hiding in her eyes and seeping through her pores. Yes, Elaina Dawson wanted to do more to me than check me off her inspection list. She wanted to hurt me, slowly. That much was finally clear.

Thankfully, Push It passed the inspection, and I was able to let out a sigh of relief. Yet there was something about Elaina's jittery response that made me uneasy, something about the way she smiled a crooked smile on the way out.

"Until we meet again, Mrs. Bryant," she said.

She said it as if our business wasn't over, as if I'd see her again.

"Right," I said, hesitating to close the glass door behind her. For a moment I wanted to confront her, but then again a part of me felt I had no right to. She hadn't exactly threatened me, nor had she even mentioned our past meeting. The only evidence I had was that she knew my maiden name, but using it wasn't a crime.

I could feel something sinister in my spirit, so I knew Elaina Dawson was still going to be trouble. I just didn't know when or how it was going to come.

Chapter Six

We woke up early on Sunday morning to the sound of pigeons cooing. The late June sun peered through the window, reminding us that it was finally summer. Keith and I held hands and prayed together before we took our showers. When I came out, I rolled over to my closet, choosing to wear an orange and brown fitted dress with matching orange pumps, while Keith chose his brown and beige three-piece suit with brown shoes, which nicely complemented my outfit. I wondered what Paul would end up wearing, since he would be attending church with us today.

Paul had been with us for one whole month already, and everyday living with him had been a challenge.

When I rolled into the living room, I saw that Paul wore a casual two-piece cotton suit that looked like it needed ironing, with a neon green T-shirt underneath. I sighed. Tasteless was what I would call that outfit, except that I had no control over it. Paul sat in Keith's favorite chair, the leather recliner, relaxing and reading one of our fitness magazines. A beautiful model in a tiny spandex shorts set graced the cover. I wondered if he was really reading the articles or if he was just glaring at the pictures.

I approached him. "Good morning, Paul."

"Good morning," Paul said.

I studied him. "Are you ready for church?"

"Yep, I'm ready." Paul shoved his hands into his pockets. "Haven't been in years, though."

"Don't worry. It's just like riding a bike." I smiled, trying to connect with this friend that was so important to my husband.

"You know, you're probably right about that. Last time I went was with my grandmother," Paul said.

"Oh, that must've been quite a while ago." I squinted as I considered what he was saying.

Paul grinned. "It was. I was just a boy then."

Trying to be cheerful, I smiled again and then turned. "Well, I'm going in to get us all some breakfast so we can be on our way."

Paul was chewing on a pencil. "Where is my buddy?"

"He'll be out in a few," I said, rolling into the kitchen.

Once I was in the kitchen, I transferred myself from my wheelchair to my walker. Then I fixed three bowls of cold wheat cereal and cut up fresh bananas and strawberries into them. I put six slices of bread into the toaster and put three eggs on to boil. I sighed because this was the most cooking I had done in weeks, and no one could argue that it wasn't my forte. Then I took my walker and trudged over to the kitchen window, waiting to hear the laughter, which came soon enough. It made me cringe to hear Paul's and Keith's voices mingling together joyfully. No matter how hard I tried, I just couldn't wrap my head around Paul Meyers.

Keith walked into the kitchen. "Need any help, babe?"

"Not with breakfast, but with everything else," I answered.

"Okay, what do you need?"

I balanced myself, then rolled my eyes. "I need our unwelcome houseguest gone."

"Shhh." Keith frowned as he gestured for me to keep my voice down. "Taylor."

"I'm sorry, Keith, but I'm tired of picking up after a grown man. Empty cans, clothes, and cigarette butts . . . I know he's not smoking inside the apartment, but why come back in with it?"

Keith shrugged his shoulders. "I know he's a little sloppy, but—"

"A little? He should be trying to fit in around here, not stand out on purpose." I took a quick breath. "We don't have maid service, you know?"

"I know."

"Does he know that my name is not *Mrs.* Paul Meyers? Thank goodness. Being the total slob he is, I doubt if anyone will ever be *Mrs.* Paul Meyers again."

"All right, Taylor," Keith said in his "I've had enough" voice.

"I'm just sayin'," I mumbled, wincing. "I'll be picking up candy wrappers and dirty socks for days. This madness has to stop."

"After church I'll help you clean up." Keith wrapped his arms around my waist and began to kiss my neck.

"No, Keith. I don't feel comfortable with Paul living here." I peeled his hands off of me and used my walker to get to my seat. "I always feel like he's sneaking around or something."

"Oh, come on." Keith put a frown on his face. "He's not like that."

"He's not like that? How is he, then?"

"If anything, he's loyal," Keith said.

"Loyal? You never spoke of him until he showed up on the scene, but then you say he's loyal?"

"Yeah, he's a loyal friend." Keith didn't blink.

"How do you know? What has he done to prove his loyalty to you?"

Keith left the kitchen without another word.

Three minutes later, everything was ready, so I called the men in to eat.

"Wow, this is a breakfast fit for a king. Thanks, babe," Keith said, watching me carefully.

"Yep, this looks very, um, uh, healthy." Paul laughed.

I wasn't sure what was so funny. "That's how we eat around here—healthy," I couldn't resist saying.

When we were done, we all piled into our car and took off down the lively Brooklyn streets. Paul sat in the backseat, of course, but I could see him watching us with his beady eyes from the rearview mirror. I couldn't wait to get to church.

As soon as we pulled up in front of the church, I saw Aunt Dorothy walking in with Daddy. Keith helped me out of the car, and I rolled up the ramp to catch up with them.

"Hey, sweetie. We didn't even see you," Aunt Dorothy said.

"Hi, Aunt Dorothy." I hugged her. "Hi, Daddy."

Daddy bent down to hug me. "Hey, baby girl."

Aunt Dorothy smiled. "Where is that handsome husband of yours?"

"He's right over there, Aunty, talking to this friend of his from college." I yawned as I pointed a limp finger at Paul, who was leaning against the car.

"Well, you don't look too happy about it," Daddy said.

I let out a deep breath. "I'm not crazy about him, but he's been staying with us, so . . ."

"Oh, say no more. An unwelcome houseguest." Aunt Dorothy laughed. "Chile, I know what you're going through."

I looked into Aunt Dorothy's eyes. "Do you?"

"Yep," Aunt Dorothy said. "Come on, let's go inside. They'll catch up."

"We know you don't want to offend Keith, so just be polite and you'll be okay," Daddy said.

Aunt Dorothy shook her head. "Be careful with those houseguests. Sometimes they like to stay forever. And most important, don't let any of that interfere with you and Keith."

"That's what I'm trying not to do," I said, looking back at Keith and Paul, who were coming up close behind us.

I introduced Paul to my dad and my aunt before we were all seated together. I settled in to listen to the praise team usher in the Holy Spirit.

I remembered when Alex used to sing with the praise team. I missed attending church with my sister. The choir started out with "Nobody Greater," and the crowds roared with praise. Then they followed up with three other equally popular selections. Paul looked restless sitting in his seat, squirming around and looking behind him. In fact, at one point during the service, he looked like he was about to bolt out the front door. But who was I to judge? That used to be how I acted before I got to know the Lord for myself.

Once the praise team and choir had the audience warmed up, Pastor Martin came forward and preached a fire-breathing sermon on resisting temptation. Keith handed Paul a Bible and tried to get him to follow along with the scriptures, but Paul looked uninterested in doing so.

Pastor Martin started with Jesus in the garden of Gethsemane, took us to Joseph in Potiphar's house, then led us all the way up to today and the many temptations we faced on a daily basis.

I had to admit that temptations were everywhere. I mean, it was hard for a sista to avoid them. Everywhere you looked, there was sin: on television, on the radio, on the Internet, and even in your face. I didn't know how many times I had been propositioned with something immoral by people who just didn't know me, or who used to know me and didn't realize I'd changed. That was why I had to separate myself from that old crowd. Old things passed away. I clapped because, as usual, Pastor Martin was preaching his heart out. I wondered if my brother-in-law, Joshua, was preaching just as hard on the other side of town.

The service ended, and as we were leaving, we ran into busybody Sister Winifred and her man-snatching niece, Yvonne. Sister Winifred was wearing a big peach-colored hat with a peach and white flowered dress and carried a big white purse. Her shoes were white patent leather, and they had a huge buckle on the front of them.

"Hello, dear." Sister Winifred put her bony hand on my shoulder. "It's good to see you're still coming to church."

"We all need Jesus, Sister Winifred," I said.

"Yes, dear, but some of us need Him more than others." Sister Winifred pushed her thick glasses up on her nose. "Your mother would've been so proud. She prayed for years, while you were out there doing your own thing, that you would come back to the house of the Lord."

I had to pray that the Holy Spirit would hold my tongue. "Yeah, well, I'm back now," I said.

"For good, I hope." Sister Winifred picked up her cane and walked away.

Why did I let that woman get to me?

Yvonne, who was wearing a skintight jumpsuit, was facing the other way the whole time and acted as if she didn't see me, and I was glad not to have to go through the motions. I knew she knew better than to try that man-stealing stuff she'd tried with my sister on me. When it came to another woman trying to seduce my husband, I wasn't *that* saved. Judging by her evil glare, I was sure Yvonne sensed that.

My family came right up behind me, and I heard Keith introducing Paul to Sister Winifred and Yvonne.

"It's my pleasure to meet you, sweetheart." That was the last thing I heard Paul say as I exited the sanctuary. I had to get through the lobby and out the front door before I gagged.

Later on at home I ordered Chinese takeout for dinner. The three of us sat around the table, eating quietly. There was no laughter. There was no reminiscing.

I turned to face Paul. "So, Paul, what kind of real estate were you involved in again?"

"Excuse me," Paul said, biting an egg roll.

"I see." I wanted to pick his brain, to find out what made him tick. "Were you a broker or an agent?"

Paul sighed. "I was a broker. I also owned a couple of properties. When the real estate market started drying up, you know . . ."

"Yes, I know." I continued to eat my chicken fried rice. "A real shame, this recession."

"Sure is," Keith chimed in.

Paul sneered. "It's a nightmare."

I had questions that I wanted answered. "So you know a lot about properties?"

"Yes, I do," Paul said.

I spoke sincerely, looking Paul straight in the eyes. "Good, because maybe in a couple of years Keith and I may be ready to buy our own home."

Keith chuckled. "My wife is always ready to jump into something."

"It would be a good investment, especially the way interest rates are low right now," Paul said with a serious face.

"Right. My sister and her husband recently purchased a foreclosed property, a three-story building," I said.

"Hmm. Interesting." Paul nodded.

"Yes, they were able to move in, renovate it, of course, rent out two small apartments, and they still have room for their church." I still admired them for that move.

"Good for them," Paul said, looking uncomfortable.

"I mean, it still needs a lot of work, and they've been doing a lot of the renovations themselves, but I figure it's still a good investment. Living, ministry, and rental income all in one shot," I said.

"That's pretty good." Paul nodded. "Unfortunately, it doesn't always end up that way, but it sounds like your sister and her husband made a sound decision."

I reached for my glass of cranberry juice. "That's what I say."

Paul started rubbing his hands together. "How much are you and Keith working with?"

"Well, not much right now, but we're working on it," I said.

"There are a few things we need to pay off before we take on the responsibility of a house," Keith said, giving me the "Be quiet" signal.

Paul's eyes started shifting back and forth. "Oh, I don't know. The lady may just be right. I might be able to help you all find something very affordable if you've got the money."

"Like I said, we're still working on the down payment," Keith said, without a smile.

"Yeah, I was just asking," I said, trying to reverse what I'd started.

"Come on now. I know Keith here ain't broke. Strike while the iron is hot, my brother," Paul said. "Hook a brother up."

I could see the wicked wheels of greed turning inside Paul's head, and I knew then what his motivation was. He didn't care whether or not we moved into a house or lived on the nearest street corner. It was money. In order to get him interested in anything, he had to have money. So I shook my head and filed this piece of information away in my brain for later use.

Paul played with the hairs on his chin. "So when do we start looking for your dream house?"

For the first time Keith seemed to be annoyed with Paul. "Not now, man."

"You know I could sure use that commission." Paul's eyes appeared to be dilated.

"I said *not now*." Keith got up and walked away.

Since I'd never seen my husband react like that before, I wondered what that was all about.

Chapter Seven

Keith

Keith didn't know whether he was coming or going lately. The conflict between his beautiful new bride and his long-lost friend proved to be a constant challenge. It was always Paul this or Paul that. Even during the private times with his wife, he found himself analyzing or defending Paul and his actions. Paul had lived with them for two months now, and there was never any peace anymore. Taylor seemed to notice and question everything. It was how she was.

Never satisfied. Then there was Paul's incessant need to sell them a property they could not yet afford, which added to the already mounting pressure between the three of them.

Keith knew living with Taylor was going to be exciting, but he didn't count on it being like this. When he first met her, he was taken aback by her straightforwardness and her abrasive personality, but those seemed to fit him. She was cute and sassy, with a well-built body and a killer personality, yet Keith sensed that there was a vulnerability hidden behind her scowl. Sure enough, he and Taylor became friends and confidants. He smiled as he remembered Taylor's attempt to string him along until she could *walk* down the aisle, before finally marrying him in an intimate church ceremony. He knew his wife was stubborn and sometimes tough, but he also knew he could handle it, because he too was tough.

He was from the streets. In fact, Taylor didn't even know just how much from the streets he was. Sure, Taylor knew that his mother had left him when he was just four years old, and that his father had raised him and his brother as a single father on the mean streets of Chicago, but what she didn't know was that his father had been an alcoholic. And that his father's lifestyle had left Keith and his younger brother scrambling on the streets more than once, trying to fend for themselves. Still, he didn't want her pity, just some understanding. He wanted her to lay off of his friend Paul, the one who had saved his life on more than one occasion, the one who knew him and the secret he was hiding.

Dysfunctional was what he called his family. Keith looked at a family picture of the three of them and missed his father and his brother, Robert. His father had been dead for some time now, and he hadn't seen Robert since his father's funeral. Keith regretted that he couldn't reach him in time to invite him to be a part of his wedding, but the truth was that Keith had no idea where to even look for him. In the first few years after his father's death, Robert had been spotted here and there, always running with the wrong crowd, but in recent years no one had heard from him at all. It seemed as if he had disappeared off the face of the earth. Keith often wondered if his brother was even alive, that is, until Paul came on the scene.

Keith and Paul sat on the royal blue leather couch together. Paul used the remote to switch the channels on the flat-screen television set. It was Saturday, and Joshua was babysitting the children so Alex and Taylor could go shopping together. That was one of Taylor's favorite pastimes, and Keith knew that his wife wouldn't be home anytime soon. The conversation up until this point had been very discouraging, and Keith sat with his head in his hands.

"Tell me again how he looked," Keith said without lifting his head.

"I ain't sure it was him, but there's a good chance." Paul put the remote down and lit a cigarette.

"That's good enough for me." Keith waved away the smoke. "Hey, man, put that out, or you'll have the whole place smelling like smoke. My wife will kill me."

"All right, all right." Paul put out the cigarette. "Didn't you say your wife used to smoke?"

"Yeah, she *used to,* as in that life is over," Keith said.

Paul shrugged his shoulders, as if he was confused. "Okay, okay. I get it, Mr. Church Boy."

"Don't make fun of my faith, man," Keith said in his most serious voice.

Paul put both his hands up. "I'm sorry. Sorry."

Keith began to nod his head. "I've got to find him. I can't just leave him out there."

"That was months ago, Keith. He could be in Timbuktu by now for all we know."

"Then I'll have to look in Timbuktu, but for now I've got an image of him still living under some bridge in Chicago."

The image of his brother being strung out on drugs, homeless, and living a pitiful life turned Keith's stomach. Although Keith felt that it was inevitable for his brother to suffer the plague of addiction, he still didn't think that it was fair.

How could his brother not become addicted after watching his father's own addiction to alcohol day after day, year in and year out?

Keith didn't know what to think about Robert's issues, how he had gotten into them, and how he was going to get out of them. He felt guilty about leaving his brother in order to pursue his education. He could have stayed at home, gone to a local college, and fought for his life. Instead, Keith chose to leave his family behind, embrace his scholarship, and fight for his dreams. But the dream had now become a nightmare, and Keith was becoming desperate.

"I don't know, dude. But if that was him, he's got to be sick, man." Paul shook his head.

"Probably strung out." Keith didn't like what he was hearing, but he knew he had to hear it.

"Yeah, the guy I saw was very thin, and when I called out the name Robert, he ran."

"Why would he run?"

"I don't know." Paul picked up a handful of peanuts from his bowl. "Maybe it was someone else."

"Maybe," Keith said.

Paul took a sip from his glass. "It was too dark, so I couldn't see very well."

"I know it might not be him, but I've got to try to get to him." Keith swallowed hard.

Paul put his hand up. "Keith, man, you can't go messing up your life for some crackhead."

"Hey, that crackhead is my brother. I've got to find him," Keith snapped.

"Man, please." Paul put his feet on the center table. "That's gonna be impossible."

Keith picked up his Bible from the center table. "It can't be impossible. All things are possible for those who believe."

"Oh, not that religious stuff again," Paul scoffed.

"It's not just religion. It's the truth," Keith said. "And get your feet off my table."

Paul sneered and shook his head as he removed his feet from the center table. "All right, whatever."

"I feel like it's my fault he's out there. I should've protected him." Keith put his hand up to his forehead, overcome with emotions.

"How? How is that your fault?" Paul drank from his glass again.

"I shouldn't have gone away to college and left him," Keith said.

"Man, you went to college to save your own life." Paul burped aloud.

"Yeah, I did, but at his expense," Keith said, looking downward.

"You're only a year apart in age."

"So?"

"So, you couldn't take care of him. He had to hold his own, like you did," Paul said.

"Yeah, but we used to take care of each other." Keith let out a long breath. "He used to depend on me. . . ."

Keith's mind began to wander back to the time of his youth. He remembered wrestling on the bedroom floor with his brother. He recalled laughing in front of the television with his brother. He even pictured racing home from school with his brother. Finally, he remembered his father's funeral, which was the last time he saw his brother.

Keith sat in the front of the church with his eyes closed. He was in shock, hardly believing his fifty-five-year-old father was gone. His mother was not there, because no one knew how to get in touch with her. There was no guarantee she would have come even if they had. The last time his dad had heard from her, she said she was waiting tables, but she wouldn't say where. Robert sat beside Keith, with bloodshot eyes since he had been crying all night. His aunt Rita sat next to Robert, trying to hold his hand. She had offered Robert the opportunity to stay with her for a while, but he had refused. He sat quietly in his Sunday best suit but refused to go with anyone.

Aunt Rita was their father's only sister, a plump, jovial lady who waved her hand and said "Amen" to almost everything the preacher said. Keith didn't know her too well, because she had rarely made herself available to them while their father was alive. Keith remembered that his father had usually run her away with his bad attitude. He wasn't sure why his father had never wanted their aunt around.

All Keith knew was that his father was gone, his only caregiver and, undoubtedly, his hero. He and Robert had watched their father slip silently into depression after years of struggling to find a job and to keep his identity. No one wanted a washed-up, middle-aged veteran who was both long-winded and short on modern-day skills. No one wanted to give him a chance, especially after he started to drink. Keith wasn't sure when his father had started the habit, but he couldn't remember a time when his father wasn't drinking. Now his father's chances were all gone, and all Keith wanted to do was sneak away and drink, to feel the only source of happiness he knew, the one he and his father had in common. He wanted to take up where his father had left off with a bottle of Jack Daniel's and a dream.

Paul interrupted Keith's thoughts of the past. "I know but—"

"I shouldn't have left him, that's all." Keith took the bottle of rum from Paul's hand and began to pour it into his glass. "You can't watch somebody drinking their life away day after day, year after year, and not be affected by it. I should've stayed."

Paul snickered. "Man, are you sure you want to drink that?"

The words made Keith think about his life and his commitments, both to his wife and to God. Then he remembered his commitment to his brother, and how he'd broken his promise to look out for him. The sting of regret filled his nostrils as he took a deep breath. "I've never wanted anything more," Keith said, drinking down the rum. *Lord, have mercy on my soul.*

Immediately after he was done drinking, he felt awful, but there was no turning back. He had already broken a vow—many, in fact. He wanted to repent, but he just didn't have it in him. He felt like he'd be a hypocrite if he did, especially since he'd enjoyed the drink. He didn't want to stop the feeling it gave him, even though he knew he should.

By the time Taylor came home, he had dried the tears, gargled, and freshened up his clothes. He couldn't let his wife smell alcohol on his breath. She wouldn't understand, and she'd make a big deal of it. But he knew what he was doing; he knew how to stop when he was ready.

He just needed a little something to numb him until he could get to his brother. Today he just needed something to make him forget. God would have to forgive him tomorrow.

Chapter Eight

It was raining hard this July morning, with big translucent raindrops landing on the hot gray concrete as the thunder roared and the lightning flashed, but thunderstorms never did bother me. Not even as a child. I used to be the wild one, jumping into puddles and dancing in the spray, at least until Mama started hollering and dragged me back inside the house, saying, "You're gonna get yo'self electrocuted, gal." Nevertheless, I continued to like storms, and this day was no different. They reminded me of me, loud and unpredictable. I stood back from my office window, watching nature pour onto the windowpane. My only concern as a business owner, though, was that my clients would be intimidated by the rain. As far as I was concerned, there was no excuse not to exercise, not to "push it."

The phone rang.

I answered it, and it was Keith. "Hi."

"Hi, babe. There is a storm out here in Manhattan, and I was calling to see if it had gotten to Brooklyn yet."

"Yep," I said.

"I've been thinking about you."

I started to smile. "Oh, what have you been thinking?"

Keith's voice was rich and smooth. "I'll tell you later."

I teased, "You're just going to tell me?"

Keith laughed. "I'll show you later."

"That's better," I said in a sultry voice.

"Unfortunately, my two-minute break is over." Keith sighed. "I've gotta get back to my patients."

"What about me?"

"I'll take care of you when I get home," Keith answered in a quiet, playful tone. I could tell that he was trying his best not to be overheard by his colleagues.

"Promise?"

"Promise," Keith said in the same tone.

"Good. See you then." I could almost jump out of my own skin with the anticipation of his touch. I loved to hear his voice any time of day, but most especially on a day that hadn't been going so well.

I put the phone down and rolled into the main room just as Paul came sloshing through the front door, soaking wet and wearing this ridiculous outfit. He wore a raincoat, a yellow rain hat, and matching rubber rain boots. Though a grown man, he looked like he was ready for a day at preschool.

I laughed aloud before I could stop myself.

Paul looked around, as if he wasn't sure he was the joke. "Is something funny?"

"I'm sorry. It's just that me and my sister used to have a getup like that back in kindergarten."

"Oh? Okay." Paul squinted his already beady eyes.

I stopped snickering. "I'm sorry."

"It's okay." Paul put his hands up in mock surrender. "My ex-wife hated this outfit too."

For a moment I felt sorry for him. "Really?"

"Maybe I should get rid of it." Paul began to take off the raincoat.

"No, it's okay, really," I said. "I mean, if you like it, there is no need to stop wearing it on my account. I just call myself a fashionista, that's all."

"You do?"

"Yeah, I do." Was he slow or something? Couldn't everyone see that in me?

"Maybe you could help me pick out some new things when I get on my feet."

"Sure, just let me know when you're ready to go shopping, and I'm there." I snickered.

"I'm sure I can help out."

Jasmine walked over to where we were standing. "If you don't mind me jumping in your conversation, she's the best."

I took another look at him and knew he would probably need more help than even I could give. As I was contemplating the magnitude of a makeover project for Paul, I caught a glimpse of a car out of the side window.

I pulled the blinds wide open. "Did you see that?"

Paul barely blinked. "See what?"

I pressed my nose against the window, looked to my right and then to my left. "A fancy sports car stopped right here and then just sped away."

"So? No big deal." Paul hunched his shoulders.

"I don't know," I said, pondering the sighting.

Paul took a deep breath, as if he had to brace himself for the foolish ranting and raving of a woman. "What kind of sports car was it?"

"A Lamborghini," I said. "I'm pretty sure."

Paul seemed curious. "You know your cars, then?"

"Yep, I do," I said. "That's one of the only things my dad taught me about when he was around—cars. He loves 'em."

Jasmine rolled her eyes and snapped her fingers. "A Lamborghini? In this neighborhood?"

"Exactly." I slapped my hands together.

"Nah," Paul said.

"No way," Jasmine concurred.

"I know what I saw. It just sped away." I rolled over to the door and peered through the front glass, checking for anything suspicious I could see from another angle.

Jasmine put her hand on my shoulder. "Are you okay, boss?"

"Yeah, but I know what I saw," I said.

Paul shook his head. "Maybe it was nothing."

"Maybe," I agreed, but in my heart I knew it was Elaina.

I hadn't seen her since the last inspection, but now she was driving by again. Was she checking up on Push It, making sure nothing was out of the ordinary, or was there more to it than that?

On Saturday I decided to take Keith up on his suggestion that I do my workout in the pool. He had been hounding me about increasing the intensity of my routines. Like I said before, I had been avoiding the pool for a while, but I thought that maybe Keith was right about me giving it another try. He was always an encourager. That was how he got me to believe in my recovery in the first place. It was his kind, soft-spoken words. They were so different from my own abrasive ones. So different from my family's judgmental ones. I had latched onto his world and had been holding on ever since.

"Let's go, babe," Keith said, snapping a towel at my bottom.

"I'm ready," I said, clutching my walker with all my might.

"I think it's time we left this at home." Keith snatched the walker away from me, and I stumbled forward but didn't fall. "Let's do this."

I wasn't prepared for that. "Keith." I cringed.

"What?" Keith ushered me out into the hallway and into the elevator without saying another word.

It was clear that he'd been thinking about my slackness. I knew I hadn't been paying as much attention as I should to my own physical therapy lately, but I hadn't noticed that it was bothering him. I'd let long hours at work and probably a bout with mild depression over my condition make me lose my focus. I used to be radical about my workouts. Now I was just radical.

The ride to the gym was quiet. We listened to an inspirational jazz CD the whole time. Keith bobbed his head to the music, and I snapped my fingers. Before we knew it, we were parking in front of Push It. Jasmine had already opened for us this morning, so we didn't have to rush through our usual morning routine. Instead, we greeted everybody and went straight back to the pool room. I pulled off my wrap skirt and was ready for action, and Keith went into the locker room to get ready.

Jacque, who sat perched in his spot, hollered, "Morning, Mr. and Mrs. Bryant."

"Morning, Jacque," I said, waving up to him.

The water looked blue and inviting, and there was only one other couple in the pool at the time. They were a couple of gray-haired senior citizens who didn't look a day under seventy, so I knew they wouldn't be paying me any attention. Besides, they were busy doing laps at the deep end of the pool. It was a perfect opportunity to get my workout in and to get over my depression about not being able to swim anymore. I took off my braces, dropped my towel, and slowly slipped into the shallow end of the pool. At first the water felt cool against my skin, but after a few minutes it began to feel good. Then suddenly I saw the couple climb out of the water, screaming and yelling all kinds of obscenities.

"What's wrong?" I yelled out to them.

"You tell us what's wrong with this dirty water," the woman said, pulling at her bathing suit with a look of disgust.

Her husband was making outrageous threats about lawsuits as I attempted to lift myself out of the pool.

"What's going on here?" Keith asked as he walked in on the scene.

"I'm not sure," I said, shaking my head.

Keith helped me out of the pool and went over to talk to the couple. Jacque came down to see what all the commotion was about.

By this time the couple were red all over, itching and scratching like they had the chicken pox.

"We were fine, sir, until we got into that pool," the woman said to Keith.

"Now look at us. This is an outrage," her husband said.

"Please, ma'am, we'll get to the bottom of this if you'll just calm down." Keith spoke calmly, trying to connect with the couple, but it was useless.

The woman spat out, "Calm down? Are you kidding me?"

"We should sue you for this negligence. There's no telling what's wrong with that pool," the man yelled.

Keith shook his head. "I assure you, sir, that—"

"We don't believe anything you say," the woman said, clutching her towel against her skin, which was becoming redder by the second.

Worse yet, a rash had started to form all over my beautiful brown skin. I covered myself quickly with my towel.

Unfortunately, it was a couple who had been members of Push It for only a few months.

They hadn't been here long enough to get a sense of our personal style and long-term dedication to our clients. They were new to the business, old in age, and they were angry.

"What kind of establishment are you running here, anyway?" the man asked Keith as he walked them to the locker rooms, apologizing and promising to get to the bottom of the situation.

They left itching and scratching, complaining of burning. And I knew exactly what they were feeling because, thanks to my husband, who had convinced me to get in the pool, I was feeling it too. Why in the world did I ever listen to that husband of mine? Physical therapists always thought they knew everything, especially when that physical therapist was my husband.

When I came out of the shower and had taken Benadryl and put hydrocortisone on my raw skin, I confronted my husband in the pool room. "It was Paul."

"What was Paul?"

"This was Paul's fault." I pointed to the pool.

"Oh, come on. Do you expect me to believe that?"

I gave him the *duh* look. "Yes, he's the only one messing around the pool."

"Because you told him to," Keith said.

"Exactly," I said.

"Exactly what?" Keith shook his head in doubt. "We don't even know what happened here."

"No, we don't know, but I'm willing to bet that whatever it is, your buddy Paul is behind it." I poked my neck out to make my point.

"That's not right, Taylor," Keith said.

I could see the veins popping out in Keith's neck.

"That's how I feel," I said. "For two and a half months I've felt this way."

"What do you have against Paul, anyway?" Keith turned his back on me. "You're always giving him such a hard time."

"Well, I'm sorry. He just rubs me the wrong way. I've really tried, but there is just something about him that I just don't like. He seems sneaky."

Keith closed his eyes, as if he were picturing what I was saying. "Oh, so he seems sneaky and that's why this pool incident is his fault?"

"No, it's his fault because I put him in charge of the pool, and he was here yesterday evening. He was the last person, besides Jacque, to have access to the pool."

Keith bit his bottom lip. "Okay, but why? Why would he do that?"

"I don't know. To sabotage us maybe," I said.

"Again I say, why would he do that when he's living with us? We're helping him."

"I don't know. Maybe he's jealous because of all you have, when he has nothing."

Keith turned to face me. "Paul is a good guy."

I cornered my husband. "Really? You've said that before. But tell me one good thing about him."

"I don't have time for this now," Keith said, walking away.

"Oh, I didn't think so. If he's so good, what's the big secret? What's so good about him?"

I taunted. "Why can't you tell me anything *good* about him?"

Before the end of the day the board of health came down to the center, taking samples of the pool water. They checked the pool's circulation and filtration system, the water's chemistry, and its disinfectant levels and pH levels. They also checked that we had a current permit, that our operator training documentation was posted, that our pool log was maintained, and that the approved water test kit was used. There was a lot on the line.

The inspector was a roundish man with a wiry-looking brown beard. "If we determine that the pH was not consistently maintained within the required limits, then positive feed equipment would have to be used to maintain the pH."

"All this because of one couple's rash," I said.

Keith nudged me with his elbow.

"You will post this placard conspicuously by all entrances to the pool," the health inspector instructed.

"Yes, sir," Keith said.

The health inspector continued. "Within fifteen days you will have a hearing with either a permit-issuing official or a hearing officer, where you will have an opportunity to prove that the pool is no longer a hazard to public safety. Until then the pool remains closed."

I spoke under my breath. "Fifteen days, huh?"

The health inspector spoke quickly. "If you fail to adhere to these regulations, this entire facility may be shut down."

The seriousness of his words stung my heart. "Yes, sir. Thank you."

"Good day and good luck, Mr. and Mrs. Bryant." The health inspector left the pool area, with Keith and me following him.

Keith went to fill Jasmine and Sharon in on what had happened. They were standing in the middle of the floor, with their mouths hanging open. Before I could recuperate, I noticed that there was a news truck outside. I met the reporter from our local news station at the front door and stood in the doorway, blocking her and her cameraperson from coming inside.

"Mrs. Dawson, can you tell us what's in your pool that's making all your customers sick?" the reporter asked and then stuck her microphone in my face. The camera was rolling.

"Ma'am, with all due respect, it was only one couple who developed a rash. I really wouldn't say *all,* and I wouldn't really say *sick,* either. We are looking for answers, though, if it's our fault at all."

The reporter tilted her head to the side. "If?"

"Yes, *if,*" I said.

"You sound uncertain, yet this all occurred at your facility. The Push It Fitness Center is your facility, isn't it?" The reporter shoved the microphone in my face again.

"Yes, it is mine and my husband's, but that doesn't mean that the Push It Fitness Center has done anything wrong." I grabbed the microphone from her hand and spoke directly into it.

"Maybe, just maybe, someone has done something wrong to us."

The reporter took the microphone back. "So you won't be closing down, then?"

"Closing down?" I blew out a long breath. "The devil is a liar!" I pushed the camera out of my face. "No more questions, please."

Keith came out just in time to close the door on them.

I couldn't believe we had given the couple a free membership for a year and had offered to pay their medical expenses, yet those ingrates had still called the board of health and the media on us.

Keith raised his eyebrows and twisted his lips. "Why did you open the door for them?"

"I don't know. I wanted to give our side of the story." I was so flustered.

Keith let out a deep breath. "Not now, babe. We'll have our chance, but not like that."

"You're right. They don't want to hear the truth. They just want a hot story." I pushed back the tears that were burning my eyelids.

"For now, stay away from those cameras." Keith held me by the shoulders. "They're trouble."

"Keith, we've got to talk about some other trouble," I said, alluding to Paul's possible involvement.

"Unfortunately, I've got all the trouble I can deal with right now. You'll have to catch me later."

Then he was gone. I didn't even know where he went, but he left the building. I spent the rest of the day trying to do damage control from the front desk. There was no way Jasmine could handle all the negative phone calls and visits after this pool scare. I spent the next few hours assuring and reassuring everyone that we were still a responsible company, that the condition of the pool would be taken care of immediately, and that everything would be back to normal in a few days. Sadly, I didn't even know what normal was anymore.

Lingering in my heart was the notion that this was all because of Paul Meyers. We had escaped one mess with the licensing department only a few weeks ago, and now we were in another mess. Since clients were asking to cancel their memberships, we were forced to give out three-month freebies, which we couldn't afford. The phone wouldn't stop ringing. Both the staff and the remaining clients appeared anxious. Everything was falling apart.

The phone rang again, and Jasmine answered it. I'd had enough business for one day, so I hoped it was Keith or my sister. Instead it was Elaina Dawson.

Chapter Nine

I took the phone when I heard Elaina's voice.

"I received a report from the board of health that there was major contamination of your pool. Is this true?"

"Yes, Ms. Dawson," I whispered. "May I help you?"

"I just wanted you to know that my office has taken note of this health code violation and that even if this is resolved, this may weigh heavily against you when it's time to renew your business license."

I felt so vulnerable and unprepared. Although I wanted to slam the phone down in her ears, I resisted the urge. "Is that all?"

"That's all," Elaina said.

"Have a good one." I hung the phone up gently.

I knew that the situation was nothing for Almighty God to take care of, so I needed some true prayer warriors on the case. I took out my smart phone and called my sister. If anyone could get a prayer through, it was Alex.

"Hello," Alex said in her normally cheerful voice.

I whispered into the phone. "I need you to pray for us, Alex."

Alex's tone changed right away. "What's wrong?"

"Spiritual warfare, that's what's wrong." My voice got stronger as I spoke.

"What? Could you be a little more specific?"

"Two of our clients got a rash from the pool today," I said, waiting for Alex's response.

"Oh, no," Alex said.

"Oh yes, and, personally, I think it's sabotage."

"Okay . . ." Alex paused.

I continued," I think Paul did it."

"Did what?"

"Aren't you listening? I think Paul did something to jeopardize the balance of chemicals in the pool."

"Okay, I know you don't care for the guy, but he's Keith's friend, so why would he do a thing like that?"

"I don't know, but he was in charge of the pool. The only other person who had any access would be Jacque. And he has been with us for almost a year. Everything was fine until Paul came on the scene." I closed my eyes in anger. The old me would have already smashed a couple of things by now. "So now we've got the board of health, licensing, and the local news on us."

Alex sighed. "I'm so sorry. I know you and Keith have been working so hard at Push It."

"Well, now we'll be working even harder to keep it. I just need you and Joshua to pray for us as we pray for ourselves," I said.

"You've got it, Tay." Alex raised her voice. "Remember, the effectual fervent prayers of the righteous availeth much."

"I know," I said, sounding almost defeated.

"We're still on for dinner tonight, right?"

"I don't know."

"Oh, come on. You'll feel better if you get out for a little while. Staying at home, pining away, isn't going to help," Alex urged.

"That's true." I sighed. "Okay, I'll see you later, then."

"I'll call you later with the details," Alex said.

"Thanks," I said, but I was heartbroken.

The local publicity was nothing to be proud of. Although it was just one news story, talk of it seemed to spread like wildfire throughout the neighborhood. We certainly couldn't afford any more negative publicity. The business had been struggling to stay afloat as it was. No one ever told me that running a business would be so hard, especially one that I loved so much.

Fitness was my passion. I loved everything about it, from nutrition to the body, personal training, the feel and handling of the equipment, everything. Call me crazy, but I even loved the smell of sweat when clients were working out. It was a reminder that everything was working as it should be. With the threat of being closed down looming over my head, I could hardly enjoy what God had blessed me with. My vision was clouded, and my heart was heavy. *Lord, please order my steps.*

That evening Keith, Alex, Joshua, and I met for dinner at the Olea Mediterranean Taverna on Lafayette Avenue. It was kind of like the old days, when Alex and I were just two giggling girls together all the time, getting on each other's nerves half the time. Funny thing about twins was that either you were tight and all right or you were at each other's throats. There was no in-between. As for our relationship, we were always a hot mess.

Even now that I was saved and sanctified, there were still things about my sister that I just didn't agree with, like the way she insisted on wearing a dress every Sunday morning, no matter how dull it was. At least that was how she dressed when we were attending the same church. Not that her dresses were too long or out of date, but I felt that a pantsuit might suit her better sometimes. She'd never hear of it, though, especially not since she married Reverend Joshua Benning.

Today her outfit held a little more promise. She wore a jazzy little black dress with rhinestones down the back and long, slinky silver earrings. Her husband, though, was another story altogether. He looked stiff in his traditional dark brown suit and basic plaid tie. Keith, on the other hand, who was wearing a slightly more contemporary plum suit, had already taken off his suit jacket and had loosened his collar. I, of course, wore a gorgeous gold-colored dress with a seashell print and matching gold flats. No, I couldn't wear stilettos anymore, because of my condition, but I still did the best I could.

The men immediately slapped hands and bumped fists. Alex and I gave hugs all around before getting settled.

"It has been a while. . . . What have you been up to, man?" Keith asked, slapping Joshua on the back.

"Yeah, you know how it is. The church, the kids . . . just busy." Joshua smiled. "I hear you and Taylor have been having a little trouble with the business."

"We've hit a few rough spots with inspection matters, but it will all be taken care of shortly," Keith said with an air of confidence.

Joshua looked Keith directly in the eyes. "Something about the pool being contaminated?"

"Just an issue with the chemical balance of the water." Keith looked directly back at Joshua, like he didn't want Joshua in his business.

"Oh, okay. Well, it sounds like you guys have got it all under control, then," Joshua responded.

"God is good," Keith said.

"Yes, He is," Joshua agreed.

Joshua gently led the conversation. Keith was no ministerial student or anything, but he could certainly hold his own. Although Keith and Joshua were not close buddies or anything, they could always talk about that male thing that united men all over the planet—sports.

As for me and Alex, despite our differences, we could talk all night. Talk was what we had in common. Our voices were similar, except that hers was a softer, more annoying version of mine. Not that Alex couldn't get tough if she had to, but with her even temper, she very seldom had to. "That's your problem, Alex. You let people walk all over you," I'd say. I, on the other hand, had to be calmed down almost every day. We enjoyed each other's company, though, despite our differences. Now that I wasn't running from God, we actually got along pretty well. I was glad too, because being bad had taken a lot from me, and I couldn't get most of it back.

After we ordered our dinner, Alex and I slipped away to the ladies' room.

Alex wasted no time once we were clear of the men. "Well, enough about business, how is life as a married woman? How are you handling making compromises, considering that attitude of yours?"

"Keith is still praying about that," I answered.

"Humph," Alex said.

"A sista couldn't show all of her flaws before the wedding," I said as I stood at the sink washing my hands.

"Girl . . ."

I shook my head back and forth wildly. "You should've seen his face when he first got a glimpse of me being ticked off."

Alex moved her finger around in my face, smiling. "You mean after you were married?

'Cause he met you when you were ticked off, remember?"

"Yeah, I mean after we were married." I giggled. "I think he probably regretted ever saying 'I do' that day."

"I bet he did." Alex chuckled.

"He said I was really something."

Alex leaned forward, hungry to hear the story. "And what did you say?"

"Well, I just told him, 'God ain't through with me yet,' and he said, 'God has got a whole lot of work left to do.'"

"Poor Keith," Alex said, washing her hands.

I pushed my braids out of my face. "What? He's okay."

Alex held the door open for me. "That mouth of yours, girl."

"I'm doing better," I said as we walked out of the restroom.

"I know that, but goodness, you're trifling."

I put my hand on one hip while balancing myself with my braces. "Trifling?"

On our way back to the table, we burst into laughter, which caught everyone's attention.

That was the way it usually was when an attractive pair of twins came on the scene, acting like they didn't have good sense.

By the time we sat back down at the table, the men were deep in conversation. Basketball was the topic, and whether or not LeBron James would make it to the play-offs. Keith actually preferred football, but basketball did come in a close second. Alex and I were happy that our husbands were getting along, since they hadn't had a lot of opportunities to get to know each other.

We'd come a long way from the days of Keith being just my overly zealous physical therapist and Joshua being my sister's uptight fiancé. Believe it or not, we were both married now and the days of romantic heartache were behind us. Given Mama and Dad's off-and-on relationship, I never imagined I'd even make it down the aisle.

"So tell me about this new houseguest of yours," Joshua said.

Alex looked at me for my reaction.

Keith answered without missing a beat. "Oh yeah, Paul is a good friend of mine from college."

"Cool." Joshua nodded his head with understanding.

"It's nice to have good people around," Keith said.

I cleared my throat. "Hmmm."

Joshua moved his fork around in the air as he tried to recall the college Keith attended. "You went to school in . . . ?"

"Michigan, Michigan State," Keith answered.

Joshua continued with his questioning. "But you're from Chicago, aren't you?"

"Yep, the South Side, born and bred," Keith answered.

Joshua looked at Keith with a serious face. "Pretty tough territory out there, isn't it?"

"Not all of it's tough. Some of it is actually pretty nice, with a lot of hardworking people that live there," Keith said.

Joshua stopped eating. "I didn't mean to offend—"

"No, I understand. It's the media. All they show are the mean streets," Keith explained.

Alex jumped in. "Yeah, that's true. They're really hard on the inner cities."

"Right. Look how they devour Brooklyn," I said.

"Interesting," Joshua said. "So this friend of yours is just visiting?"

Keith looked across at Joshua. "For now he is, yes. He's had a few rough breaks, and well . . . he might want to settle down here."

I looked up from my plate. That was bad news all around as far as I was concerned.

"Oh, I see," Joshua said.

"So, anyway, Paul has been helping us out at the gym," Keith said before taking a big bite of his chicken.

"Oh?" Joshua looked surprised.

I sucked my teeth. "Oh, he's been helping us out, all right."

Alex kicked me under the table to interrupt me.

"Hey, man, good friends are hard to find." Joshua nodded.

Keith looked at me as if he were laying down the law. "That's true, but actually, Paul is more like a brother."

And that was what scared me the most.

Chapter Ten

"It's just not fair," I said, slamming the newspaper down onto the counter.

Keith sat with his elbows on top of the chrome and glass table. "What isn't?"

"As if getting a citation from the board of health wasn't bad enough, we had to be in the news too."

"I know." Keith reached out for my hand. "Don't worry."

Easy for you to say. You've still got your day job, I thought.

Although I wasn't in the best mood, I was glad we had the apartment to ourselves for a change. Paul had left the night before and had not yet returned. I could only imagine what scandalous escapades he was involved in. Though he had not bothered to call, I was totally content in his absence.

It was Sunday morning, and the July sun shone brightly against the cyan painted walls of my fully equipped kitchen, creating the perfect balance of light. If I were a cook, my kitchen would be a dream come true with all its stainless-steel electric appliances. It had grayish modern cabinetry, matching gray marble countertops, and ceramic floor tiles. I had added my own red accents to make it my own, yet these were merely for the purpose of style, not for function. Since cooking wasn't my thing, I had little interest in the kitchen, except for eating and occasionally passing through.

"Imagine an old couple getting a rash that could've been caused by anything and then stirring up so much trouble," I said, taking a Golden Delicious apple from a fruit bowl and biting down into it.

Keith shook his head. "I know."

"I just don't know," I said.

Keith didn't look up from his health magazine. "It's okay."

"No, it's not okay," I replied, pouting.

Keith finally looked up. "Well, we've been praying about the situation, but what else can we do to counteract all of this negative publicity?"

"I don't know. Seems like every time we start going forward . . . bam . . . there's a problem," I said, sulking.

"Yeah, I know it seems like that, but it's just a trial." Keith squeezed my hand and smiled. "This, too, shall pass."

I leaned forward so I'd be closer to Keith. "I know, but it's rough going through this mess, especially feeling helpless."

"You're never helpless," Keith said, starting to read again.

Suddenly an idea came to mind. "Why don't we do a fitness challenge?"

"A fitness challenge?"

I could feel myself becoming full of excitement. "Yeah, we can map out the details later, but the bottom line is we get the whole community involved. Get people checked out and weighed in. Make the whole community know we care about their health and fitness."

"Okay, okay." Keith squinted his eyes as he pondered what I was saying.

"We'll get a few doctors to volunteer their time on the day that everything culminates, and we'll have just one big health fest—the Push It Fitness Center's Health Fest and Fitness Challenge." I grabbed a note pad and pen from my purse.

Keith started nodding his head. "All right, all right. I'm feeling ya."

"You can ask a couple of your physical therapist colleagues to pitch in. . . ."

"Yeah, I can do that," Keith said.

"And since the media wants to pry into our lives, let's get them involved too. We'll let them televise everything live, and we'll sell stuff, advertise, collect monies." I scrambled to write all of these ideas down.

Keith snapped his fingers and pointed toward me. "Yeah, and how about the proceeds go to charity?"

"Right, right." My ideas just kept flowing. "And maybe, just maybe, we might be able to get a celebrity endorsement."

"Now, that might be a stretch," Keith said.

I shook my head and poked out my lips. "Not for our God, it's not."

"True. True." Keith slapped me a high five. "We'll go for it."

I gave him a pound. "Now you're talking. Are you with me?"

Keith grabbed my hands and kissed my knuckles. "Yeah, I'm with you. What would I do without you?"

I laughed. "You'll never have to find out, now will ya?"

"Nope, not if I have anything to do with it," Keith said, looking at the plans we'd written down so far.

There was a time, not so long ago, that I doubted that we'd ever be together. I thought Keith was too good for me, because he wasn't like the men I usually dated. The ones who were scheming and conniving from day one. Keith was different. He was special, and I didn't want to burden him with my baggage. Thank goodness, I got over that real quick and in a hurry, or he'd be gone.

So I wasn't able to glide down the aisle like I'd dreamed about, but I did get down to my groom with the help of my braces and walker. I had to put all pride aside in order to answer the call to be his wife. I had to accept the fact that life wasn't predictable and I couldn't calculate or manipulate every detail in my future, but I knew I wanted Keith to be in my future.

I kissed his kissable lips.

"What was that for?"

"Just for being you." I got excited all over again. "I say we make this thing big. I'll get Alex and Joshua to help."

"Sounds good," Keith said.

I was on a roll now. "I'm sure Pastor Martin can put it in the announcements, and maybe he'll even throw it out over the pulpit. You never know," I said.

"You're right. You never know." Keith tapped on the table with his pen. "I think this will work to help everyone who participates and get our reputation cleaned up. So people can get to know what Push It is really all about."

I put my hands on my hips. "Yeah, and they need it, because people around here are way too big."

"Taylor," Keith said in his stern "Stop it now" voice.

I grinned. "I'm just sayin' . . ."

"Don't insult the people." Keith put his fist down on the coffee table. "That's not cool."

"Okay. I'll be *less* me."

"Good. Just a little *less* you," Keith said.

I brushed up against him. "Are you ashamed of me, Mr. Bryant?"

Keith just stood with his hands in his pockets, shaking his head. "No, but that mouth of yours can get us into trouble sometimes."

I picked up my note pad and hit him with it. "Say what?"

"Ow, that hurt." Keith rubbed his shoulder.

"There is more where that came from." I picked up my pen and started writing. "I need to start getting sponsors."

"There is so much to do and so little time," Keith said. "Wait! We haven't even set a date yet."

"Well, we can't wait too long, or it will lose its momentum. We've got the women's conference coming up soon, so I say we set the date for mid-September. Two months should be enough time." I was glad that would give me something to look forward to, since our lives had settled into something of a rut lately.

"Cool," Keith said, giving me a high five.

I waited to hear more. "That's it? Just cool?"

Keith looked at me like I was crazy. "Yep, it's cool."

"And?"

Keith looked puzzled. "And what?"

"I don't know." I sighed. "You're in charge, aren't you?"

"Since when? I thought you were in charge."
Keith reached over, grabbed me, and tickled me down to the floor.

"No, stop," I begged, giggling. "I surrender."

"I'll never stop," Keith said, smothering me with his kisses.

"We've got to get out of here, or we'll be late for church," I said, looking over his shoulder at the wall clock.

Keith and I rode out to Missionary Church. Sister Winifred and her scandalous niece Yvonne sat on the second row, right behind Sister Trudy and Aunt Dorothy. I didn't see my father in his usual spot toward the back. Maybe he was under the weather, I thought. The usual people were in the choir stand, and the clergy sat on the front row. As always, the service was lively, and the unhindered Word of God went forth from the pulpit, through the sanctuary, to the congregation. Pastor Martin certainly had a way of delivering a message. He preached about being grateful and about how God inhabited our praise, that our breakthrough was in our praise. Keith and I sang, danced, and shouted like never before, praising God for our many blessings, including each other and the fitness challenge idea. We believed it would be enough to save Push It's reputation, and we believed that the outcome with the board of health would be favorable.

Later that evening we sat on the thick blue carpet on our bedroom floor, working on the details for the fitness challenge. Keith used his expertise as a physical therapist, and I used mine as a physical trainer to put together the plans for our community to get physically fit. We were both in good physical shape, and together we made an awesome team. I often pondered what a better team we'd make if I could walk and bend and move like I used to. I used to be the best physical trainer in Brooklyn, priding myself on whipping people into shape, even the hardest of cases. That thought used to motivate me to work harder, but now it just made me sad.

I closed my eyes and remembered what it was like to use my body in a dynamic way, what it was like to jog around the block, swim across an Olympic-sized pool, or merely use the treadmill. I was always running and moving, even when I was little.

Mama used to complain that I couldn't stay still, that I wouldn't behave. The truth was that I liked motion. Staying still never interested me. So Mama let me join the junior high school track team and the cheerleading squad. Those activities channeled my energy for a while, until I started getting into trouble. By high school I had stuck only with cheerleading, because I could jump and leap and look a little cute at the same time, but it wasn't enough.

"Girl, slow yourself down," Mama would say, but I kept on moving. Even now I felt trapped with these braces and walker and hoped that one day I'd be free of them.

Keith looked over at me. "Are you okay?"

I was all choked up. "I was just thinking how good it would be to have my legs work again."

Keith stood up and grabbed my arm to help me up. "Let's do some exercises now."

"Keith, no, not now." I pulled my arm away from him.

"Why not?"

I was ashamed because I'd regressed. "Because I'm tired now. I just can't."

"Can't?" Keith looked puzzled.

"Yes, I'm actually drained."

Keith sat back down beside me. "Okay, but we'll do it tomorrow."

"All right," I said, not wanting to disappoint my husband again.

"Taylor?" Keith looked into my eyes.

I tried to avoid his gaze. "Yes?"

Keith ran his finger gently down my cheek. "You will walk again. I promise."

I just nodded, not having the courage to say anything more, and understanding that faith required me to agree with him.

"You will," he said, holding me in his arms.

I will, Lord.

Chapter Eleven

That next day could have been an ugly one, except that I refused to let it be. We met with our attorney to discuss the legal implications of our pool contamination case. Then we had our hearing with the hearing officer. The board of health had determined that our pool's chlorine levels were too high, and since we had automatic feeders, we had to prove that our feeders were functioning well. Thanks to our fast-talking attorney and the A1 mechanical report we received on the feeders, the board of health's investigation was dropped. The incident had been labeled a mystery, an isolated incident that might have been the result of human error and/or interference. They recommended that we question our staff thoroughly to eliminate the possibility of a repeat episode. They were going to do a follow-up in the next few weeks.

"Thank you, Jesus," I hollered as we left the building.

"Hallelujah," Keith said.

We slapped each other five and climbed into the truck, praising God for His grace and His mercy. Keith dropped me off at Push It, then went off to run a few errands.

Relieved about the reinstatement of our pool license and excited about our idea for the fitness challenge, I continued to make plans on Monday. I filled the staff in on the details, and I spent the remainder of the afternoon brainstorming and assigning tasks.

"Jasmine, I'm putting you in charge of publicity because you love being in the limelight." I hardly looked up from my clipboard.

Jasmine smiled. "Okay, publicity, got it."

"Sharon, your schedule fluctuates, so you can conduct the neighborhood surveys. That's something you can do anytime." I had to assign her the least important duties because she was so unreliable.

"All righty," Sharon said, sounding a little disappointed.

"Jacque, you'll pound the pavement, rallying up support from local businesses, because you're good looking, personable, and always dependable." I gave him a big grin that said I was pleased with his work. "Keith and I, of course, have the responsibility of using our fitness expertise to bring it all together and make sense of this whole project in two months." I looked at each of them and shook their hands. "Everyone has their roles, and this will be no easy undertaking, but I'm sure that with God's help, we can pull it off in time."

In the back of my mind, there was Elaina using her position to destroy me because of what I'd done to her, and there was Paul sneaking around for reasons that were still unknown to me, but destroying me just the same. "No weapon formed against me will prosper," I whispered to myself. I just knew that this event would bring Push It to its former glory and beyond, teaching all the haters not to mess with a child of God.

Keith picked me up as usual, and I couldn't wait to get in his truck. I always liked riding, but I especially loved riding with Keith; my tall chocolate-mocha man was laid back behind the wheel of his truck. There couldn't be a sexier sight than the way his highly defined biceps trembled as he drove. His body was an absolute masterpiece, and best of all, it was all mine.

Since Paul was supposed to have plans of his own for tonight, I was actually looking forward to spending some time alone with my husband.

We arrived home, parked, and took the elevator upstairs to our apartment. I heard the sound of the television before we turned the key in the door. I knew Paul wouldn't have crossed the line by bringing company into my home. Knowing Paul, however, I prepared myself for the worst.

When Keith flung the door open, my hopes were crushed. Paul sat alone on the couch, wearing an old, funky T-shirt and sweatpants, watching television, slurping down Pepsi and chomping on Doritos.

"Hi, Paul," I said with less enthusiasm than I'd have if I were getting a root canal.

"What's up? I thought you had a date," Keith said.

"Yeah, well, it didn't work out," Paul said, dipping a chip into a bowl of dip.

I became nauseated at the sight of his dirty-looking hands in the dip.

Humph, I said to myself. I could understand that.

Before I knew it, Keith was sitting next to a sad-sounding Paul, trying to console him, advise him. I gave up and retreated to the bedroom after eating some leftover veggie lasagna from the night before. I took a quick shower and then plopped down on my bed. Instead of having a quiet, romantic evening with my husband, I was left alone.

Frustrated with our living arrangements, I went to bed early but tossed and turned the whole night. Sometime around midnight, I heard Keith and Paul leave the house together. Soon after that I began to dream.

I was flipping upside down in a burning car. My legs were on fire.

"No, not my legs!" I screamed, but no one heard me.

The fire burned my legs to a crisp, until they were two charcoal-looking stumps. Then the car finally stopped spinning, and I fell out onto the street. When I looked up from the ground, Elaina and Paul stood over me, laughing.

I woke up shivering and covered in sweat. No fire had not consumed my legs like in the dream, but they were almost useless nonetheless. I sat on the edge of the bed. I felt Keith's arm reach around my waist, pulling me back, but I resisted.

"Good morning, beautiful," Keith said, stroking my hair.

"Good morning."

Keith sat up in bed. "What's wrong?"

I sighed. "Everything."

"Then let's bring everything to God this morning," Keith said in a comforting tone. "He'll know how to fix it."

Keith gave me a peck on the cheek and immediately plunged to his knees. He was always the first one to suggest prayer as a solution. He was my rock.

Keith reached for my hand. "Now, what exactly are we praying about?"

"The first days after the accident when I was paralyzed, I didn't know what would happen to me. I thought my life was over. Then, after a few weeks and then months, when I had gotten a little better, I thought that maybe my injury was temporary. I thought that maybe I would wake up one day and know it had all been just a bad dream, that I could still lunge and leap like before." Tears began to run down my face. "But after weeks and weeks, when that didn't happen for me . . . I . . . "

"I know." Keith tried to hold me.

I pushed him away. "No, you don't know. As understanding as you've been, you don't know."

"We'll get through this together." Keith dried my tears with his hands.

"I know that. It's just that I'm not used to having bad dreams, and I want them to stop."

"Don't give up, Taylor. Don't let your bad dreams drain your faith."

"My faith could use a recharge lately," I said, smiling.

Keith smiled. "Yours and mine both."

Keith held my hand as we prayed together.

Nothing had ever scared me as much as the thought of permanently losing my ability to walk. The only thing that had ever even come close to terrifying me that much was the thought of losing Mama.

She had been so sick and so weak. All the church folk surrounded her weekly, cooking for her and praying for her. The Lord knows I didn't believe in any of that stuff back then. I just stood on the sidelines, dumbfounded by this outpouring of what the saints called love. I didn't call it love, though. I thought it was phony and that it was only for show. All I could see was that her body was failing and falling away from life. Still, Mama was steady, talking about her Jesus even as her body turned cold and her eyes rolled to the back of her head. Death hadn't scared me before, but Mama's did.

Now I was faced with something similar, the fear of losing my legs, my mobility—the death of my dreams. I closed my eyes as I decided to fight for both.

Chapter Twelve

August finally came, bringing with it the sweltering Brooklyn heat. It was so hot, I could almost fry an egg on the sidewalk in front of my building. Children played happily in the spray of open fire hydrants and park sprinklers, while adults remained agitated by sweat. I couldn't wait to get up to Maine for Missionary's annual women's conference. I looked forward to the potentially milder temperatures. I'd heard about Maine's pleasant coastal breezes.

The day before the big event, I spent the whole day preparing for my trip. Alex took me shopping for a new traveling outfit during my lunch break. When I returned, I made all my phone calls pertaining to business. I made sure to give Jasmine, Sharon, and Jacque their last-minute instructions. I also gave a few instructions to my handsome business partner. I had never been away from the business for more than a day before. Although Keith had assured me that he could, I wasn't entirely convinced that he could handle things without me while I was gone. He wasn't around on a daily basis, so he didn't know Push It like I did. In any case, I needed to get away for a few days, away from the drama.

Alex and I rented a car to drive up to Bangor, Maine, for the women's conference. We left at five o' clock in the morning in order to get there in time. We didn't want to be bothered with the charter bus this year, especially with Sister Winifred being in charge of the trip. We were afraid she'd have us seated under the bus if she could. The drive started off pleasant enough, with us pulling away from my apartment, heading down toward eastern Long Island, and going over the Whitestone Bridge. Alex was a little nervous about being away from her baby overnight for the first time. She kept going on and on about how Joshua might forget to do this or that. Then she kept calling Joshua to check on the kids. I guess she forgot that Joshua was a single father long before she ever came on the scene. I'd say she was a nervous wreck if you'd asked me.

"Relax," I told her. "The kids are with their father. They'll be fine."

"I'm not sure if Joshua can handle it," Alex said as she picked up her cell phone to call once again.

"I think you're the one who can't handle it," I said, laughing along with her.

Alex always amazed me with her maternal instincts, and I wondered when in the world mine might kick in. She was a great mother, and since we were twins, I hoped that some of that might rub off on me when and if it was ever needed. She drove, while I looked over the map. Even though we had a GPS system in the car, I enjoyed looking at maps. With all those roads and highways, maps were like a way to escape for me. We rode onto the Hutchinson River Parkway toward New Haven, crossed into Connecticut, then merged onto the Massachusetts Turnpike somewhere between Hartford and Boston. We did all of this before passing through New Hampshire and finally crossing into Maine. We talked and we laughed more than we had in months, or at least since she became a mommy of three.

Since little Josh was born eight months ago, Lilah joined them when Alex married Joshua fifteen months ago, and Kiano just joined them a few weeks ago, it seemed like I hadn't seen my sister a lot. She balanced all these kids along with the full-time responsibility of being a first lady, building a new church with her husband, being a landlady to the two tenants she now had in their new building, and running a young wom-

en's ministry. All I could say was that my sister
had her hands full. It was a wonder we were able
to see each other at all, and it was because of this
that I didn't take this trip for granted.

It was an eight-hour trip to Maine, so with
a couple of rest stops in between, when we
arrived on Broad Street in Bangor, it was already
one-thirty. We were staying at the Charles Inn,
a local bed-and-breakfast, which was now the
first hotel in town to have an art gallery. It had
its own visitors' welcome center and was located
right in the center of downtown Bangor. There
were boutiques, restaurants, and museums all
within walking distance. I imagined that the
convenience of its location was why Sister Martin had chosen this particular place for us to
stay.

We hurried to the front desk to get checked in,
admiring the hotel's old European charm along
the way. I looked all around me, taking in the
scenery, but I must admit I was a little confused
about the whole gallery thing. I guessed art was
that important to some people. I did like the
particular pieces of art that lined my walls down
at the gym, but that was about the end of my
art appreciation. In any case, Missionary ladies
were everywhere, roaming the halls, claiming
this art gallery as their own. There were big hats,

big purses, and Bibles everywhere. Missionary was here, and everyone knew it.

Aunt Dorothy was possibly the loudest, not on purpose, but that was just how she was . . . friendly. She went around hugging people, giving out peppermints, and talking to everyone, whether they were with the conference or not. She just liked talking to people about the Lord, and before we knew it, she had invited a good portion of the hotel to our event. "Everybody needs an experience with Jesus," Aunt Dorothy said. No one could argue with that.

Once we were in our room, we took a few minutes to freshen up before we were on our way out the door. The service was being held at a place called the Spectacular Event Center. It was twelve thousand square feet of sophistication and elegance. There were three meeting rooms, separate dining areas, temperature-controlled ballrooms, and I figured all of that out just by reading the brochure. We followed the crowd into our designated meeting room and took a seat.

This year the guest speaker was Minister Mariah Baldwin. She was clearly in her fifties at least, with fair skin, light brown eyes, and medium-length dark brown hair. She was a medium-sized woman with thick legs and ankles, yet she wore very high heels. She wasn't graceful like last year's speaker, and she certainly didn't dance for her audience, but she did deliver a word from the Lord that had me thinking for days.

As always, Sister Martin came up to the microphone first, thanking everyone for coming and introducing herself as the MC for the day. Then she gave a brief introductory speech about the annual tradition of the women's conference and how it had blessed her life, as well as women all around the country. Sister Martin wore a long white beaded gown, and just as a first lady should, she looked very elegant. When she was done, two women from our choir came forward to sing a duet.

The next voice we heard was that of the guest speaker. "Good afternoon, ladies," she said. She took the platform slowly, easing her way up to the microphone. Dressed in an all-black two-piece ensemble with a string of pearls and matching earrings, she appeared to be very conservative. The audience listened intently, waiting to see what pearls of wisdom this year's speaker would unleash.

"Today I want to talk to you ladies about your enemies. Not the kind that come and rob your house or steal your car. Not those strangers. I'm talking about the kind you know, the kind that come in sneakily, chatting, smiling, and stabbing you in the back. Oh, you know the ones I'm talking about, like Delilah was Samson's enemy when she betrayed his love. Like King Saul was David's enemy when he offered David his unfamiliar armor to fight in so he could take all the credit. Like Jacob was Esau's enemy when he stole his birthright. Like Joseph's brothers were his enemies when they threw him into the pit, and like Judas was Jesus's enemy when he offered his life for thirty pieces of silver.

"You see, it's the people who you allow to come close to you. Not always the ones who are mere passersby, but the ones who live in your house and lay on your couch, sleep in your bed, are all up in your face, and eating up your food. Sometimes they're wolves in sheep's clothing."

The crowd went wild, clapping and shouting.

"Amen, sister," Alex said.

I must admit that she had my full attention.

I saw Alex waving both of her hands in the air as if she were going to take off.

"Hallelujah."

"Enemies, my sisters. They come to you one way, but God will have them flee from you many ways. They pretend to be your friends. They offer their hands in friendship, pretending to be helpful, pretending they don't want anything from you, or some of them pretend they're so needy, but all along they have ulterior motives. They're not pure in heart. They have jealous and wicked hearts. They want what you have, your money, your job, your husband, your business, your house, or your anointing. Yes, they're smiling in your face, but they want what you have. They don't want what God has for them. No. They're enemies to the Kingdom of God because God said, 'Touch not my anointed and do my prophets no harm.' They're out to get you one way or another."

The crowd was overwhelmed with praise and worship. One lady in front of me stood up to do a ten-second holy dance. Some were shouting. Others were quietly crying. Everyone looked like they were having an experience with God that night.

Minister Mariah went on. "You see, what God has for you is for you. Nobody can take it, shake it, or fake it. Nobody can touch it. But your enemies try to come close. They know all your secrets, all your hurts. They know you from the inside out. Guard your heart, my sisters. Guard your heart. Don't let just anybody into your inner circle, into your holy of holies. Watch carefully the people around you so you can properly discern who your enemies are. Who has what's best for you in mind? Who is just using you as a means to an end? Watch your enemies, sisters.

"But when you find them, like Satan, they have to restore you sevenfold. Don't try to get back at them. 'Vengeance is mine, I will repay, saith the Lord.' God said He'd repay. Don't you try to repay. Wait on the Lord, and He shall renew your strength. Just be mindful of your enemies. Pray for them. I said pray for them because God knows how to take them down, and in His timing and in His way, He will. He's a just God. Oh yes, He's a just God. Let's give Him praise and glory for our enemies, because they cause us to get stronger."

After the service we shuffled out through the crowd, and I couldn't help but to ponder the word Minister Mariah had preached. It was powerful. Had I allowed enemies to manipulate me and take over my life? Two immediately came to mind. Had Satan truly been able to sneak in?

Alex and I walked out of the building to experience the sights and sounds of New Orleans right there in downtown Bangor. It was funny that I never knew that Maine had anything in common with New Orleans. We walked a little farther, found a nice little seafood place, and ordered the poached salmon. It was one of our favorite dishes, and one of the few that we actually agreed upon. There were so many different varieties of fish on the menu; it was almost as if we were literally in the ocean.

"Minister Mariah was right about the whole enemy thing," I said.

"Yes, she was." Alex lifted her hand as if to say "Amen."

I looked right into her eyes. "I've got one that I've got to get out of my house."

Alex let out a long breath. "Not that Paul thing again?"

"Yeah, that Paul thing again."

"Okay, what if he's really innocent and he didn't do anything to sabotage the pool?"

"First of all, I don't believe that, and secondly, it's deeper than just the pool. It's how he has come into my husband's life and turned everything kind of upside down."

"How so?"

"I mean, Keith is out with him all the time. We have no privacy at home, or anywhere else, for that matter. We're always arguing about him. He's rude and out of order. And most of all, I feel like Keith is hiding something from me, something that only Paul knows about," I said with a hint of whining in my voice.

"Oh, so that's what it is?"

"No, it's everything with him." I used my hands to demonstrate my point. "Not one thing, but everything."

Alex shook her head as she continued to devour her meal. "That's too bad, because if that's your husband's best friend, you're in for a real fight."

I put my fork down and put my fists up. "Oh, I know that. But I've never been one to back away from a good fight."

"Taylor," Alex said.

"Well, I haven't. Keith can't expect me to keep on living with the enemy indefinitely. Me and Paul don't get along at all." I threw up my hands. "And I'm his wife."

"I understand. I just hope you are right about Paul and are not throwing an innocent man out on the street, because then you'll be accountable for that."

"I'll take my chances." I took another bite of my salad. "Believe me, there is nothing innocent about Mr. Paul Meyers."

When we arrived back at the hotel, we were able to relax in a room that was both clean and comfortable. Alex showed me, like, a million new pictures of her kids. Then she took out her laptop and logged on to Facebook to keep in touch with her young women's ministry. Thankfully, they had free high-speed Internet available in the hotel room. It was inspiring the way she and Joshua were dedicated to the ministry. Even though Keith and I loved God and knew we owed our lives to Him, it was clear that we really hadn't found our place yet in the church. I lay back against a pillow and dialed my husband's cell phone.

I was excited to hear his voice. "Hi, Keith."

"Hi, babe," Keith said.

I heard music and laughter in the background. "Where are you?"

"Oh, Paul and I are at this wing place, watching the game," Keith said.

"Oh, I see. You sound like you guys are having fun."

Was it my imagination, or did Keith's speech sound slightly slurred? I heard Paul in the background singing.

Keith cleared his throat. "Yeah, we are. What about you and Alex? How is the conference going?"

I paused. "It's great. We're having fun."

"Okay, babe. I gotta go." Keith laughed. "They're bringing around the wings."

"Okay then. Bye," I said.

Then I heard silence. I couldn't believe that they were out on the town again, and that he had hung up on me before he even said good-bye. That wasn't like him at all. I definitely didn't like the effect this Paul person had on my husband. I'd have to address things when I got back.

I spent the rest of the night thinking about Keith and Paul, wondering about the secret bond they shared. Finally, exhaustion overtook me and I lapsed into much-needed sleep.

The next day we enjoyed a continental breakfast before we left for the Spectacular Event Center. The message was just as riveting as the one yesterday; it was a continuation of the theme of how to guard your heart. The minister spoke about the issues of life coming out of your heart. This time she discussed spiritual enemies, like doubt and unbelief, unfaithfulness, and sin. Alex and I both left with repentant hearts, ready to give more of ourselves to God. I wasn't sure how much more of my sister there was to give, but it was nice to have her along for the ride.

Since the conference was officially over, we were free to do some sightseeing, so we did just that. First, we grabbed something quick to eat at a diner that was within walking distance. Then a couple of the local folk suggested that we do a drive down the Schoodic Scenic

Byway, so we started on our way. Sure enough, it was entertaining as we traveled along the Eastern seashore, looking at the unspoiled landscape, the mountains, coastal islands, historic buildings, and lighthouses. We even stopped to hear the history of the Schoodic Peninsula. All in all, we saw traditional fishing villages, such as Winter Harbor, epic coastal villas on the rocky coastline, and small towns. We made one last stop at the Bailey Island Bridge, which connects Bailey Island to Orr's Island. There was water all around us, clams, lobsters, and fishing boats everywhere. It was a beautiful place to visit, but Alex and I agreed after our tour was over that we wouldn't want to live there.

Back at the hotel, we loaded our luggage into the rental car. It was an American economy model, not much unlike Alex's car, except that it was newer and more reliable.

"This is a nice car," I said as I climbed into the passenger seat.

Alex smirked. "Yeah, I guess so."

"Seriously, though, when are you going to get rid of that heap of junk you have at home?"

"Don't make fun of my little car." Alex put her finger right in my face. "I love that pink car."

I moved her finger and laughed, because only she could get away with doing something like that to me. "I know that. You've loved it ever since college. Maybe it's time to love another car."

She ignored me, popped a CD in, and started singing along to a familiar Donnie McClurkin song. Before I knew it, I was singing along with her, and we were rolling speedily down the highway, heading for home.

When we were singing along with Byron Cage, I looked behind me and caught a glimpse of a big black Range Rover right on our tail. I didn't say anything to Alex at first, because she looked so happy. But I watched the truck nervously from my side-view mirror until one time it came so close to us, I had to say something.

"Wow, that truck behind us is following too closely," I shrieked.

"Maybe a little," Alex said matter-of-factly.

"I think it's Elaina," I gasped.

"What? You're tripping, girl."

"No, I'm serious."

"Way out here?" Alex peered into the rearview mirror and shook her head. "No way."

The more we talked, the more I knew in my heart that it was her. It had to be Elaina. She was all up on us by now. She was bearing down on us hard. Questions swirled through my head.

How did she get all the way out here? How did she know about the conference? Or did she just follow us all the way from New York?

We were swinging around the curve, trying to shake her.

I didn't remember Derek telling me that his wife was psychotic, just that they were separated, and that he couldn't deal with her anymore. Maybe this was what he meant. Nah! He was a self-proclaimed baller, plain and simple. He wasn't concerned with his wife's emotions or mental status at all. All he ever cared about was partying.

I continued to watch the truck behind us as it gained speed.

"Speed up," I said.

"Are you crazy?" Alex smirked. "I'm already going as fast as I can. I'm not getting a speeding ticket for anybody."

"I know, I know, but you need to push it." I was convinced it was her, even if it wasn't.

"This chick is crazy."

"Are you still on that? How do you know it's her, anyway? Maybe it's just some other road-rage lunatic," Alex said.

"I just know," I said.

Same vehicle. Same dark tinted windows.

Alex reached for her reading glasses in the glove compartment. "If we could see the tag, then we could report it."

"Drive. Drive! Put the pedal to the metal, or we won't live to report it!" I shouted.

"Maybe you should just call the police." Alex began to look panicked. "What if she or whoever runs us off the road?"

"Oh, so *now* you believe me?" I felt guilty for getting her involved in this mess. She did have three children waiting for her at home. I had none.

Alex looked panicked. "I'm just saying, what if it is her?"

"Yeah, you're right. I'm dialing nine-one-one," I said.

Just as I began to dial, the truck mysteriously veered off to the right and exited, almost as if the driver had heard our conversation. That was even more scary.

I was glad to finally be home. Keith looked like he was glad to see me too. I sat him down on the couch and told him about our experience on the road. I also told him that the business license inspector, Elaina Dawson, was Derek's wife. He was surprised and confused at first, but after I explained that she came to visit me in the hospital right after my accident, he understood. I also told him that, although I had no proof, I suspected it was Elaina who had tried to run us off the road. *Enemies*.

Keith thought I was being paranoid, that I had been watching too much Lifetime on television. Deciding to choose my battles, I left the Elaina issue alone.

"Now that I've told you my theory about one enemy, let me tell you what I think about another," I said, putting my hand atop his. I proceeded to present a case against Paul, incident after incident, suspicion after suspicion.

Keith frowned. "I've had enough of your conspiracy theories."

"Theories?"

Keith bit into the apple he'd been holding. "Without proof, that's all they are."

"I've got proof."

"Circumstantial evidence." He didn't even stop chewing.

"Oh, so now you're his attorney?"

"No, but maybe he should have an attorney just to defend himself against you," Keith proclaimed.

"Why does he even need defending, though, Keith?"

Keith stopped eating for a moment. "Look, there is no reason for Paul to want to do that to me. None."

"Maybe he's jealous." I shrugged.

Keith arose from the couch and stood over me. "Paul is not like that. We used to be very close. You know that."

"Actually, I know nothing. You've told me nothing, really, except that you two went to college together."

Keith bit his bottom lip, as he did whenever he was upset. "He stood by me when no one else would."

My voice went up a little higher. "Why won't you hear me? What is it about this Paul that's so special?"

Keith grabbed his keys off of the marble center table and walked out while I was still talking.

Chapter Thirteen

The next morning was typical of a summer day in Clinton Hills, Brooklyn. I could see the downstairs activity from my window. Children played outside on the stoop. Cars zoomed back and forth through the streets, and familiar vendors were already outside hustling. Keith had gone to the supermarket to get a few groceries. I watched him hit the sidewalk and take off jogging down the street. I turned over in my bed and picked up my Bible. I read Psalm 37 to stabilize my mind before I made a move. Then I took a quick shower so I'd be fresh and clean for the task at hand.

"This is it," I said to myself. "It's been long enough." Paul had been living with us for three whole months, and within that time, our lives had virtually fallen apart.

I put on my nicest jeans and a short-sleeved royal blue blouse so I would look my best. It was silk, so I put on an extra coat of deodorant, hoping I wouldn't sweat under the arms. I decided to use only my braces this morning. Since I was on a mission, I didn't want to be slumped over in my wheelchair when I did what I had to do. I wanted to stand tall when I had to wrestle with adversity.

As usual, Paul was already on the couch, watching television, with his feet on my marble center table and his sticky hands holding a sandwich and touching my furniture. I gawked at the crumbs that rolled down his shirt onto the floor. I took two deep breaths before I spoke. *Lord, please give me the words to say.*

"Good morning," I said.

"Morning," Paul said, using his mayonnaise-covered fingers to flip the channels on the remote.

He hardly looked at me, not realizing what was coming. Why should he notice anything strange? He looked like he was having the time of his life. He wasn't out looking for a job or volunteering to do something positive. Instead, he was wasting time and money, keeping my husband out at all hours of the day and night for his own selfish pleasure. He was drinking and hiding bottles in my trash can. He was living rent free and carefree. No, he didn't look at all like a man who had any intentions of leaving.

He looked comfortable and very much at home. Keith had made sure of that.

In my business tone, I began, "Paul, may I speak to you for a minute, please?"

"Sure, go ahead," Paul said, stuffing the entire remainder of his sandwich into his mouth and then wiping his mouth with his sleeve.

"I'm sorry, but I can't do this anymore." I came up close to him.

"Do what anymore?"

"This." I pointed to the couch. "I want you out."

Paul continued to flip the channels on the remote. "You want me to leave?"

"Yes, because . . . I mean, things aren't good between us, and I think it's best that you leave before things get worse."

Paul chuckled. "This is about me hanging out with Keith, isn't it?"

"No, this is about you and me. I just can't live with you anymore. I'm sorry."

"You're sorry?" Paul put down the remote and started to pay attention. "Why are you kicking me out on the street, then?"

"I'm not saying you've got to go this minute. I'm giving you time to find a place to go, but . . . I can't stop thinking that you tried to sabotage us with the pool incident," I said.

Paul turned his whole body to face me. "And just why would I want to do that?"

"I don't know, but things have been pretty rough since you came." I was sure that I wanted him gone. He had brought nothing but confusion when he set foot in our apartment.

Paul looked me up and down. "And that's all my fault?"

"Look, I think we'd all be better off if you found somewhere else to stay."

"Just like that?" Paul snickered.

"Yeah, just like that," I said.

Paul had the nerve to lean back on the couch. "Okay, does Keith know?"

"Does Keith know what?" Keith entered through the front door and put down three bags of groceries.

I wished that I could alleviate the tension that was thick in the room. But my words were out, and just like my husband had said before, sometimes my mouth caused trouble. It was too late to go back. I could only go forward.

Paul sat up straight. "That your wife is just putting me out."

Keith frowned. "Taylor."

"What? I told you I wanted him out." I hunched my shoulders.

"Taylor, you shouldn't have done that without talking to me first."

"I've been talking, Keith, but you haven't been listening," I said. "I don't trust him. I know you do, but I don't."

"I know him." Keith looked back and forth between me and Paul. "I've known him for years."

I still couldn't believe they had been friends for so long. Paul was nothing like my husband, and besides the sporting events they shared, I couldn't imagine what would possibly draw them to each other. Keith's friends usually weren't loud, rude, and unruly. They usually didn't take him for granted the way Paul did, either. Since Paul had come to town, Keith hadn't even had time or energy for his other, "civilized" friends.

"Well, it's really hard to live with someone you regard as the enemy." I looked Keith right in the eyes. "And whether you believe me or not, he is the enemy."

Paul barked, "Oh, so now I'm the enemy just because your pool chemistry got messed up somehow?"

"Taylor Bryant, you're out of control," Keith said.

"*Somehow?* I put you in charge of the pool. Nothing was ever messed up before you got here," I yelled, ignoring Keith's comment.

Paul's eye began to twitch. "So?"

"So we have automatic timers on the pool. There was no reason to have unacceptable levels of chlorine. No problems at all with the pool until you came," I said.

"That's a coincidence. Why would I want to mess up my best friend's business?"

"That's what I want to know." I leaned forward. "Keith has done nothing but try to help you, and this is how you've repaid him, by tearing down what we've worked so hard for."

"I haven't torn down anything," Paul yelled.

I snapped my fingers. "Not because you haven't tried."

Paul started laughing. "Oh, don't be such a drama queen."

"Drama queen." I lunged at him, but Keith caught me by the waist. "Oh, I'm a drama queen all right." My husband knew me too well.

"Look, that's my wife, so don't go there, man," Keith said to Paul abruptly.

"Oh, so now you're defending her?" Paul stood up and began to gather his belongings.

"All right, that's cool."

"I'm sorry, but if you two can't get along, then maybe it's best if you go stay somewhere else, buddy," Keith said to Paul.

"Okay, I see how it is. I thought you had my back, man," Paul sneered.

"I still have your back. I'll help you get a room down at the Y. And I'm sure old man Tony can use some help down at the car wash until you get on your feet."

"Whatever, man," Paul said, walking to the guest room.

While Paul gathered his belongings, Keith and I continued to argue. After what seemed like forever, Paul came out, carrying all of his luggage.

"I'm really sorry things went down like this." Keith looked over at me with an evil glare.

"Right. I'll see you around, man." Paul grabbed his bags from the closet and walked out, slamming the door.

Then Keith turned to me, and the scene that followed was nothing pretty.

Keith pointed his finger in my face. "Taylor Carter-Bryant, you're my wife now."

He had seriously crossed the line.

I crossed the line too. "And what is that supposed to mean?"

"Nothing to you, apparently," he said.

"That's not fair. Don't make me out to be the bad guy when I've been putting up with all this mess all along."

"Okay, so he's a slob, but that still doesn't mean he contaminated our pool."

"He's sneaky too. I never told you this, but I found a bottle of cognac in our kitchen trash, all wrapped up in a plastic bag. I thought it was maybe a one-time thing, but now I don't think so."

"What do you mean?"

"Now I think this is just the real him, sneaky and reckless," I screamed. "I think he's a drunk."

"You don't even know him," Keith said, walking away.

Frustrated, I followed him around the room. "And why are you always defending him?"

"He's just been a good friend, so—"

"All I ever hear is how good he's been, but you never tell me what he's done that's so good. You hardly mentioned him at all before he showed up at our door. Then you welcome him with open arms and throw him down at the gym on me."

"All I did was suggest—"

I nodded my head repeatedly. "Oh, come on, I didn't want to work with him at all, and you made me do it. Now it's a big mess, and you want to blame me for it."

"I didn't say I was blaming you." Keith's nostrils flared. "I'm just saying that you don't know Paul."

"You're not convincing me, and at this point I think I know enough." I started to hobble away. "No, I know way too much."

"You're impossible," Keith grunted.

"I'll tell you what's impossible. Not only has this man sabotaged our pool, but he has also done everything to sabotage our relationship."

"Oh, come on," Keith huffed.

"You don't believe it? Look at us now."

We continued going toe-to-toe, with both of us saying harsh things we probably didn't mean, until Keith ended up walking out on me. Twice in one day I had the door slammed in my face, and I was getting tired of it. Back in the day I would've thrown a straight fit and come out swinging, but I wasn't the old Taylor anymore. So instead of acting the fool, I decided to pray. "Father, take hold of my life. Deliver me from my enemies and deliver me from myself. Help me to get along with my husband and not to get ahead of myself. Help my husband with whatever he's hiding from me. Help our marriage to get stronger in spite of the pressure we now face. Work through my life, Lord, so that I may bring glory to your name. In Jesus's name, amen."

Even though Paul was gone, he had left a residue in my home, and I knew he'd be back, if not in the flesh, then in the spirit.

Chapter Fourteen

The next day was Sunday. The light breeze flowing through the window caressed my skin as I yawned, stretched, and opened my eyes. However, I woke up to an empty bed. I knew I'd heard Keith come home last night, but I didn't remember him ever coming to bed. I went out to the living room but saw nothing. Then I went into the kitchen and found Keith with his head down on the table. There was a bottle of gin in front of him, and he smelled like alcohol. Oh, I was familiar with the smell because of the life I used to live. I used to kick back at least a pint of gin sometimes. So I now knew that Keith had been drinking too, and not just Paul alone. But why? I didn't understand why Keith would jeopardize his relationship with God by doing something he knew he shouldn't be doing. Why now? I'd never seen or heard of him drinking before.

"Keith Bryant, I don't believe this," I yelled.

Keith lifted his head and opened his blood-shot eyes. "Tay."

"Ugh," I said in sheer frustration.

Keith just groaned and fell back onto the table.

Obviously, he was in no condition to go to church, so I left him there, promising myself that I'd take care of him when I returned. I got ready quickly, throwing on a plum skirt suit. Then I called for a cab to take me down to Missionary.

Once I arrived at Missionary, the cabdriver was nice enough to help me get out of the car and onto the curb in front of the church. Some did help out, and believe it or not, some didn't. That was the nature of New York City cab-drivers. When he pulled away, I struggled to balance my Bible case and purse with my braces. Usually, I had Keith at my side to hold them for me. I sighed as I thought of Keith at home in the alcoholic stupor he was in. None of it made any sense. Keith had never even touched a drop of any alcoholic beverage since we'd met. He was serious about the things he put into his body and about his walk with God. No matter how many times I mulled it over, it just didn't add up.

When I walked into the building, Sister Winifred was the first to notice Keith's absence.

"Is the honeymoon over already, dear?"

Again, the Holy Spirit soothed me and kept me from jumping on old lady Winifred. Yes, I was a changed woman. She just didn't know how on the edge I was. Others were nice enough to ask how Keith was doing, and some were wise enough not to ask anything at all. I managed to avoid Aunt Dorothy and my father for the most part, because I didn't feel up to answering any of their questions. All I wanted to do was to hear the word, which I desperately needed, and get back home to handle my business.

Unfortunately, that was easier said than done. Just as I was about to get away after the service was over, Sister Trudy caught me at the door.

Sister Trudy practically ran over to me. "Taylor, I'm glad I caught you."

I tried to hide my disappointment. "How are you, Sister Trudy?"

"I'm fine, baby. Just fine. Now I need your help," Sister Trudy said.

I looked around, as if she couldn't possibly be talking to me." How may I help you?"

"It's the birthday committee," Sister Trudy said.

"Oh . . . I, uh . . ."

Sister Trudy put her hand behind my back as if she were holding me in place. "The committee only meets once a month. The mission is to help the members feel loved by having the church celebrate their birthday with them."

"Oh, okay," I said, trying to sound interested. "How nice."

"Everyone will receive a birthday card, a small gift, and a phone call," Sister Trudy continued.

I began to shake my head in disagreement. "Sounds good, but I don't know if—"

"I know you're busy with your business and everything, but if you could just help us out with the phone calls." Sister Trudy looked down at my legs. "I hope you're up to it."

Now she had offended me. What did my walking have to do with anything? "I'm up to it."

"Good. Now, just get with Mother Williams, and she'll give you the rest of the details," Sister Trudy snorted.

I fidgeted. "The rest?" Hadn't she just talked for ten minutes nonstop?

How did I get caught up with that? All I wanted was to get back home. Before I could blink, she called over Mother Williams to sign me up for the committee and had three other ladies with wide-brimmed hats talking to me about some other women's auxiliary. I smiled and nodded, trying hard to slip out of the conversation, but each time someone would bring me back in again. They had to be kidding me. I wasn't ready for that.

"That's a lovely blouse, dear. Just a little too snug around the bustline," Mother Williams whispered in my ear.

"Oh, I . . ." I was embarrassed, but at least she was discreet, unlike mischievous Sister Winifred.

When the ladies announced that they all had to use the restroom, that was my chance to get away. I was sure I'd receive a phone call from one of them, but that was better than doing this in person.

When I finally got home, I was so drained, I felt like I'd run a marathon. I climbed out of the cab with my last strength and took the elevator upstairs. Mrs. Faison from the fifth floor waved to me as I was going into my apartment. I waved back, but the sad way she looked at my legs I could've lived without. Friendship I could do, but I didn't want anyone's pity.

The apartment was empty, and I wondered where Keith had gone on a Sunday. I went to my bedroom, stripped out of my church clothes, dropped down on my bed, and waited for Keith to come home. I grabbed a granola bar from my side table drawer, washing it down with a bottled water. I kept a supply of both next to my bed for those times when I was hungry or thirsty yet too lazy to make my way to the kitchen. I watched reruns of my favorite sitcoms on television until I heard the front door open. That was when I sat up straight in bed.

"Hi," I said when Keith walked in the room.

Keith avoided my eyes. "Hi."

"Everyone missed you at church this morning," I said, then waited for his response. I needed more than petty conversation.

"Oh?"

"Yeah, even Sister Winifred asked about you," I smirked.

"I'll bet," Keith said, stepping out of his pants.

I couldn't hold it in anymore. I had waited long enough. "Do you want to explain why you were drunk last night?"

"It was just a one-time thing," Keith said quietly.

I wasn't sure I believed him. "A one-time thing?"

Keith didn't look at me. "Yes, I'm sorry."

"Since when do you even like to drink?"

"I don't," he insisted. "I just did it."

"I'm glad you don't, but there has got to be more to it than that," I said, badgering him.

Keith held up both hands. "What do you want me to say?"

"Everything happens for a reason. No one starts doing something new for no reason whatsoever," I said.

Keith's voice became louder. "I told you it was a one-time thing."

"That's not a reason." I made my voice louder too. "That's a description."

Keith walked away from me, so I let it go. Unlike the old me, who was always down for a good rumble, I didn't feel like having another round of arguing.

We did a pretty good job of avoiding each other for the remainder of the day. Later on in the evening I made Caesar salads with cheddar cheese and honey-smoked turkey for dinner. We sat at opposite ends of the table, eating and twiddling our forks in silence. Keith walked up behind me while I was washing dishes. He wrapped his arms around my waist and told me that he wanted to talk. I told him I thought he owed me at least an explanation for his change in behavior, and surprisingly, he agreed with me. He helped me to sit back down at the table. Then I waited while Keith made strawberry-banana smoothies in our blender. He returned to the table with the delicious treat in his hands, sat close to me and, seeing my arms folded, wasted no time getting started.

Keith started playing with his thumbs, something he did whenever he was nervous. "I got drunk because I've been struggling with something."

"What is it, Keith?"

"Something I've been dealing with that I never told you about," Keith said.

My heart pounded as I prepared myself to hear the unknowable. "Okay. I'm listening."

Lord, brace me.

Keith took my hand and lowered his head. "My brother is missing."

"You told me about that when you couldn't get in touch with him for the wedding."

"I told you I couldn't find him, but I didn't tell you why he was missing," Keith said, looking away from me.

"Why is he missing?"

Keith looked down. "Because he's a drug addict."

"Oh, I'm so sorry." I reached over to touch his hand. "How long has he been—"

"He's been hooked for years. No one had seen him for a long time until Paul . . ."

Immediately I shrank back. My guard was up. "Paul? What has he got to do with this?"

"Paul thinks he saw him a few months back." Keith began using his hands for emphasis.

"Thinks he saw him?" The worst thoughts immediately came to my mind, like maybe Paul was lying. "Are you sure Paul saw him where and when he said he did? I don't want to sound negative, but are you sure that he saw him at all?"

"It's a long story, but Paul thinks that he saw him." Keith had a faraway look in his eyes.

"He wasn't close enough to him to know for sure."

"I see." I hugged him tight. "I'm so sorry."

Keith cleared his throat. "I need to find him."

"Right," I said. "Now, when was the last time you saw him?"

"At my dad's funeral," Keith said. "He kept in touch with my aunt for the first few years, but after a while he stopped communicating with anyone."

"So you lost touch with him right after the funeral?"

"He went off on his own, and that was that. I went back to college and then on to graduate school."

I put my arm around Keith. "So you never came home?"

"There was no home to really come to. My father was gone. My brother was gone. My uncles and my aunt and I were never really close. It was what it was."

I imagined my husband all alone in the world, with no family of his own. I realized that God had protected him even when he didn't know he was being protected. A tear ran down my face. "That's a real shame."

"Yeah, but my brother got the rawest end of the deal. Now I've got to find him."

I rubbed Keith's back. "I understand, and I'll help in any way I can."

"I should've never left him," Keith said.

"It's not your fault."

"It is my fault," Keith said as he left the kitchen. "And I'm going to fix it."

I didn't know exactly what my husband meant by "fixing it," but the wild look in his eyes made the hairs on my skin stand on end.

Chapter Fifteen

As soon as the sunshine came through our bedroom curtains and I felt a knot in my stomach, I knew I didn't feel up to going to Push It that morning. I was glad that Keith had agreed with me when I said I needed a break. Keith stretched as he came out of the shower, wearing only a terry-cloth towel around his waist.

"Don't worry," Keith said. "I'll hold it down for you today, babe."

"Thanks." I smiled as I slipped back underneath the covers. I was in no mood for business drama today. I'd let my husband deal with the issues.

After Keith finished dressing, he brought me a blueberry muffin and a cup of freshly squeezed orange juice. How he was able to do it all, I'd never know, but I was glad he did. Then, with a banana in one hand and his keys in the other, he kissed me good-bye. Minutes later I heard him drive away from the parking spot he had been fortunate enough to find out front. I would've started up the laptop, but I had promised myself not to think about work today. Clearly, that was going to be easier said than done. I was looking forward to seeing my sister, though, and spending a quiet afternoon with our dad, if quiet was even possible.

When I finally crawled out of bed, I peeked out front, at the spot where Keith's car had been parked. A strange black car was parked in its place. I couldn't readily identify the make or model, but the car looked very expensive and shiny. I stood up straight with the help of my braces and peered at the vehicle, waiting to see someone get in or out, but I saw no one anywhere near the car. People hustled back and forth on the sidewalks, and cars raced through the streets. Children walked and played nearby, but that car remained still. After getting a better look at it, I determined that it was probably a Ferrari, not exactly a common sight on the streets of my Clinton Hills neighborhood. By the time I managed to get to the bathroom and come out, I heard footsteps by the front door.

"Who is it?" I asked as I approached the door, thinking that maybe Keith had forgotten something.

There was no answer. I waited for Keith to enter with his key.

I stepped closer to the door to see if I could hear anything. "Keith, is that you?"

I heard only breathing. I backed away from the door, nearly falling over backward. I made my way to my bedroom window to look outside, and by that time, the mysterious car was pulling away.

I went back to the front door and put my ear to it. When I heard nothing, I cracked the door to my apartment open. I looked in both directions, but there was no one in sight. The only thing left in the hallway was a lingering scent. It seemed to be the same Ralph Lauren perfume that Elaina wore. I had a good nose for that kind of thing. After what I'd gone through the past few weeks, I'd recognize that scent anywhere. I didn't think it was a coincidence, so I kept my guard up for the rest of the morning. I went through the apartment, praying that the hands of the enemy be bound and that divine safety and protection would be loosed on earth as it is loosed in heaven. Prayer was the ultimate solution to any problem, no matter how big or small. I'd learned that from Mama.

Fortunately, nothing else strange happened before Alex arrived for our visit to Dad's house. By the time I heard my cell phone ringing, I was already on my way downstairs in the elevator. Alex met me at the main entrance and helped me to slide into her small car. It was her idea that we pay our dad a visit, because I never thought about things like that.

As soon as I was buckled up, I said, "Elaina was at my apartment this morning."

"What? No."

"Yes."

Alex looked at me for a moment. "Did you talk to her?"

"No, but it was her MO—a very fancy unidentified car and then a mysterious knock on the door."

Alex took one hand off of the steering wheel. "So?"

"So by the time I got to the window, the car was pulling away. And when I opened my apartment door, the hallway smelled like Elaina's perfume," I said.

"I'm no lawyer, but all of that sounds very circumstantial to me," Alex said, continuing to look straight ahead.

"I know it does, but not if you're being stalked by a madwoman." I rubbed my hands together. "I know Elaina's after me. I just don't have enough proof yet."

Alex pulled up in front of Dad's house. "What are you going to do?"

"I don't know, but please don't say anything to Dad about it," I said. "I don't want him going to jail for killing Elaina at his age."

Alex chuckled. "Yeah, I know better than that."

As it turned out, our dad was recovering from a serious bout of his asthma. When we first entered the small house, we could smell the Vicks VapoRub in the air. Dad was famous for smearing it on his chest when he couldn't breathe well, along with using it in the vaporizer.

"Hi, Dad," I said, hugging his lumpy body.

"I've seen your sister, but you haven't come by for a while. I was beginning to worry," Dad said to me.

"Oh, Daddy. You know you and me ain't never been tight like that," I smirked.

Dad coughed and rubbed his chest. "True, but I'd like to think things have changed."

"I'm sorry. I didn't mean it like that," I said.

Dad stopped rubbing his chest to listen. "What did you mean, then?"

"I've just been really busy with the gym, and then I had that houseguest, which was causing all kinds of problems between me and Keith, so . . ." I said.

"You want me to talk to him?" Dad chuckled. "You know I have always liked Keith."

Alex jumped in. "And not Joshua, Daddy?"

"Now, I didn't say that." Dad scrunched up his wrinkled face. "Don't go putting words in my mouth."

"No, I don't need you to talk to Keith for me." I let out a quick breath. "I'm grown, and I'm his wife. I'll handle it."

Alex put her hands on her hips. "But I've been married longer, and I've never heard you say you like Joshua."

"You know Joshua's all right with me, a little stuffy, but that's just his way. He's family now." Dad coughed roughly. "It's his parents I don't care for."

"Daddy," Alex said.

"Well, it's the truth." Dad walked over to his worn-out recliner and sat down.

"Okay, you two, stop it," I said.

"I'm old now, so I speaks my mind," Dad said, wrinkling up his face.

"You sound like Mama." I laughed.

Dad pulled open his newspaper. "If your mama was here, I'm sure she'd be saying the same thing. I like them both, but all I've got to say is they'd better take good care of my girls."

"Daddy," Alex and I said in unison.

"It's the truth," Dad said. "Speaking of which, Mrs. Taylor Bryant, when are you going to give me some grandkids?"

"Probably never, Daddy," I said, wincing.

Dad shook his head. "Gal, you're out of line."

I looked him straight in the eyes. "I'm out of line?"

"Come on, you two," Alex interjected.

"Don't push it, Dad," I said. "We're just starting to get along."

Dad looked up from the newspaper and over his glasses. "You just started to get along with *everyone* now that you got them demons out of you."

"Did he just say 'demons'?" I turned to my sister.

"Yes, I said 'demons.'" Dad put the paper back up to his face.

I playfully lunged toward him as Alex pretended to hold me back. "Okay, I've got your demons, Dad. . . ."

"Stop it now." Alex held up her hands. "Both of you. I'm tired of this fighting and foolishness."

"Whatever," I said.

"Can't we have a nice dinner without a grumpy old man and a hot-tempered young fool?" Alex remarked.

Dad looked directly at Alex. "Who are you calling old?"

"Who are you calling a fool?" I stepped back and got into a fake fighting stance.

"Don't worry about it," Alex said.

I put up my two fists and aimed them at my sister. "Just 'cause I'm saved doesn't mean I won't fight you."

"God fights my battles for me." Alex pretended to tend to her fingernails, as if she wasn't worried, while I hovered around her like a bee, bouncing as much as I could under the circumstances.

"Really?" I giggled. "Well, you'd better thank Him now, 'cause I was about to whup yo'—"

"Shut your mouth," Alex said, chuckling.

"Sometimes my girls, pretty as they are, don't have a lick of sense," Dad said.

Alex and I burst into continuous laughter and fell into our dad's arms.

Not that long ago I was too angry with him to even give him the time of day. I blamed him for walking out on Mama and us, for not being around much when we were little, and for coming back into our lives just in time to give Mama cancer. Yeah, for a long time, I believed the cancer was his fault. I thought it was the adultery, the abandonment, the aggravation, and the betrayal that eventually weakened her immune system and took her out. I didn't understand how she could have ever taken him back after all he'd put her through, and I didn't mind showing my disapproval, right up to the day she died. But something changed inside me when Jesus became my Lord and Savior. I learned how to love, really love, and that changed the way I felt about everything, including my father. I guess I realized that everybody needed forgiveness. Lord knows I did.

Chapter Sixteen

It was bright and sunny on the day of Missionary Church's end of the summer picnic at Prospect Park. Keith and I left our apartment wearing matching red and white shirts with jeans and red and white sneakers. It took some convincing to get my husband to agree to the outfit, but he finally gave in.

"I'm looking forward to spending a day away from home or work," I said.

"Yeah, I guess it'll be fun," Keith said with little enthusiasm.

This attitude wasn't like Keith at all. He was usually full of optimism. I hoped that this outing would help him, help us.

After we parked, Keith gently took my arm and led me through the park's entrance. The park was extraordinarily beautiful with its lush landscaping and its pools, waterfalls, and streams that flowed into a sixty-acre lake. Then there were the rustic shelters skirting the lakeshore, the newest of which was the arbor set on the bank of the Lullwater. I'd heard about the meandering body of water connected to the lake, but I hadn't visited the park in quite a while and I'd missed all it had to offer.

When Keith and I finally caught up to our group, they were already settled in. We hugged Alex first, who had been invited by Pastor Martin personally. Alex wore a beautiful carnation-pink sundress with a matching headband. She held Joshua Jr. in her arms, so I kissed his little plump cheeks before sneaking a hug from Lilah and Kiano, who were by her side.

Joshua sat around talking with the other ministers, so we just waved at him across the grassy field. Then we went over to speak to Dad, who sat with the other seniors, including Brother Tate, who liked impromptu whistling, and Brother Morris, who liked to tell sad war stories. Immediately, Sister Trudy came over.

"Chile, you've just got to try some of my peach cobbler," Sister Trudy said, holding the pan up to my face.

"Thanks. I'll get some as soon as I get a plate," I said.

Keith just smiled and shook his head to say "No thanks."

"Y'all don't forget." Sister Trudy set the pan back down on the table.

Then Aunt Dorothy walked over with a pan of potato salad. "You know you want some of this."

"We do," I said, nudging Keith in the ribs.

"Oh yeah," Keith said, careful not to hurt Aunt Dorothy's feelings.

"Now, give me a hug, you two," Aunt Dorothy said, hugging us both at the same time while balancing the pan behind our backs.

"We'll be right back," I said, putting up one finger to get away.

Before we could get far, Sister Winifred stepped up. "Well, isn't it nice to see you two together again? I was beginning to think you were having trouble," Sister Winifred squawked.

Nosy, nosy Sister Winifred, always in someone's business. Her ridiculous niece, Yvonne, came forward wearing a white shorts outfit that should've been banned from the picnic, and even from the park. With her skin overflowing atop her clothes, she had single-handedly made our innocent little outing look like Hoochieville, USA, but that was nothing new for Yvonne.

"Come on now. Try my baked beans. It's my grandmother's recipe," Sister Winifred said proudly, taking the pan from Yvonne.

"We promise to get some as soon as we get a plate," I said, trying to keep a smile on my face.

Keith looked at me and then said, "Let me get us two plates now."

I couldn't believe how we were being bombarded with food before we were even greeted.

Did we look that hungry? Or was this picnic just a competition for all the cooks?

After we filled our plates, we could hardly find a place to sit because there were so many people lounging around, casually taking up more than one seat. Keith and I walked through the crowd, with Keith carrying both of our plates. It wasn't easy using the braces on the grass. I preferred concrete.

Keith found two empty lawn chairs on which we could sit and eat. From there we could see everything. The deacons barbecued the ribs, hamburgers, hot dogs, and chicken wings on the grill. Alex, of course, had volunteered to help with serving the lemonade and sweet tea, in between keeping an eye on her own three children. The young women sang and played cards, while the younger men started setting off the fireworks. Some of the children played kickball or hand games in the field. Others had relay races, running speedily across the grass.

I missed running. It used to be my favorite thing to do because I was so fast. At one time I was the fastest runner in my whole elementary school. After years of running on the middle school track team, where I developed strong legs, thighs, and calves, training under slave driver Coach Glenn, I left the track team for cheerleading. I never stopped running, though. I continued to jog all through high school and even as an adult. I could run and forget everything else in the world while I was doing so. I'd have my headphones on and a pair of my favorite running shoes, and I could tune out the world and all of its mess while I did laps around the block. My neck stiffened as my mind came back to the present and I remembered that running was no longer an option.

Not knowing what else to do, I stopped watching the children and spotted a group of women who were about my age. "I'm going to help them fold napkins," I told Keith and stood up.

"Cool," Keith said. "I'm gonna help Brother Curtis with the good ole gospel music."

"Yeah, you handle that." I laughed as I thought about my husband attempting to play amateur DJ.

I settled down with the women, although this kind of female bonding really wasn't my style, but eventually Alex came over with her kids. Kiano and Lilah were everywhere, running, playing, and knocking over stuff, while baby

Josh refused to leave her arms, whining and crying the whole time.

I frowned. "Like I said before, you've really got your hands full."

"It's not as bad as it looks," Alex said.

"I know." I chuckled. "It's worse."

We burst into a chain of laughter that affected all the women and lightened the mood of the group. I didn't know if it was like that with all twins, but it was always that way with the two of us.

Several mosquitoes, ants, and random bugs irritated us off and on as we ate, but we enjoyed ourselves, anyway. Throughout the day, I noticed that Keith's mind seemed far away.

He barely said two words to me the whole time. I noticed that he spent a short time with Joshua, while he was eating a slice of watermelon, and a few minutes with Dad, when they were cutting the red velvet sheet cake. At one point Keith sneaked away from everyone and went to sit by himself under a big shade tree. After about twenty-five minutes I figured he'd had enough separation time. I hobbled my way over to him.

By the time I reached the tree, I was tired. "Are you okay?"

"Yeah, I'm fine," he said.

"Okay," I said.

"Okay." Keith began walking back to the picnic area, leaving me behind.

I knew something was bothering him, but I couldn't pinpoint what it was. I stood by the tall oak tree and touched one of its lower branches. It was so peaceful, I could see why Keith had sought refuge there. What an absolutely beautiful day I was basking in.

I felt a tap on my shoulder. I whirled around to grab Keith, to tell him I loved him, that I was glad he was here with me. But when I reached my whirling destination, it wasn't Keith.

Instead, I stared into Elaina Dawson's eyes. I stepped back and gasped for air. My heart pounded in my chest.

"Hello, Mrs. Bryant," Elaina smirked.

I stuttered," W-what are you doing here?"

"I'm here for my son's soccer practice." Elaina grinned, displaying perfectly white teeth.

"Oh," I said, observing a child up ahead.

Elaina sneered," I came over to deliver a message about Push It."

"What is it?"

"Your days are numbered." Elaina winked before walking away.

Within seconds, I heard Aunt Dorothy making her way toward me, hollering, "Chile, what are you doing all the way over here by yourself?"

"I'm sorry, Aunt Dorothy," I said.

"First, Keith disappeared, and now you," Aunt Dorothy said once she reached where I was standing.

I continued to watch Elaina walk into the distance.

"Did you want to invite your friend to the picnic, dear?"

"Oh, she's no friend, Aunt Dorothy." I turned to walk toward the crowd. "No friend at all."

Chapter Seventeen

Keith

It was Labor Day, and the neighborhood sports bar was full of intrigue. It was decorated with slightly worn mahogany tables and chairs, wall-to-wall sports memorabilia, and a wrap-around bar that seated fifteen at a time. Keith sat on a bar stool, with a giant blow-up bottle of Budweiser towering over him. There were a few pool tables and dartboards in the back, where random customers competed, oblivious to whatever was going on around them. There were fifty-inch flat-screen televisions on every wall, except on the back wall, where a movie-sized screen was displayed for his viewing pleasure. Every sport of the season was shown here, particularly the championship games. The bar also had a small stage, where they sometimes offered live entertainment, but not tonight. Tonight it was barren, like Keith's spirit.

He looked around the smoke-filled room at his counterparts. Most of them were sulking, heads down, seemingly hiding in their drinks. Others were talking loudly, pretending to be important. Loose women roamed the room, looking for prospective partners, someone to buy them a couple of drinks, have a couple of laughs with, and then keep them warm through the night. The men were looking for a way to forget the problems they had left at home, and consequently, embraced the fantasy that good liquor could provide. Lonely, misguided people, that was who they were, and Keith didn't really want any part of it. Yet he didn't know how to break away from it.

Paul leaned over to Keith and whispered, "How is that feisty wife of yours?"

"Leave my wife out of this." Keith burped. "It's bad enough that I'm here."

Paul continued," Okay, if you say so. But I say you need to get your woman under control."

"Yeah, whatever, man," Keith said.

"No, I mean it. It's time you showed her who the man is."

"Look, my wife knows who the man is." Keith grabbed Paul by his already wrinkled collar and lifted him up. "And I don't need you telling me anything about my wife." Keith put Paul down, then dropped his own head on the counter.

Paul straightened out his collar. "All right, all right. I didn't know you'd get so sensitive. Goodness."

Keith didn't respond. He did not like Paul talking about his wife, even though he was still his friend. Keith sympathized with her about everything she was going through. He knew Taylor was concerned about Elaina's subtle intimidation, that she might be trying to sabotage Push It, and that she'd shown up at the picnic the other day. He also knew that Taylor wanted, more than anything, to walk again. She also wanted him to stop drinking, and yet he had made no promises to her. She seemed to want so much, but he was empty.

Within minutes the waitress delivered their order of buffalo wings, and they ate them leisurely. Keith kicked back his drinks like it was water. The bartender kept offering to refill his glass. And each time Keith fell further and further into the abyss that was his addiction.

It was crazy how one drink made Keith feel empowered, like he was king of the universe.

The buzz he felt seemed to stretch his soul, or at least it made him feel like it was already stretched, where honesty and boldness met with passion. The alcohol could take him further in his mind than he had ever intended to go, and the hope of it would linger for hours.

"I'm out of here," Keith finally said after throwing back his last glass of gin.

"Let's go." Paul was always agreeable when it was time to leave. He didn't have the same longing as Keith did. He didn't have a pull inside him.

Keith stumbled onto the street at three o'clock in the morning. He and Paul had been there almost all night. Thank goodness neither of them had to drive home. Paul was staying at the YMCA a few blocks away. Keith's head ached, and his mind wandered. He sang a happy little tune as he walked, yet deep inside he knew he wasn't happy. He had failed his wife, himself, and more importantly, he had failed God. No matter how hard he tried, he couldn't shake the feeling that his life would never be the same.

When he arrived at his building, he was really too tired to climb the stairs, but he made his way up the front steps and onto the elevator. It was hard for Keith to focus enough to get the key into his apartment door, but he refused to ring the bell, waking up Taylor. He slipped through the living room and headed to the kitchen. As he moved around in the dark, forgetting where the light switch was located, he bumped his knee against a corner table and ended up limping into the kitchen.

The bright light in the kitchen hurt his blood-shot eyes. There he found his bottle of vodka hidden in the cabinet, behind the flour and corn-meal. He knew that since his wife didn't cook, she would certainly never look for those sup-plies. He reached for it, pulled it down, and held it against his chest like it was his baby. He mixed it with orange juice. That drink used to be one of his favorites. Then he sat on a kitchen chair and drank it straight down, without stopping to breathe, without having a second thought. He tried to wash away all his bad memories and all his hurt. He gulped down half of it as it burned his throat like fire.

Keith remembered the first time he ever took a drink, which was at his cousin's wedding.

It was a small sip of champagne he was of-fered, and he was only twelve years old, but he thought he had resisted long enough. It was never the taste of it that lured him, but it was the feeling it gave him, intensifying some senses and dulling others. Unfortunately, his father was a shining example of the false happiness alcohol could provide. And in his loneliness and con-fusion Keith began to secretly mimic his father. It started with just a drink every now and then, whenever no one else was around. He'd sneak into his father's secret stash for just a taste, then fill the bottle back up with water so his father wouldn't notice it had been touched. This little game went on indefinitely. His drinking didn't escalate until his last year in high school. By then he was full of rage, and although he was, miraculously, a good student, he found solace every day in a bottle.

College only worsened his habit, with the constant fraternity parties and popular trips to the neighborhood bar with Paul and his other frat brothers. They had seen him at his drunkest, vomiting, waking up in strange places, and not remembering where he had been. One time Paul pulled him from a garbage bin close to the campus. He didn't know how he got there, and Paul claimed not to know, either, but he was naked and cold when he was found. That still wasn't enough to instill fear in him. Before long Keith found himself drinking several times a day, although he managed to become better at hiding it. When his father died, everything fell apart, and his drinking began to consume him.

He couldn't get the images of his father dying in his own blood out of his mind. He couldn't get his own craving for alcohol out of his system. And to top it all off, his brother was on and off the streets, sometimes disappearing for weeks at a time, and other times showing up to ask for

money from their aunt. Keith tried to reach out
to his brother whenever he heard he was around,
but Robert never returned his calls or showed up
when he was supposed to. Keith wanted to numb
the pain that he was feeling. So he didn't drink
just at social events anymore, but also in secret.
Sometimes Paul drank with him, and other
times Paul rescued him from the wrath of his
drinking. That was how it went for the next year
and a half. How he managed to finish college
with the amount of alcohol he had in him on a
daily basis, he would never know. It was only by
the grace of God that he was even alive.

However, he did realize that he needed help
and checked himself into an alcohol recovery
program before he started graduate school.
He finished the twelve-step program, moved
to an apartment off campus, and didn't look
back. Only Paul knew the truth about his addiction. Only Paul knew he was an alcoholic.

Keith didn't leave the kitchen chair until he
had gulped down half the bottle of vodka. Then
he left it on the table when his vision began to
blur. He stumbled into his bedroom.

Taylor was already asleep, of course, so Keith
tried hard not to wake her. However, he tripped
over a pair of shoes and made a loud noise.

"Keith, is that you?"

"Yeah, babe." Keith held up his hand. "It's me."

Keith came close to his wife.

Taylor sat up in bed. "You've been drinking."

"Right," Keith groaned.

"You smell terrible," Taylor spat out.

"Oh, come on. It's not that serious," Keith said.

"Are you kidding me?" Taylor rolled her eyes. "It's very serious."

"It's not," Keith said, kneeling down next to the bed.

"You told me it was a one-time thing. Now, obviously, that was a lie."

Keith sighed. "It wasn't exactly a lie at the time."

"Not exactly a lie? What's going on?"

Keith lifted himself to a standing position. "Nothing is going on. Can't a man just come home without having to hear your mouth?"

"Yeah, a man can, but not to *this* home. We're children of God, and you know better."

"I don't know anything anymore." Keith dropped down on the bed.

"Oh, I see. Is this about your brother?"

"What? What if it is?"

"You can't live his life for him or give up yours for him, which is what it looks like you're doing," Taylor said.

"I'm not doing anything. Just trying to get some sleep." Keith rolled over on the bed.

"Don't you see you're drowning in alcohol?" Taylor pushed him. "You're killing yourself."

"No way. I ain't killing no one." Keith stood up and held on to the bed for balance.

"You're wrong about that. You're killing me and killing you," Taylor said.

"I'm okay."

"You're not okay. You're dying, Keith." Taylor closed her eyes for a moment." If you don't let this go, you'll die."

"I won't die," Keith said.

Taylor hit him on the head with his pillow, and he fell over. "You will. You're just too drunk to know it."

"Argh."

"You've turned your back on God. Please come back to us." Taylor started to cry despite her attempts not to.

Keith struggled to get up from the floor, then passed out on the bed.

Deep in his subconscious Keith remembered the twelve steps he had pledged himself to many years ago: he had admitted to his power-lessness, believed that God could help him get back to himself, turned the situation over to the hands of God, searched his moral character, admitted his wrongs to God and others, said he was ready for change, humbly asked for change, made a list of those he needed to make amends to, made amends to those on his list when it was possible to do so, continue to admit when he was wrong, prayed and meditated, and promoted spirituality to other alcoholics.

Although the twelve steps emphasized God, Keith didn't seek a real relationship with God until years later. Somewhere along the line something went wrong with the recovery plan. It was supposed to be foolproof. It was supposed to be forever. Maybe he'd stopped implementing the principles. Maybe he'd started trying to handle it all on his own, without God's help. Maybe that was what had led him back to this plague.

Keith tossed and turned for the rest of the night, tortured by voices in his head. *Keith, come back.*

Chapter Eighteen

Keith hardly wanted to get up the next morning, though it was a beautiful morning.

When I shook him, he moaned and rolled over on his stomach.

"Keith, get up," I shouted.

He ignored me by putting a pillow over his head.

Then I hopped into my wheelchair, made my way to the bathroom, filled a cup with cold water, rolled back into the room, and poured the cup of cold water on his face.

Keith jumped out of bed. "What did you do that for?"

"Are you kidding me? We're going to be late for work," I said.

I just sat back and watched him hurry to get himself together, tripping over furniture, flinging clothing here and there, and mumbling to himself. I had my signature "This is what you get" look on my face as I waited for him to be ready. I'd never dreamed my husband would

have a hangover, of all things. I was totally unprepared for it.

The drive to Push It was quiet. I was sure that
his head ached, but I didn't care. I didn't know
what the problem was, but I wanted this foolish
behavior to end. I just wanted *my* Keith back.

"I'll see you later," he said.

"Right." I wasn't going to give him the
satisfaction of thinking for one moment that
everything was okay when it wasn't. I hopped
out of the truck, and he sped down the street.

As if I didn't have enough to deal with at home,
I had to work on solutions for saving our Push It
Fitness Center. We had only a couple of weeks to
go. We had lost so many of our clients since the
pool scandal. The good news was that signing up
participants for the fitness challenge was easy
once it was announced on the radio, but recruit-
ing volunteers to help us was not as easy. People
started pouring in from everywhere to sign up,
so much so that we hardly had room enough
to contain them. We collected the five-dollar
entrance fee from them, weighed them in, and
also measured their muscle mass. There were
those who were obviously overweight, those who
were mildly overweight, and those who weren't
overweight at all. Some participants just needed
additional toning or wanted to become more fit
and healthy.

We explained to everyone that they had to commit to changing their eating habits over the next thirty to sixty days, to doing some structured cardio and strength routines, to stretching and being more flexible, to staying active throughout the day, and to making time for relaxation. It was a tall order, and some participants looked at us as if we were asking for their firstborn; nevertheless, these activities were necessary for their total body experience.

I was forced to speak to the crowd. "You see this challenge is designed to motivate you to exercise or lose weight. It's about changing the way people live, eat, and schedule their time," I said with a big grin plastered on my face.

"I, for one, know what getting off track can do to your body," Jasmine said. "Look at my thighs."

"Oh, please," Sharon smirked.

"No, really. I'm not the same size as I was in high school," Jasmine insisted.

"No one is, honey." Sharon was tall and lean, with random freckles on her face and long, wavy black hair, which she kept ponytailed when she was working. She was a mix of Greek and African American, which was reflected in her golden complexion.

"I know I'll be bench-pressing seventy-five pounds of weight," I announced. "That's my goal."

"Good for you, boss. I don't know if I'm ready for that." Jasmine giggled. "Maybe I'll walk a hundred miles. I could stand to burn at least five thousand calories."

Sharon smirked, "Only five thousand calories?"

"At least five thousand," Jasmine smirked back.

"I may do the bike challenge," Sharon said, throwing her head back and releasing her thick, shiny black hair from the ponytail so that she looked like a model for a shampoo commercial.

"Sounds good." I bit my lip, wishing that I too could do the walk or the biking.

"Swimming is what's gonna do it for me. I was a three-time state swim champion in college," Jacque said, flexing his muscles.

"Nice." I was ready to change the subject now. It was always painful to remember the categories I could no longer compete in.

Where was Keith? It was Saturday. Was he working, at home, or was he with Paul? He was supposed to be here to help with the sign-ups. He used to be dependable, but after last night I just didn't know what to think. How could he do that to me, to us?

We spent the next few hours registering all the walk-ins. Then there were the online sign-ups. If we could keep this momentum going and

get full support from the community, I was sure
we could turn Push It's reputation around.

When the crowd had left and the gym was
quiet again, I went to my office to relax. We had
succeeded in at least getting the word out about
the challenge. It had been expensive, with the
commercial slot, but it had been worth it. We
had made a lot of the money back from the entrance fees. I was more than grateful for that. I
took my Bible from my desk drawer and began
to meditate on God's goodness. There, in that
office, I bowed my head and folded my hands.

"Dear Lord, I put everything in your hands,
my husband, this business. I know the plans you
have for me, plans to make me prosper, not to
harm me, to give me hope and a future. Lord,
I love you. Show me what to do in every area of
my life. And, Lord, no matter what I think, don't
let me stand in the way of your will. Your will be
done in my life, Lord."

At the end of the day I glanced through the
blinds at the occasional passerby and noted
the beauty of the streetlights beaming onto the
dark pavement. An old lady walked by in raggedy clothing, clutching several paper shopping
bags. Her face looked wrinkled and thin. When
I looked at her feet, I immediately recognized
her from the last church gala we had to feed the
homeless. She stood out because she wore these
beautiful purple alligator-skin boots. It was so

unlikely for a woman of her stature in life to have such exotic-looking boots. They looked like they might have been designed by Nine West, Kenneth Cole, or Steve Madden. In any case, she had told us that a woman took them off her own feet and gave them to her.

I remembered being so touched by the story that I wanted to give to her also. But she wouldn't accept anything from us, no help, no money, nothing. The only thing she wanted was food. And that day she had her fill of that. But although many other things in her life were missing and broken, she refused to accept any other help. She was still a proud woman. Mama used to say, "Gal, pride always comes before a fall." My guess was this lady had already fallen to the bottom. *Lord, be with her.*

Before Keith came to pick me up, I called him to suggest that we go out for dinner.

"Sure, that's cool. Where would you like to go?" he'd said.

"Let's do Madiba, since it's in the area. Besides, we haven't been there in a while."

"Sounds good," he'd said.

"Good."

I couldn't wait to get him in a public place, where he couldn't run or hide. Then I'd confront him about his volatile behavior, and he'd have to answer me. He wouldn't ignore me at Madiba.

Chapter Nineteen

Keith and I walked into Madiba, a restaurant that specialized in South African food and culture. Its decor was that of the informal dining halls in South African townships. It had authentic music, eclectic cuisine, and arts and crafts. It was brightly colored and decorated with art on the walls. The tables were lined up adjacent to each other, with green table tops, and apple-red chairs. We came here often because of the restaurant's good food and atmosphere. Since it was only two blocks over from Push It, its convenience was irresistible as well.

Even though it was our first night out alone together in a long time, the mood was somber. Attempting to make the night as normal as possible, I wore my red silk dress with a moderately plunging neckline and a short white jacket over it. I also wore my favorite little bobbed wig. Keith's eyes didn't dance with excitement, as they usually did when I wore this outfit. I ordered Organic Chicken Wings Peri Peri, marinated in spicy dried pepper oil with garlic and vinegar, a favorite of mine. Then I ordered Chocolate Indulgence for dessert. Keith ordered the Oxtail Potjie Kos Bredie, which was oxtails slow cooked in a traditional rich stew, and a side order of curry and rice. We seldom ate such big meals, but when it came to Madiba, all the rules went out the window.

The live band played soft native South African musical selections as I stared into Keith's eyes. I didn't have time to play games, so I started in on Keith right away. "What's going on with you, Keith? With us?"

He sighed. "Can't we just enjoy our dinner without getting into all of this?"

"No, we can't."

"Then what's the point of us coming here if we're just going to fight?"

"We had to continue with our normal plans, even though you haven't been acting normal."

"What do you mean, I haven't been acting normal?" Keith pointed to himself. "I'm the same me."

"No, you're not the same you," I said with just a hint of sarcasm.

Keith didn't miss a beat. "Whatever."

"At least here at this restaurant there is nowhere to hide." I looked all around me. "I've got to know what's going on with you."

Keith frowned. "I've got a lot on my mind."

"Okay, so have I, but I'm not lashing out at you," I said.

"Oh, you're not? Then what do you call this? A friendly inquisition?"

"You know what I mean."

"No. I don't." Keith banged his fist on the table.

A couple across from us turned around to look at us. Keith made an apologetic gesture while I smirked at him.

"See what I mean? You're drinking and acting different. You've been skipping church. You won't talk to me. You won't pray."

"How do you know what I do?"

"Oh, you're right. I don't know what you do. Okay, you don't pray with me anymore, so I don't know what to think."

Keith put his hand up. "Don't think anything. Why don't you just leave me alone?"

"See what I mean?" I slapped his hand down. "You used to not be this way."

My own temper was rising up in me. I didn't have to sit here and take this disrespect. I didn't have to sit here and watch him squirm and listen to him make excuses. I had better things to do, and I deserved better than this cold treatment. The way he talked to me reminded me of how Dad used to talk to Mama before he got his life together, how he'd tell her off and then leave. He'd leave and be gone for months or sometimes years at a time, only to return and do the exact same thing. I wasn't going to get stuck in that cycle. I was not the one.

Keith stared at me. "What way?"

"Cruel and hard," I said.

"Oh yeah, you're right. That was your job."

"Don't do this, Keith," I said. "I can't help you if—"

"Help? The only help I need is to find my brother so he doesn't end up dying on the street like—"

I pushed him because I had no choice. It took everything in me to not jump on the table and start screaming. With the help of the Holy Spirit, I remained calm. "Like what?"

Keith coughed hard. "Like my dad did."

I opened my mouth wide. "You never told me your dad died on the street."

"No, he didn't die in the street. He died at home," Keith blurted out.

"Okay?"

"He died at home, in front of us, because of his life in the streets," Keith said.

"What do you mean?" I squinted my eyes. "You told me your dad died of natural causes."

"Well, if you're an alcoholic like he was and you die, it *is* natural," Keith said matter-of-factly.

I didn't buy his excuse. "An alcoholic? But why didn't you tell me?"

"It's not exactly first-date conversation."

"This is not our second date." I held up my hand with the wedding ring. "We're married, for goodness' sake."

Indeed, I remembered our wedding day. Alex had driven me and Dad down to Missionary Church. I wore a beautiful powder-blue gown with a matching veil. I didn't have the heart to wear white, even though I was told that I could. The church was decorated with blue- tinted carnations and white ones. Alex was my maid of honor, and she wore a powder-blue dress. Dad walked me down the aisle slowly since he had a bad hip. The entire church was invited to the ceremony, although not everyone attended. Sister Winifred and Yvonne weren't there. *Haters,* I thought to myself. Aunt Dorothy made the wedding cake, which was served right after Keith and I took communion, knelt down to be prayed over, and then recited the vows we'd written. Finally, in front of family and friendly onlookers, Pastor Martin pronounced us man and wife.

"It's not the kind of thing you want to bring to your wife," Keith said.

"If not me, then who?" I tried to hold back the tears. "You just hold it in until it destroys you?"

Eventually, the waiter delivered our food and we began to eat.

Keith covered his face with his hands. "It was never supposed to end up like this."

"What do you mean?" I pulled his hands away from his face.

"Nothing. I—"

The band's music switched to a livelier note. I noticed an older lady, who sat at the table in front of us, tapping her foot.

"Keith Bryant, talk to me."

"I was supposed to go away to school and come back to help everybody. My brother, Robert, was supposed to follow me to college."

"But he didn't?"

Keith swallowed hard. "No, he didn't."

"What happened?"

"I left him with my dad. That's what happened. He ended up with the wrong crowd and dropped out of school." Keith shook his head.

"That's not your fault. That's no one's fault."

"No, it's my fault." Keith swallowed hard.

The waiter stopped by to ask if everything was okay, so I smiled a fake smile and told him that everything was great. Unfortunately, the conversation I was having with my husband was not great. If only he could do something about that.

After the waiter walked away, I continued. "What happened, Keith?"

"On Christmas break of my junior year I came home to visit. I hadn't come home for Thanksgiving, because I had dinner with my girlfriend's family." Keith paused. "Anyway, home was no welcome place. My dad was sprawled out on the couch in his underwear with a bottle of Jack Daniel's in his hand."

"Wow. That must've been tough."

I imagined my own dysfunctional family, with my absentee father and my "trying to hold it all together" mother, who was sometimes too harsh because of her own pain. I remembered how Mama tried to mask her issues by hiding in the duties of the church, even before she became saved for real. I remembered the male suitors she put her hopes in before she met Jesus for the first time. And the lonely nights Alex and I sat home by ourselves, wondering when Mama would get a grip and get over the fact that Dad was gone. Somewhere between her pious pretense and the many hours she spent volunteering at church, Mama caught hold of the Word of God. She was never the same again.

"Yeah, it was tough. There was no Christmas tree, no presents, just garbage everywhere, and believe me, it was a far cry from the campus life I had become used to. College had become a home away from home. My scholarships afforded me that luxury."

"I can understand that. I kind of felt like Alex abandoned me when she went away to college."

"I wanted a better life for myself, and I wanted a better life for my brother too."

"What did he want?"

"Nothing. He had dropped out of high school and had been running wild ever since."

"Oh," I said.

"Worse yet, I had to confront Robert about some rumors I heard, and he denied everything. I was relieved, even though I wasn't sure if I believed him or not."

"Rumors about what?"

"Being in a gang." Keith balled up his fist and hit it against the palm of his other hand. "I knew that if things didn't change, he'd be locked up or killed."

"Right. Okay . . ." I hung on to Keith's every word. I wanted him to know that I was there for him, that I would always be there for him.

"I wanted to change everything those few weeks when I was home. I wanted to get help for my dad, even though he said he didn't want help. I tried everything, but do you know what my dad told me?"

"No. What did he tell you?"

"To leave him alone, that he'd never stop drinking. That his bottle was better to him than I was." Keith sniffled and wiped his nose with his sleeve.

I shook my head. "I'm sure he didn't mean that."

"Yes, he did. He did," Keith said as the bitter memories came rushing back. "One night, while we were sleeping, Robert and I heard a loud bump coming from the kitchen. We both ran barefoot to the kitchen."

"What was it, Keith?"

"We found our father crawling around on the floor, moaning in a pool of his own blood. I'll never forget the thick, dark texture of it." Tears began to freely fall down Keith's face.

"Oh my goodness. You had to be scared."

"We were. We tried to help him, tried to get him some help, but by the time the paramedics arrived, it was too late. Within minutes they pronounced him dead."

"I'm sorry to hear that," I said. I felt my husband's pain as he told me the tragedy that apparently had left him changed forever. I rubbed his hair gently and tried to speak soft words, but I knew that none of that could erase the trauma he had suffered. Only God could do that.

"Cirrhosis of the liver took him out." Keith dried his face. "That's why I've got to save Robert. I promised him I'd do better by him. I can't let the same thing happen again."

At least now I knew what he was up against. "Okay . . ."

"That's why I've got to go. . . ."

"Go where?"

"I've got to go find him," Keith said.

Chapter Twenty

Keith

Keith and Taylor arrived at JFK Airport early Friday morning.

Nothing could stop them from catching their flight. Determined to find his brother, even if he had to circle the globe, Keith had secretly packed their passports just in case there were any unexpected developments. Taylor's eyes were puffy and swollen from crying the night before, and Keith felt sorry for her. She had begged him not to let his brother's disappearance come between them, not to let it destroy him. Still, he hadn't had it in him to stop her tears. This was something that he had to do, and nothing but the hand of God could stop him. They checked their luggage and boarded the aircraft.

Keith couldn't wait to get to Chicago. He didn't have a plan, but he felt confident that once he arrived in Chicago, he would know what to do. *The steps of the righteous are ordered by the Lord.* His mind was clear, but his heart was hurting. If only he could have just one drink on the plane. Taylor wouldn't stand for that, he thought. He knew she'd turn that plane upside down if he so much as said he was thirsty for alcohol. So he ignored the flight attendant passing through the cabin with her cart of snacks and turned his head toward the window.

He wanted to stare at the clouds, to become lost in his thoughts. His wife sat next to him, holding his hand, and he was grateful that she had volunteered to come with him. He wondered if she was genuinely concerned or if this was just an attempt to keep an eye on him. Either way he didn't really want to be alone on this trip, so he was glad his strong-willed wife had joined him. He quietly prayed that God would settle everything concerning them and that he would find his brother alive and well.

When they got off the plane at O'Hare International Airport, Keith's aunt Rita was there to meet them. She was an older woman with dark chocolate–colored skin and deep dimples in both cheeks. She had a somewhat plump build and skinny legs. She wore her silver-gray hair slicked back and had medium-sized gold hoop earrings in her ears.

"Keith, it's so good to see you, chile," Aunt Rita said.

"It's good to see you too, Aunt Rita."

"This must be your beautiful wife. I didn't know she had a disability. I could've brought a chair for her. I've still got your uncle Willie's chair at home." Aunt Rita reached out to hug Taylor. "It's good to meet you, honey."

There it was again, her disability. Before people noticed her smile or her winning personality, they noticed Taylor's equipment. Taylor sighed and then hugged her back. Keith hugged her too, taking in a whiff of vanilla and Blue Magic hair grease.

"Yes, this is Taylor. Taylor, this is Aunt Rita," Keith said.

"It's nice to meet you too," Taylor replied.

Aunt Rita signaled them to keep moving. "Well, we'd better get going. I know y'all didn't travel all the way across the country to chitchat in the lobby of the airport, so let's go."

Keith and Taylor followed her out to the parking lot and hopped into her big car.

Chicago's South Side was just as Keith remembered it, a section of the city with much potential, despite its harsh exterior. They even passed by the area where the infamous Robert Taylor Homes used to be. Keith noticed that a number of the buildings had been demolished and had been replaced by nouveau Victorian houses, complete with mowed lawns. Still, he knew there weren't enough of these homes to house everyone from the public housing buildings that had disappeared, and he wondered what had happened to the displaced residents.

He leaned over to whisper to Taylor while his aunt Rita answered her cell phone. "The Robert Taylor Homes used to be right over there. About twenty-eight identical towers."

Taylor nodded, displaying a quiet sensitivity. "You mean the ones we saw on the documentary?"

"Yep," Keith said. "Those are the ones."

The documentary had been on the decay of the community as a result of poverty, gang violence, cop shootings, and drug addiction. They had watched it together, with Keith almost in tears, although he didn't say much. He had never shared with his wife how close he lived to this area.

Before long they arrived at Aunt Rita's house. Keith remembered it vaguely from his childhood, not that he was there often, but he did remember attending a few parties there and spending the night once or twice. Whether it had been a cousin's birthday bash or a backyard barbecue, Keith remembered always feeling welcome in Aunt Rita's home. Her house was a modest three-bedroom, split-level brick house, complete with one and a half bathrooms and rickety steps that led to the front door.

Inside the house the Victorian-style furniture was covered with plastic seat covers.

"Come on in and sit down. Make yourselves at home," Aunt Rita said.

"Thanks," Keith and Taylor said in unison.

Keith looked around, recalling his childhood visits, as he stepped onto the oriental carpet.

It was like going back in time. Everywhere he looked, there was antique furniture and trinkets.

There was a mahogany grandfather clock in a corner of the living room, and a mahogany china cabinet containing ancient-looking dishes, some of which Keith was sure were crystal, stood in the dining room. There were porcelain sculptures of ballerinas and little French girls in petticoats. There were lace Priscilla curtains on the windows. The lamps were all porcelain and shaded. The walls were covered with pictures of the family, especially Aunt Rita and her three sons. There was one picture in particular of Keith, his parents, and his brother that interested Keith. Seeing his mother, who had abandoned him when he was four years old, was bittersweet. He had so few memories of her. Keith swallowed his emotions and focused in on his aunt.

"Let me get you two some tea," Aunt Rita said before disappearing into the kitchen.

Within minutes she reappeared with a silver tea set and offered us chocolate-covered raisins.

Aunt Rita sat down on the arm of the flowered couch. "I know what you're going through, feeling like you could've done more for your brother. I feel the same way too sometimes."

Keith raised his eyebrows. "What do you mean?"

"Well, I always stayed away, and if you ever wondered why I didn't get involved in your lives more, it was because your father didn't want me to," Aunt Rita said.

Keith took Aunt Rita's hand. "Why not?"

"He was always fussing and cussing, and I didn't like it. I'd always get on my brother about doing the right thing in front of you kids. I kept praying for y'all, but I just couldn't deal with your father's mess. He'd kick me out sometimes when I came by. Didn't want to hear anything I had to say about changing his life," Aunt Rita said, sniffling, as though she were about to break down any minute.

"I can believe that. He was very stubborn." Keith did not crack a smile.

"Yes, very. Darn near stupid." Aunt Rita shook her head. "It's a crying shame all that old fool wanted was a bottle of that darn Jack Daniel's."

"Yep, that was Dad," Keith said, smiling a sickly smile.

Aunt Rita sighed. "It was him, all right. But sometimes I think I should've pushed my way in more. Maybe Robert would be around here today if I'd pushed more."

"You can't blame yourself, Aunt Rita," Keith said.

"Like *you* can't blame *yourself,* either," Aunt Rita whispered.

"Smart," Keith said. "You were always so smart, Aunt Rita."

"Uh-huh. God gives me wisdom. Now, we'll look for your brother as best we can, since you had an eyewitness that spotted him, but that's really all we can do besides pray. We can still pray that the angels will protect him and that someday God will bring him home," Aunt Rita said, lifting herself off of the couch.

"I've missed you, Aunt Rita," Keith said.

"I've missed you too," Aunt Rita said. "You know, the older you get, the more you look like your mother."

Keith didn't answer. He just smiled. He hardly knew Aunt Rita. He didn't remember his mother at all.

There was a record player in the corner of the living room and a stack of records beside it.

Taylor got up and walked over to it. "Wow, my mom had one of these, but she pawned it one day while my sister and I were growing up." Taylor took one of the records in her hand and felt the vinyl against her fingers.

"Ooh, I'd never sell mine. It's priceless. As you can see, I still have a big record collection." Aunt Rita shook her head.

"I see." Taylor held a few of the records in her hand. "My mom used to love Mahalia Jackson."

"Well, I used to love me some James Brown," Aunt Rita said as she walked out of the room.

Keith leaned over and whispered to Taylor, "I used to come over here and pretend this was my house, pretend Aunt Rita was my mom, and that my dad wasn't a drunk."

"I'm sorry," Taylor whispered back.

Keith swallowed hard. "I'm okay. I've just got to find my brother and make this thing right."

"We'll find him," Taylor said softly.

Aunt Rita served them hot spaghetti and meatballs for lunch, and then Keith set out along an unknown trail. Upon Keith's insistence, Taylor stayed at home with Aunt Rita.

It was Friday night, and the streets were alive with activity. Keith didn't know where to look first, so he started with the pool hall by his old home in Bronzeville, which was just a bus ride away from Aunt Rita's house. As soon as he approached the street, he took a deep breath.

He hadn't been back to this street in so long. He saw the elementary school and junior high school he attended, the corner church where he was baptized along with Aunt Rita's three boys, the three-story apartment building he grew up in, and the raggedy little pool hall.

Although it was run by a fairly decent old man, he remembered that they used to run numbers in the back room, and that it was always a haven for drug addicts and petty criminals.

Yet the police never shut it down. As an adult, Keith had wondered if the police had been on the payroll themselves. In any case, Robert used to work for old man Wilson from time to time, running errands and doing miscellaneous tasks around the business. Keith had always worried about the unsavory characters that liked to hang out in there, though. He couldn't dictate which people were allowed to play pool or video games, but he didn't like it nonetheless.

Keith asked around the pool hall. No one admitted to seeing Robert at all.

"Naw, man. I haven't seen little Robert in years," old man Wilson said, pulling his beard.

That news was very discouraging to Keith because Robert loved to shoot pool. He'd thought that this might be the first place Robert would come to if he were in the area.

Keith's next stop was the liquor store around the corner. It used to be his father's favorite hangout, as well as that of his degenerate buddies, so he figured stopping there was worth a shot. No luck there, either. He even stopped at the neighborhood barbershops. Then Keith walked around the entire neighborhood until his feet hurt, looking in abandoned cars and checking behind Dumpsters. The only places he didn't dare venture into alone were abandoned buildings. He was well aware of the goings-on in those. For that kind of search, he would need backup. Maybe Aunt Rita could convince one of his cousins to help.

Keith took the train down to Monroe Street and Millennium Park. He remembered that the twenty-four-and-a-half-acre park was another hot spot for the lonely, homeless, or disenfranchised. He figured it might be easy for Robert to hide out in this beautiful park and find refuge after hours if he needed to. Although the park had garnered awards for its art, music, architecture, and landscape design, he knew this fact probably wouldn't matter to someone who was strung out on drugs. As soon as he hit the corner of Monroe Street and Michigan Avenue, which was the southeast corner of Millennium Park, he could see the Crown Fountain, consisting of two fifty-foot glass blocks at each end of a reflecting pool. Water spewed out from the video images of mouths displayed on the two glass blocks, just as he remembered. He took a deep breath and kept walking. Then he went down to Navy Pier.

Keith was tired and discouraged, but he was afraid to stop looking. He was also afraid of what he might find if he didn't.

Chapter Twenty-one

While Keith was out looking for his brother, I stayed back at the house with Aunt Rita. It was clear that she was Keith's family from her dark skin, her deep dimples, and the way she twitched her nose when she laughed. She told me all the stories about Keith and his brother when they were children, and I enjoyed hearing them. She told me about how Keith and Robert used to love pretending that they were pirates, and how they'd hid under the stairs one time, pretending that it was a pirate ship. She also told me how Keith had always loved to read, how he was very good at sports, and how all the neighborhood girls flocked to him when he was a teenager. I figured as much, but she could have left that one detail out, I thought to myself. Regardless, it made me feel closer to him to hear about his childhood exploits. Then without warning, she brought up what I figured she had been curious about all along.

Aunt Rita took a seat in the armchair directly across from me. "So how did you hurt your legs, sweetie?"

"It was a bad car accident," I said, twisting uncomfortably in the chair.

"Must've been something, huh?"

I sighed. "Yes, it was. The driver was drunk."

"Mercy." Aunt Rita shook her head and waved her hand in the air. "Oh my. It's so unfair that such an irresponsible person would crash into you."

Without eye contact, I said, "Actually, it was my date who was drunk and crashed into someone else."

There was a beat of silence before she responded. "Oh, I see."

I could see the concern on her face, and I could imagine what she was thinking. What was her precious Keith doing with a messed-up woman like me?

Finally, we settled in front of the television. We watched sitcom after sitcom, until I was bored beyond belief. I hadn't watched that much television since Mama was alive. Before the next show could come on, I suggested that I go out to buy us dessert.

"Are you sure, dear?"

"Yeah, I'm sure," I said. *Sure I'm bored out of my mind, that is.*

"But maybe you should wait for Keith. I mean with your . . . I mean."

"I'll be okay. I'm a New Yorker, Aunt Rita. Believe it or not, I'm used to getting around by myself," I said. That was only partially true. Yes, I was used to getting around by myself, but that was mostly before the accident. The accident had taken away a great deal of my independence, more than I was ready or willing to admit.

"Well, I don't know." Aunt Rita had an expression of pain on her face.

"I need to get out for a while," I said. "I'm restless sitting here waiting for Keith."

"I understand, but, but I . . ."

"Don't worry." I took up my braces and hopped over to kiss her plump cheek. "I won't go far. Besides, I have my cell phone with me."

Before she could stop me, I was out the front door and dragging myself up the street to the corner store.

The people looked just like most people in the inner city, tired and rough. Fortunately, I was used to it, so that alone couldn't scare me away. I had to help my husband find his brother.

I went inside the store and purchased a pint of Häagen-Dazs chocolate chip ice cream.

When I exited, I turned left instead of right, which would've taken me back up the block to

Aunt Rita's. Two teenagers stood in front of an abandoned building. One wore a bandanna around his head, and the other wore a dirty baseball cap. Both had sagging pants, which seemed at least two sizes too big, and I thought about Joshua's sermons. He frequently pointed out that the origin of the sagging pants was prison, and that wearing one's pants this way was originally supposed to be a kind of homosexual mating call. As I stumbled past them, I heard them snickering. Were they laughing at me because of my condition, or was it just a private joke they were tickled by? Maybe I was paranoid. In either case, I wondered if they were good kids who went to school every day and took care of their business, or if they were gang-bangers, destined for jail. I certainly couldn't tell just by looking at them, and I avoided direct eye contact nonetheless.

Then I saw it. It was a café called the Road Dog, which I remembered Paul bragging about one night, when he was rambling on and on about his days in Chicago. The Road Dog Café looked rough from the outside, like a dilapidated old brick building that had all but been abandoned. The sign was falling apart, with the *a* in *Café* missing. The windows were tinted, so I couldn't see inside. I slowly slipped through the

front doors. As horrible as it looked on the outside, the atmosphere was everything Paul had
said it was on the inside, with rich smells of food
lingering in the air, a line of people waiting to
be served, and smooth jazz playing in the background. It was not unlike a few places I had been
to in New York.

I squeezed past a young couple and a middle-aged lady, then took a seat at an empty
round table, placing my braces next to me.

A short, shapely waitress with multiple ear
piercings bounced over to me. "What do you
want, honey?"

"I'm looking for someone," I whispered. "Well,
two people, really."

"Two people?"

"Yep, sort of," I said. I wasn't sure if this was
the right way to go about looking for someone
under these conditions, but I had nothing to
lose.

"Well?" The waitress smacked her gum.

I leaned in closer to the waitress. "Do you
know a Robert Bryant or a Paul Myers?"

"Sorry. I just started working here last week."
The waitress pointed straight ahead. "But you
see that guy over there by the door?"

"Yeah, I see him," I said.

"He's a regular in here and has been for a long time, they told me. Maybe he can help you." The waitress walked away before I could ask anything else.

"Okay, thanks." I struggled to stand up, took hold of my braces, and walked over to the man she had pointed out.

The man looked like he was in his mid- to late sixties. He wore a tight orange and brown outfit that just screamed the seventies, brown wing-tip shoes, and he smelled of cigar smoke. After I introduced myself and asked if he knew my brother-in-law, he told me that he did remember Robert, that he was a good kid. The sad part was that he told me that he did not know Robert's whereabouts and that he hadn't seen him around in a couple of years. When I asked about Paul, however, he seemed more interested. I was glad that I had struck a nerve.

"So you do know Paul, Mr. . . . . uh?"

"Uh-huh, and call me Mack." He chuckled.

"Well, what do you know?" I said with a little street savvy mixed in with a little apprehension.

"Not much, 'cept your boy Paul is a con," Mack said, twisting his jaw back and forth, as if he were trying to get food out of his teeth.

"What do you mean?"

Mack squinted his eyes before speaking. "Paul Meyers is a no-good con man."

I leaned in a little closer. "Okay . . ."

"Yeah, word around here is that he had his own woman out here on these streets one time," Mack said.

I blinked my eyes uncontrollably. "What in the world?"

"He's a real loser, you know?" He just shook his head. "You're not interested in him for yo'self, are ya?"

"No way." I put both hands up to demonstrate a definite no. "But I thought he was into real estate?"

"Yeah, I guess he was, if you consider women property. Then again he did used to own a couple of tenements over on Elm Street." Mack peered around him. "He was a real slumlord."

"So he was no businessman?"

"Nah, but he was a slumlord and a con. Everybody round here was glad when he left."

Mack chuckled right before we ended our conversation.

"Thank you, Mr. Mack," I said.

"Just Mack, darlin'." Mack grinned, revealing some missing teeth. "I ain't that old yet."

I walked back to Aunt Rita's with no news about Robert but with a newfound lack of respect for Paul. I knew he was shady, but I never imagined that he had a street rep as well. The only thing I was concerned about was telling Keith about his good friend. Keith had been so close-minded where Paul was concerned, I was almost afraid to go there. Almost.

When I got back, Aunt Rita was nearly hysterical. "Girl, don't you ever scare me like that again! I tried calling your phone, but no answer."

"I'm sorry. I didn't hear it, because I forgot to take it off vibrate," I said. "Did Keith call?"

"No, and I'm glad he didn't. He would've been worried sick."

"I didn't mean to worry you. I just decided to stop in at the Road Dog Café to do a little investigating myself." I was actually rather pleased with myself, whether she knew it or not.

"The Road Dog? What do you know about that place?"

"Not much, except that Keith's friend Paul mentioned it was nice."

"It's all right. Nothing special," Aunt Rita said.

I studied Aunt Rita's face for her reaction. "I wanted to ask around about Robert, and I also decided to ask about Paul, since he claims to be the last one who saw Robert."

"Hmm. Claims? You don't trust this Paul, do you?" Aunt Rita held her gaze on me.

"Not as far as I can throw him, no," I said. "Do you know him?"

"No, chile. Never met him," Aunt Rita said. "Your husband kept his private life very private once he went off to college. He never brought any of his friends or girlfriends by to meet me. Don't think he brought anyone home to meet his father, either."

"Well, this Paul person showed up on our doorstep not too long ago, down on his luck, and stayed with us for three months." I sighed as I remembered the horror. "In that short time more bad stuff happened than you can imagine."

"Whaaat?" Aunt Rita sat with her mouth opened wide.

"I'm not blaming him for everything we've gone through, but I have some suspicions about him and his intentions."

"How so?"

"I think he's trying to ruin Keith, but I just can't prove it yet. And Keith is not on my side with this at all. He doesn't believe it."

"Oh, I see," Aunt Rita said.

"He loves me, but he thinks I am paranoid and am overreacting. I think I'm right on point. I think, just like I heard tonight, that Paul is trouble."

A couple of hours later, Keith returned, empty-handed.

Aunt Rita prepared the guest room for us, and we slept comfortably through the night, not discussing anything until morning.

Early the next morning, we went out to Lincoln Park Zoo, the Garfield Park Conservatory, and Skydeck Chicago. Keith thought it would be fun for us to check these few places together and to enjoy the tourist attractions while we searched for Robert. Since I was tired of being cooped up in Aunt Rita's house, I didn't argue. Sadly, we had no luck finding Robert.

On the way back we bumped into an extraordinary church building that was for rent. It was a bona fide gem in the midst of decaying and abandoned buildings. It appeared to be open for some reason, so we decided to take a look inside. It had arches detailed with angels, a choir loft on the upper level, mahogany pews, a mezzanine, and windows encompassing the third-floor level. There were two enormous sliding frosted-glass window panels and a curvy hallway, which made the space seem like a giant maze. Wherever there was no carpet, there were hardwood floors. Since the building was once a Catholic church, there was even a vestiary.

"This morning was fun," I said, once we had finished our tour of the church. "I'm sorry about your brother, though."

"I just don't have any more leads. I don't know where else to look."

"Did you check with any of his old friends?"

"That's what I did first, and most of them were from the old neighborhood, but no one has seen him recently," Keith said, with more than a speck of disappointment in his eyes.

"Wow. No one?"

Keith nodded. "No one."

"I just don't understand. How can a grown man just drop off the face of the earth without anyone seeing him?"

"I don't know," Keith said. "He must know we'd be looking for him by now."

I hated saying it, but it had to be said. "Maybe he does know you're looking for him, but maybe he doesn't want to be found."

Keith looked at me with droopy eyes, and immediately I regretted ever saying it.

"Maybe. Either way, it's time for us to leave." Keith put his arm around my shoulders as we headed for the train station.

Keith's aunt Rita drove us to the airport in her 1992 Cadillac Eldorado. It was a big car that provided a comfortable ride. As she whizzed through the treacherous streets, she told us how we were going to be missed, and she invited us to come stay with her again. Aside from her cheerful chatter, the ride was quiet. Keith and I answered her, threw in an occasional chuckle and a head nod when necessary. I could tell that Keith was writhing about his still missing brother, yet no one dared to mention Robert's name. Our entire trip had been a failure, and I could see the discouragement on Keith's face.

"Honey, don't stay away so long." Aunt Rita hugged my husband after we climbed out of the car at the airport.

"I won't," Keith said.

"Good." Aunt Rita let him go, then grabbed his hand and squeezed it.

Finally, she gave me a hug that reminded me of my mother. It was warm and smooth, and she smelled of cinnamon. I remembered that Mama often smelled like baked goodies herself. A lump formed in my throat afterward.

Keith and I were on our way back home from Chicago, checking in at O' Hare International Airport. We hadn't found Robert, but I had gathered valuable information about Paul, and although there was tension between Keith and me, it was worth the trip just to tell him about Paul. We had arrived at the airport an hour earlier than our flight just to be on the safe side.

While we were waiting in the boarding gate area, Keith received a call from his aunt Rita.

I sat on the edge of my seat as I heard bits and pieces of information that sounded promising. As soon as he ended the call, I pounced on him.

"What?"

Keith stared straight ahead of him, as if he were in a daze. "Aunt Rita said a young girl came by the house."

"Okay . . . so?"

"Her name is Maria, and she said that Robert went to Mexico with her sister, Lupita, a month ago."

"What? Lupita?" I braced myself for the rest of the story. "Okay . . ."

Keith explained, "According to her, they've been dating for the past six months and . . ."

"And what?"

"And Aunt Rita said she had a picture of the two of them together. She sent a copy of the picture to my phone." Keith pressed a few buttons and handed the phone to me.

Sure enough, there was a scrawny, rough-looking man who badly needed a haircut and a shave. He looked much older than his years, and he had his arms around a pretty Mexican woman. She looked like she was in her early twenties, and she looked healthy, unlike Robert.

I passed the phone back to Keith. "How did she know we were looking for Robert?"

Keith was smiling again. "I put the word out, and you know how word on the street spreads."

"Yeah, like wildfire," I said, chuckling.

"We can't go home now," Keith said.

"Why not?"

"Because we've got to go to Mexico."

I shook my head. "I don't know. This sounds like a long shot to me."

"Maybe, but do I have a choice?"

I pulled myself to stand up. "I don't mean to sound insensitive—"

"Then don't," Keith snapped.

"It's just that we've got so much going on with the business and this fitness challenge coming up soon, and the media, and—"

Keith didn't blink. "I know about the business stuff, but I've got to do this."

"Sometimes you sound like you don't really care at all about the business," I said, concerned that we might be going on another wild-goose chase.

"I didn't say that." Keith's jaw tightened.

I backed up against the wall and put one hand on my hip. "Like you don't care about our livelihood."

"No, *your* livelihood," Keith said sternly.

"Oh, is that what this is? You don't care, because you've got your career in physical therapy? Well, this is the only income I have, Keith, and—"

"I'm sorry. I didn't mean that. It's just that the business has taken all of our money, and it hasn't even turned anything near a profit yet."

I rolled my eyes. "So?"

"So, you know I care about Push It. It's my dream too, but I'm frustrated. And I've got to at least try to find my brother. I've got to know I did all I could to help him, or I'll never forgive myself."

"Even if it costs us everything?"

"It won't." Keith grabbed both of my shoulders and leaned in close to me. "Just trust me."

"I do trust you," I said. It was just that my trust in him was waning under the weight of our issues.

Before I knew it, we were on a flight headed to Houston so that we could connect with a flight to Mexico, compliments of a credit card we reluctantly decided to max out. First, I called Alex and begged her to keep an eye on the business for me. Then I called Jasmine and told her that she would have to be in charge for a few more days. She was happier than ever for the added responsibility, but I wasn't. I had never been away from my baby, Push It, for this long, and an extended vacation was never my plan. However, despite my concerns, and they were many, my husband had to come first. In any case, the fitness challenge was just a few weeks away, and I knew that I would have to prove to the entire community, including my husband, that Push It was here to stay. *Lord, please guide us.*

Deep inside I wondered if we were making a big mistake, if we were wasting our time and the last of our emergency credit and cash reserve. I guessed this did kind of qualify as an emergency. After all, if my brother-in-law was as strung out on drugs as Keith suspected that he was, then his life really was in danger.

I looked over at Keith and saw the lines of worry across his forehead. I gently rubbed his forearm before placing my hand into his strong one. He squeezed it gently, as if to assure me that we were doing the right thing.

The ride was three hours and fourteen minutes, and Keith fell asleep about forty-five minutes into it. Although I put my head on Keith's shoulder, I couldn't sleep at all. My head was filled with questions, not only about Robert, but about Paul and Elaina too. With a vengeance-filled inspector like Elaina and a sneaky so-called friend like Paul, I didn't know whether I was coming or going. I could feel the anxiety rising up in my chest.

Chapter Twenty-two

After the long ride, our flight arrived in San Luis Potosi in Mexico. The first thing that we noticed when we departed the plane was that it was very hot. People all around us wore sombreros, and our bare heads were practically scorching. When we left Ponciano Arriaga International Airport, we headed toward the heart of San Luis Potosí in a complimentary shuttle bus. Thank goodness the driver spoke fluent English, because the street Spanish I picked up from the old neighborhood was a little rusty.

"How long will it take to get to downtown San Luis, sir?" Keith's Spanish was much more polished than mine because he'd studied it in college. Still, he spoke in English.

"About ten minutes," the driver said.

The bus was packed with people. The driver was a small man with a wide mustache. He not only drove but played the role of tour guide as well, announcing that San Luis was the tenth largest metropolitan area in Mexico and that it was a major commercial and industrial center. I could almost see that from the window. There were beautiful classically designed buildings lined up along open streets.

"Please take us to the Holiday Inn on Carretera Central," Keith said.

"Holiday Inn San Luis Potosí Quijote," the driver said.

"Sí," Keith said.

The driver answered, "Only about eight miles, senor."

Within minutes we arrived at the hotel. We checked in, dropped our bags, and were out on the streets again in no time. This time we took a taxi. We were told that it was only a twenty-minute drive to where Lupita, whose last name was Sanchez, and Robert were supposed to be staying.

As the taxi drove through the streets, we began to see haciendas and donkey-drawn alfalfa carts. There were loose dogs roaming everywhere and children casually riding on the backs of trucks. It was funny how only a twenty-minute drive took us from a thriving cultural center to the simplest of rural life. We arrived at the hacienda where Robert and Lupita were supposed to be living, and I had to admit it was much larger on the inside than it looked on the outside. However, it didn't take long for us to realize that we had the wrong address. We were at a dead end, and we didn't have much time. Our money was running low, and we knew that we both had to return to work soon.

I tried not to sound frustrated. "What do we do now?"

"Let's just go back to the city and follow the other leads we have."

"What other leads?" I was truly getting frustrated. I had always wanted to see Mexico, but not like this.

"Aunt Rita gave me one other address. It's supposed to be one of Lupita's friends. But first we'll check the university where Lupita is enrolled."

By this time, we were hungry, however, and decided to stop to eat. We chose a restaurant, and the owner, who looked quite happy that Americans had decided to patronize her establishment, recommended her specialty, *enchiladas potosinas*. This dish turned out to be bright orange enchiladas served with refried beans and guacamole. Keith and I both loved authentic Mexican food, so we thoroughly enjoyed our meal. When we were finished, we went up to the owner.

"*Muchas gracias, señora,*" Keith and I said in unison.

"*De nada,*" the owner answered. "*Adiós, mis amigos.*"

"*Adiós, señora,*" we said as we left the establishment.

San Luis was an interesting place, complete with waterfalls, thermal baths, green grass, and shade trees, yet the plazas made the biggest impact on me. They were everywhere downtown, surrounded by historic buildings. We took a taxi through the city, stopping at a few key points along the way.

First, we checked the Universidad Autónoma de San Luis Potosí, where Lupita allegedly attended college. We passed by the San Luis Potosí Regional Museum. Next, someone suggested we stop at the Theater of Peace, Teatro de la Paz, because it was a good place for students. We found out that the second floor of the theater told of its history, and that there was a gallery installed on the left side. There was also a good coffeehouse, called Café del Teatro, there, but there was no sign of the mysterious Lupita. We passed by the Plaza de Armas, located downtown, and could hear the state band playing. It was surrounded by the Catedral de San Luis Potosí, the Palacio Municipal, and the Palacio de Gobierno. We even checked an Internet café along the way. When we reached the second and only remaining address we had, it was a town house.

The young woman inside was named Camila and was also a student at the Universidad Autónoma de San Luis Potosí. She told us that she and Lupita had been friends and had even been roommates in the past. The key words were *had been* and *in the past,* as in past tense; they were no longer roommates or friends. Before disappointment could set in, though, she offered to take us to where Lupita now lived. Keith and I followed her as she led us to a rooftop casita that sat on top of a fairly modern apartment building near Tangamanga Park. Then she said, "Adios, amigos," and walked away.

"Okay, thanks. I mean, *gracias,*" Keith said anxiously as he stared at her as she disappeared down the street.

When we finally caught up with the mysterious Lupita, we could see why Robert might be enamored with her. She was young, pretty, and smart, with bouncy dark hair and big brown eyes.

"*Hola,*" Lupita said.

Since Keith was the one who spoke basic Spanish, he said, "*Hola, Lupita. Habla inglés?*"

"Yes, I speak English. I have family in the States." Lupita squinted her eyes at us and paused. "Who are you? What's going on?"

"My name is Keith Bryant," Keith said, extending his hand.

Lupita raised her thick eyebrows. "Bryant?"

Keith let his hand drop down to his side. "Yes, I'm Robert's brother, and this is my wife, Taylor."

"*Hola,*" I said, feeling uncomfortable with the language.

"Oh." Lupita stumbled back in shock.

"I didn't mean to surprise you like this, but we're looking for my brother," Keith explained.

"*No comprendo.* I don't understand." Lupita ran her hands through her long hair. "Why did you come to me? How did you know about me?"

"We were in Chicago, asking around about Robert, and, uh, a friend of yours told my aunt about you, that you and Robert were pretty close, and that he had come back to San Luis with you," Keith replied.

"Come in." Lupita opened the door wide.

"Thank you," Keith and I said in unison.

We walked through her neat and colorful apartment, following her onto a tiled terrace overlooking the city.

"Honestly, I don't know where Robert is," Lupita said.

Keith looked shattered. "But I thought he was here with you?"

Lupita motioned for us to sit down on the outdoor chairs. "He was here for a while, but then one day I woke up and he was gone."

Keith and I sat together on one seat, and she sat on another.

I felt her pain. "So he just left you?"

Lupita looked down at her hands. "Robert has a bad habit, you know."

"I know." Keith looked desperate. "But why did you bring him here with you?"

"I love him, and I think he cares about me, but he loves those drugs and the streets more than me." Lupita's eyes began to water. "I paid for his passport and for his ticket to come here. I wanted us to have a life together when I finish school, but—"

"Robert couldn't hang," I said, completing her sentence.

Lupita wiped the tears from her eyes. "No, not for long. Not at all."

Keith put his hands on his forehead as he processed the information. "Do you know if he went back to the States?"

"I don't know. Maybe. Maybe not. There are six major parks that are walking distance from here, so he could be hiding out in one of those, or he could've gone back."

"When was the last time you saw him?" Keith asked.

"It has been over a month, and he took all of his things," Lupita answered.

"I'm sorry," Keith said.

"Yeah, I'm sorry too. But it's okay," Lupita said.

Lupita offered us some tacos and burritos, which were freshly made, but we turned them down.

"If you see him, please tell him that I'm looking for him and give him my number."

Keith handed her a piece of paper with our contact information on it.

Lupita reached out to take the paper.

"You can also call me, us, anytime if you hear anything at all from him," Keith pleaded.

"I will." Lupita twiddled the paper between her fingers.

Then we hugged her and said good-bye before leaving her apartment.

"Adios," Lupita said.

That dead end marked the end of our time in Mexico, so we went back to the hotel. Since the night was clear and the air was fresh, we stood under the open sky, looking at the stars. The next day we woke up late, ate our complimentary breakfast, then left our hotel room and headed to the airport around noon, passing by businesses that were closed for the traditional siesta time. It was funny that we'd always heard about it in textbooks, but now we were able to experience it for ourselves. We were on our way back to our lives in the States, back to Brooklyn, New York, without a trace of Robert.

Chapter Twenty-three

The alarm clock went off on schedule. As soon as I opened my eyes that morning, I had a strange feeling. I immediately began to pray quietly and declared that my day would be a blessed one. I tapped my husband on the shoulder and climbed out of our queen-sized bed, yawning. It was our first day back since our little out-of-town adventure, so Keith was noticeably down. I slid into the shower with my pear shower gel and cleansed my body, but I could not wash away the feeling that had come over me.

"I've got the feeling that something is going to go down at work today," I said after stepping out of the shower.

"Don't worry. Everything will be okay." Keith kissed me on the lips.

"I hope you're right," I said.

Keith and I got dressed for work. I wanted to wear something lively in light of my mood, so I chose a bright red workout outfit I hadn't worn in years. Red was clearly my favorite color, because I thought it went with my fiery personality. My outfit consisted of a sporty spandex halter top and matching spandex pants. We ate a breakfast of oats cereal, an all-bran muffin, and fresh fruit. With one last spritz of my body splash, we were out the door.

Keith dropped me off as usual, helped me unlock everything, and turn on all the lights.

Nothing was unusual. I locked the door behind him when he left and looked around the entire building. Nothing seemed to be out of place. Everything looked normal, and I sincerely hoped that everything was. I didn't know if I could take any more surprises. I went to my office and waited for Jasmine to arrive.

At eight o clock Jasmine arrived like clockwork and got straight to work. Jacque arrived shortly after and immediately went to the pool area, even though he was early. Jasmine filled me in on everything that had happened while I was away, how two people had enrolled, how our supplies had been delivered on time, and how no one had complained about the pool. Thank goodness there had been no major catastrophes. Everyone had done their part while we were away, including Sharon, who was usually missing in action. Everyone had shown up on time and completed their assignments, and my sister, Alex, had overseen it all. I smiled because it was good to have a twin in my corner.

Three of our regular clients came in, and one of them, with towel in hand, headed straight back to the pool room. It was good to see that some people still believed in us and hadn't been persuaded by the negative publicity.

The phone rang, and I answered it, happy to be back at my place of business, until I realized it was a reporter wanting to do a follow-up story.

"Come down to our fitness challenge and I'll give you your follow-up," I said before carefully hanging up the phone.

"Good for you, boss." Jasmine held out her hand for a high five.

I slapped her a high five before we got started on our inventory. Just as we were tearing open the cardboard boxes that were stored in the corner of the room, we saw Elaina drive up in her Range Rover. She double-parked across the street because of the alternate side of the street parking rule.

I was standing right next to Jasmine at the time Elaina walked right into the building.

She looked like a million bucks, and I still hadn't figured out where she'd gotten all that money from. She was swinging a genuine Gucci bag, not one of those imitations you picked up at the flea market, but the real deal. She also wore diamond earrings and a matching bracelet. I could tell they were real by the sparkle. Besides, I had spent a lot of years studying the kind of jewelry I would demand from men. And her suit looked like she had just stepped out of the window at Lord & Taylor. I was an expert in the fashion department too. A sista was obviously rolling in money. But what did she want with me? I wondered. I had only a minute to gather my thoughts and my words.

"What can I do for you today? Is there another code violation I don't know about? Or are you making one up along the way to destroy my business?"

"What? I'm not the one who destroys everything." Elaina pointed her perfectly manicured index finger at me. "You are."

"I beg your pardon," I said.

"Don't beg, sister. It won't help you," Elaina said.

I shook my head. "I'm not your sister."

"You're right about that. My sister would've never killed my husband, Derek."

I looked at her like she was crazy and shook my head. "I did not kill Derek."

Elaina squinted her eyes. "Yes, you did. You killed Derek."

"I did not kill Derek." I didn't flinch. "He killed himself."

"You saw he was drunk, and you let him drive," Elaina spat out.

"Look, Derek was not a child, and I couldn't stop him from driving. I didn't want him driving, either. As you can see, it turned out bad for both of us." I looked over at Jasmine, who had been listening the whole time, and I was ashamed. This was no testimony for the young girl I was trying to mentor. This was just the hard, cold truth.

"Not bad enough for you," Elaina said.

The old me was trying to come forward. "Excuse me?"

"You deserved to die too. You took my husband from me. You cheated with him, stole him from me, and then you killed him," Elaina said.

I shot Jasmine a look that said "Be prepared for everything." I was glad Jasmine was from the streets too and would definitely know what to do when being attacked. "I did not steal him. He left you, and believe me, that had nothing to do with me. When I met him, he told me he was separated from his wife and was getting a divorce. Now I know that's wrong. I know that now, but I wasn't trying to—"

"Shut up." Elaina appeared disoriented and began to suddenly wipe her eyes. "I don't want to hear anything you have to say. You're guilty."

"I am innocent. I'm a different person now. I've been cleansed by the blood of Jesus, and I'm brand-new." I was really glad that this was true. As dirty as I used to be, I needed God's grace and mercy in a big way.

"Good! Let Jesus save you now." Elaina scowled.

Out of the corner of my eye I could see Jasmine moving closer to her cell phone. It wasn't my intention to evangelize to her, but without my knowledge or permission, it just came out. "Jesus already saved me, Elaina. He can do the same for you."

"Don't try to play mind games with me. I know what women like you are all about. You use people, especially men. You use them for their cars and their money. You use them up, and then, when you have no more use for them, you throw them away. After they've broken the hearts of their wives and children."

She was right. The woman she was describing was the old me. And, yes, I would've used Derek up and thrown him away. It was my MO back then. "I didn't kill your husband, though."

"You killed my marriage first. Then you killed my husband. He should've been home that night with me and his son."

"That's true, and I did play a part in it, but that's not entirely my fault. I am sorry about what I did, though," I said.

"Do you know what it's like to have a child all the time asking for his daddy and you don't know what to tell him, 'cause you don't know where he is?" Elaina swallowed. "It ain't funny."

"I know it's not—"

"I said, 'Shut up.' I don't want to hear anything from you. No pleading. No begging. No mercy." Elaina came right up on me.

I tried to remember some of my old defensive moves, but nothing would come to mind. I could feel her breath in my face. "Elaina—"

"Don't say my name," Elaina said calmly.

"All right, your husband was drunk. He drove with poor judgment, crossed over into the wrong lane, and ran into a big truck that night. Now, I'm sorry for your loss, but we all lost that night." I reached for the phone.

"You didn't lose enough, though. I'm going to make sure you do." Elaina turned and walked out the front door as easily as she'd come in.

My heart continued to beat fast.

"That was too scary. I think you should report that lady." Jasmine stopped smacking her gum for a minute. "Who was she, anyway?"

I closed my eyes and took a deep breath. "Just a remnant from my past. God has washed away all my sins, but Satan is an accuser of the brethren, so he tries to condemn me by bringing up my past mistakes."

Jasmine looked confused. "Huh?"

"I used to date that woman's husband, just like she said I did," I admitted.

"Oh," Jasmine said, trying to hide her flushed cheeks with her hands.

I sighed. "But that was a long time ago, and I'm not like that anymore."

Jasmine was silent.

"Unfortunately, we were involved in a wreck that messed up my legs and took his life. I guess she never got over it," I continued.

Jasmine stopped chewing. "How long has it been?"

I couldn't believe I was explaining my sordid past to my employee. "It has been about three years."

"She sounds crazy to me," Jasmine said.

"Yeah, maybe, but I'm cool." I pretended to dust myself off and straighten out my clothes. "I know how to handle women like her."

Jasmine didn't look impressed. "I don't know. Maybe it's something the police should handle, Mrs. Bryant."

Jasmine had probably sensed my apprehension when Elaina was in my face. That woman had a lot of nerve. Back in the day that would've been it for her. I would have popped her right in the eyes and would have taken her down. Back in the day I would've laughed at her weakness and taunted her until she surrendered. My roughneck crew would've cheered me on. But I was different now, and the sad thing was that no matter how bad she seemed, I could actually feel the woman's pain. The old me had really hurt her. *Lord, help me.*

I shook my head. "Well, nobody got hurt, and she didn't really do anything, so . . ."

Jasmine smacked her gum as she usually did. "Sounded like threats to me."

"Maybe, but I don't want to deal with cops. Where I come from, they can sometimes be the enemy."

"I know what you mean." Jasmine started giggling and couldn't stop.

Talking with her reminded me of the carefree times I spent with my sister, giggling for hours over the silliest of things. But this Elaina issue was truly no laughing matter. Whether I liked it or not, something had to be done to stop her. I called Alex to vent.

"Look," Alex said, "you need to relax."

"Relax? Yeah, right," I huffed.

"No, I'm serious. Why don't we see if Cute Cutz can take us this evening? It's about time for my touch-up, and it would be fun."

I sighed. "I don't know if I'm in the mood for it."

"Oh, come on. Be spontaneous."

"You're telling me about being spontaneous? Now, that's funny," I said.

"Maybe, but Joshua will be home tonight. He can watch the kids, and we can go get our hair and nails done." Alex paused. "You know you'd feel better."

"Yeah, you're right." I sighed. "I would feel better."

"So I'll call to get us on the schedule, if possible. You call Keith and let him know it's ladies' night. You deserve it," Alex said.

Suddenly, I remembered my marital problems. "Call Keith? I don't even think he'd notice I was gone."

"Oh, come on. It can't be that bad." Alex chuckled, not taking my comment seriously.

"It's worse," I said.

"Hang tight," Alex said in her usual bubbly tone. "Let me call Cute Cutz. If they can fit us in tonight, then it's on."

Chapter Twenty-four

That evening Alex picked me up at work for our hair appointment at Cute Cutz Hair Salon. The salon was a medium-sized room with pale pink walls with a burgundy and pink flowered border, burgundy salon chairs, and matching furniture. It smelled of fresh lilies and licorice. The lighting was kind of dull, reminding me of the supper clubs I used to frequent with the gentlemen of my choice, sometimes legitimately mine and other times stolen. Yeah, before Jesus came into my life, I was nothing to be played with.

We loved how they treated us at Cute Cutz. It was almost like we were celebrities. They greeted us at the door and offered us coffee, water, or tea. Soft jazz tunes resounded from the surround-sound system. For the first time in a long time we were getting our hair done together.

"What are we getting? Braids?" I looked at Alex. "Diva weave?"

"I was thinking of a nice conservative cut."
Alex pinched a lock of her hair.

"Oh, come on, you already have that," I
squealed.

"No, I want something shorter," Alex said.

I rolled my eyes. "Oh, please. You ain't fooling
nobody. I didn't come in here to get some granny
cut."

Alex threw her hand up. "Well, I didn't come
in here to get some freak-of-the-week hairdo,
either."

"Oh, no, you didn't," I said.

"Yes, I did, diva. Please, what?"

I burst out laughing. "Okay, let's compromise,
then."

Alex narrowed her eyes. "What kind of compromise?"

"I'll get a short cut if we can get a honey-brown
dye. What do you think?"

"I don't know." Alex looked skeptical.

"Come on. We're twins, and I'm the one giving
up my hair. The least you can do is give me some
color." I pouted.

Alex laughed. "All right, I'll do it."

"Good. You won't regret it," I said.

Alex rolled her eyes at me. "I don't know
about that."

Lashonda, the stylist, took me in her chair. Rae Rae took Alex in hers. Alex and I gave each other a serious look, rolled our eyes, and started laughing.

It was just about time for a new look, anyway. I never did like to keep one style for too long. Staying the same never failed to make me feel boring and unattractive. The truth was, I was glad to be getting a sassy cut. I told Lashonda to feather it at the ends and part it down the middle. Alex told Rae Rae to do the same. We sat in the styling chairs, chatting like schoolgirls, anxious to see what masterpieces these talented ladies would bless us with. We had confidence in their abilities because we had used them many times throughout the year. Even though their salon was fairly new, it had earned our respect.

While I was sitting under the dryer, I had an irresistible urge to use the restroom, so I hopped to the back and quickly squeezed into one of the stalls. There I felt an even more urgent need to pray, so I did. *Lord, keep me.*

Afterward, I went back to the dryer. By the time Alex and I were each in styling chairs, I decided to do some impromptu marketing.

"You've got to come down to Push It for the fitness challenge on the twenty-second," I said to Lashonda.

"I've heard about it, but I don't get down to Fort Greene very often," Lashonda said. "That G train is something serious."

I clapped my hands together. "No worries. You can also sign up over the Internet."

"Really? Cool. I could sure stand to lose a few pounds," Lashonda said, stopping to twirl around.

"What about that five-dollar charge? I don't know about all of that," Rae Rae said.

"It's just to help buy the supplies and pay the staff. The challenge is a whole wellness campaign." I folded my firm arms. "I'm gonna stay fit regardless."

"You do look good, girl," Rae Rae admitted. "I guess I'll just have to pay the fee, then."

"It's a good investment," I said.

"It's well worth it, if you ask me," Alex agreed.

"I just wanna tighten up my abs." Rae Rae stopped combing Alex's hair to snap her fingers and do a neck roll.

A heavyset lady who was sitting under a dryer poked her head out. "Me too."

"Since I had my son, my weight has been out of control," Alex said, patting her tummy bulge.

"Mine too," Rae Rae agreed.

"Girl, yeah. Me too," another stylist said.

"That's why I'm not having any kids," I said, snapping my fingers.

Alex pretended to choke. "Yeah, right."

Lashonda raised her eyebrows. "Does your husband know that?"

"Nope." I twisted my lips and held two fingers up for the peace sign.

"Girl, you ain't serious," Rae Rae smirked.

"Oh, I'm serious." I fluttered my fake eyelashes to emphasize my point.

"I thought you loved Keith," Alex teased.

I burst into one of Tina Turner's songs. "What's love got to do with it, got to do with it?"

"I heard y'all was having some trouble with your pool," a customer from the back shouted out in a loud, shrill voice.

Her accusations didn't shake me. "Don't believe the hype. Our pool is safe. Push It is in better shape than ever."

"Really?" Rae Rae coughed. "Why all the media attention, then?"

"One word, Rae Rae." I cleared my throat. "Haters."

The entire salon started to laugh aloud.

By the time our hair was done, Alex and I had the honey-brown color that I wanted and the sassy short cut that Alex wanted. We had our nails done in a bright, glossy melon, drank two cups of cappuccino, slapped everyone a high five, and left with the promise that they'd all sign up for the fitness challenge online.

It had just begun to drizzle. Alex grabbed her umbrella while we were still standing under Cute Cutz's decorative awning.

Alex smiled. "Well, my sister, you did it again."

I stopped in my tracks. "Did what again?"

"Like you don't know." Alex chuckled.

"I don't," I confirmed.

"You won those people over in there, and that's a tough crowd," Alex said.

"You got that right." I shook my head, thinking of the ghetto mind-set I'd just had to face.

"I've got no doubt that you'll win back your clients and the whole community too."

"Thanks, sis." I hugged her before she left to get the car, which was parked two blocks away.

While I waited, I covered my hair with the collar of my jacket and my rain hat. Then through the raindrops I caught a glimpse of something crazy. I saw Paul Meyers and Elaina Dawson walking by together, talking.

They never even noticed me, but even though their faces were blurred by the rain, I'd recognize those two anywhere. They walked past the salon, but I couldn't hear what they were saying. Then they got into a cab and sped away.

When Alex finally pulled up, I told her what I'd seen.

"I didn't hear what they were saying, but they were talking," I explained.

Alex's eyes became two sizes larger. "Wow."

"And they were together. That proves Paul sabotaged the pool." I punched my palm with my fist. "I knew he was scandalous."

"Yeah, you were right," Alex admitted.

"I knew he contaminated our pool. I just wasn't sure why. Now I know why. It was Elaina all along."

Alex glanced over at me while we were stopped at a red light. "So you think they're together as a couple?"

"I don't know. Anything is possible," I said, with the very thought of the two of them together turning my stomach.

"Elaina with Paul?" Alex laughed. "That's a scary thought."

"I know," I agreed.

"When did they get together, though? And better yet, why?" Alex kept shaking her head in disbelief. "It doesn't make sense."

"I don't know if money is involved or romance, but either way, I'm going to find out."

Alex poked out her bottom lip as she analyzed the situation. "I wonder what Keith is going to say."

"Lately, dumping bad news about Paul on my husband is the norm. It's not what he's going to say that worries me," I said. "I'm worried about what he's going to do."

Chapter Twenty-five

I went to my sister's church today because I couldn't endure the questions and stares from the Missionary folk. Not today. It had been a month since Keith had attended, and I knew they'd noticed. I was not in the mood to answer questions about my usually dedicated husband's slacking church attendance. Not only that, but even Pastor Martin had asked about him the last time. It was inevitable in a small church like Missionary.

The Faith and Freedom Christian Church was located on the first floor of Alex and Joshua's new property, while the second and third floors housed their tenants and themselves.

With its many renovations, it was beginning to look like a sanctuary, but Joshua claimed not to be worried about appearances. He said he was trying to break away from the stereotypical ideals of the church, particularly those of mega churches like Kingdom House, where his parents pastored. He said he was trying to step out into unchartered waters. He wanted a different kind of church, where pews were replaced by soft couches with matching love seats, and where the pulpit was merely a laptop stand with a place for his Bible. I must admit when I first heard my brother-in-law's radical ideas, I was more than skeptical, but now that they seemed to be catching on, at least with the younger crowd, he had my respect.

Three teenagers greeted me at the door with hugs and a program that said "Welcome to freedom." There was no dress code, little formality in the way of greetings, and his choir didn't wear robes. In fact, they wore black slacks and bright blue Jesus T-shirts. His preaching was done on the same level as the congregation, instead of on a platform. Joshua said he wanted to be an in-your-face kind of preacher, and that he was.

I looked for my sister, who, as the first lady, would normally have had a special seat up high in the front. Instead, my sister was seated right in the middle of the congregation, leaning back in something that resembled a beanbag chair. So I sat right next to her. She looked over and hugged me. I hadn't told her that I would be visiting her church today, so she looked pleasantly surprised. The praise team sang in the background.

Alex did a double take. "What in the world are you doing here?"

"Well, hello to you too," I smirked.

"You know what I mean." Alex turned around in her seat to face me. "Why didn't you tell me you were coming?"

"Last-minute decision," I whispered.

"Keith acting up on you again?"

I grunted. "Yep, and I'm not in the mood to have to explain my business to the likes of Sister Winifred."

"Humph, I don't blame you with that one. But you can't run away from church because you're having problems," Alex said, looking very serious.

"I know. I know. I'll be back next week," I reassured her. "Just needed a break, that's all."

"Okay." Alex grabbed my arm and held on tight.

Once I was settled in, the choir, which consisted of six individuals of all ages, came to the front to sing. They sang two fairly modern selections before being seated back in their comfortable chairs. I looked around the room. Everything was so easygoing and peaceful. There were no big hats, no stuffy suits, and no fashion statements being made anywhere in the sanctuary. I was definitely the best dressed person there, but that was because I don't ever take half steps, not because I didn't know there was no dress code. There were no ushers dressed in white, either. Instead, the youth helped to direct each person to the seat of his or her choice, not theirs, and made sure everyone was comfortable. When it was time to pray, everyone dropped down to their knees. Some people even dropped flat on the floor in front of their seats.

When it was finally time for the word, Joshua came forward casually, with no grand ceremony or music. He spoke and strode among the congregation during his sermon, which seemed more like a chat with an old friend. He used the laptop on more than one occasion to check his notes, yet he still referred directly to the Bible when he read scriptures. I kind of liked his style, which was not necessarily better than Pastor Martin's, but it sure was entertaining. Who knew that my humdrum brother-in-law could keep my attention for over an hour without even breaking a sweat? Maybe if this kind of church had been an alternative when I was running from God, I would have reconsidered sooner. It was definitely a different approach to worship.

After the service, we left Joshua with his members and went up to Joshua and Alex's apartment, where we had time to talk. Alex breast-fed baby Joshua, made peanut butter and jelly sandwiches for Kiano and Lilah, and then put them all down for a nap.

As soon as we were alone, Alex started in on me. "Why are you looking so defeated?"

"I'm thinking about giving up on physical therapy and going back to my wheelchair."

"What kind of foolishness is that?"

"It's just easier," I said.

"That's garbage, and you know it. Now, what's really going on?"

"I don't know, Alex. I've just gotten too comfortable, I think. I don't know what it is, but I've just stopped caring," I said in a lower volume than I was accustomed to using.

"I don't think you've stopped caring," Alex responded. "I think you're just scared."

"You're crazy. I've never been a scaredy-cat a day in my life."

"I think you're scared that if you try harder, it just might not be enough, that you'll fail."

"Well, what if that happens? What if I fail? I must admit I've stopped begging God for my legs."

"Listen to yourself," Alex admonished. "You never had to beg in the first place."

"I know but—"

Alex continued, "You ask and He hears your prayer. Then you hold on to it, confess it, believe it."

"I know, but I remember Mama died believing for her healing." A single tear escaped from my mascara-clad eye.

"Are you still tripping about Mama?"

"I'm not tripping," I said. "I'm just wondering why she had to die."

"Taylor, God's ways are not our ways. Just because Mama died doesn't mean you can't live. I really believe Mama was ready to go."

I blinked away the tears that threatened to come. "She suffered so much."

Alex put her hand up to her forehead, as if she was stressed out. "I believe it was her time. She wanted to go to heaven."

"Yeah, I know. I know." I waved my hands in agitation.

"God is a healer. Mama's destiny is not yours." Alex came right up on me and gave me a bear hug. "Keep believing."

In just a few months my life had been transformed from a dream to a nightmare.

It wasn't so much that it was perfect originally, but it was the expectation I had of my life being something different than it was. I guess I was in denial until the ugliness I'd tried to run from caught up with me, threw me down, and looked me right in the face. Needless to say, I didn't like what I saw. Even though I wasn't the person I used to be, the distorted reflection seemed to chase me. In my heart I begged it to let me go. But it wouldn't.

Chapter Twenty-six

It was an unusually overcast day. The September clouds were dark and heavy with rain.

Temperatures felt below normal as a cool breeze blew against my skin. I stood outside, leaned against the building, taking in the busyness of the city.

It was time for more than my typical early morning routine. I decided to push myself. I went from the rowing machine to the free weights to the barbell combo bench with leg developer. I wanted to remind everyone, including Elaina, that I was no pushover.

"Wow, boss. You're really moving this morning," Jasmine said, the gel in her blond spiked hair glistening in the light as she passed by.

"Thanks." I grimaced. "I've got to keep my body operating like a well-oiled machine."

Jasmine stopped in the center of the room and looked back, with one hand on her hip. "I hope I look that good when I'm your age."

My age? How old did she think I was? "Get to work, Jas. Chop, chop." I had run her off.

My age, my age. I was less than ten years older than she was. *Please.*

Not since my years on the track team, when Coach Glenn commented on my extra bulge and made me do five extra laps around the track, had I ever slacked off on exercise. Food wasn't mandatory, but exercise was.

Sometimes I didn't like being who I was. Being tough had its drawbacks, because people always expected me to be hard. Not to cry, not to feel, not to be vulnerable. But sometimes I just wanted to be me. And maybe that meant punching someone one minute and crying the next, but that wasn't what was expected of me. So I masked so much for so long. After a while it was hard to know what was even real anymore. I prayed God would reveal the real me. Tears began to well up in my eyes.

It was time to unlock the front door for the morning clients. So I hopped off the combo bench and into my braces. I remembered the conversation I had had with my sister the day before about not being afraid, about not giving up. One thing was for certain, whether I'd win or not, I was not a quitter. About halfway to the front door, something came over me and I decided to put down my braces and attempt to walk across the rest of the floor. I started out strong, catching a firm footing. I took two baby steps before I lost my balance, slid, and fell right by the glass front door.

Jasmine came running over. "Are you all right, Mrs. Bryant?"

As I scrambled to get up, I looked right into Elaina Dawson's eyes. She was standing outside the glass door, laughing at me. It was the most humiliating moment of my life. I tried to slide away from her view and get behind the counter so I could brace myself. I really wanted to curl up behind the counter in a fetal ball and cry. *Why me, Lord?* What was she doing here, anyway? Hadn't she hurt me enough already?

Jasmine assisted me with getting my bearings, and I was able to retreat into my office for the rest of the day. Was I a coward? Maybe Alex was right. Maybe I was defeated.

Why did I have to lose my legs? On the inside I cried out every regret I'd ever had about my life and the way I was. I cried about my injury and the muscles in my leg, which just weren't strong enough. In my spirit I tried to believe I would walk again, but every day my experience told me I wouldn't.

I'd prided myself on my physical beauty and fitness. Now that the physical had failed me, I had only the spiritual. I closed my eyes and let the memories fade.

I wanted to walk, run, and do aerobic dance. I wanted to be me again. I wanted to be whole. *Please, God, make me whole.*

I tried to call Keith, but his voice mail came on. I didn't bother to leave a message.

Instead, I kept a very low profile until three o' clock and then left work early, allowing Jasmine to lock up. This was something I'd done only once before, when Alex had emergency surgery to deliver Joshua Jr.

My cab pulled right up to the doorway.

Jasmine held the door open for me. "Don't worry, Mrs. Bryant. I can handle it."

"I know you can," I said.

"I hope you feel better," Jasmine said, with the worry on her face showing.

"I'll be fine," I answered, but I was sure she could see sadness on my face.

The driver, seeing my condition, came over to help me get in. Before long we were on our way to East Flatbush. I had to take a cab because I couldn't deal with trains and buses anymore. They were just too much trouble, especially when I had to squeeze past folks with my braces. Not that I was ever crazy about public transportation in the first place. In fact, I used to prefer riding in luxury cars. They just never happened to belong to me. Riding in fancy cars was important to me back then. Not driving them.

I wanted to buy a beef patty for lunch and stop and shop in my favorite discount store.

Shopping always made me feel better, and discount items were all I had the budget for right now, considering our business woes.

East Flatbush was a thriving neighborhood with street vendors on every corner and everywhere in between. The smell of international foods was in the air, and the expressions were those of everyday people whose hopes and dreams were similar to mine. *Lord, help me to survive.*

I went into the discount store and started browsing through the aisles. There were beauty products, socks, discounted lingerie, cooking utensils, toys, and other miscellaneous items. I loaded my cart, wondering how I was going to manage these packages when it was time to go.

After paying for my items, I stood in front of the front door, waiting for the cab I'd called. A dollar cab pulled up beside me instead.

The driver spoke with a heavy Caribbean accent. "Dollar cab, miss?"

"No thanks." I waved him away as I watched him load all the bus-stop passengers into his van. He would drop them off at the train station for the cost of just one dollar.

After that encounter, I decided to step back closer to the wall so I wouldn't be in the way. From my obscure spot near the wall, next to a fruit stand, I could see the whole street.

I watched a woman from the shop next door walk over to a beat-up Honda and put coins in the parking meter it was parked in front of. She wore torn-up sweatpants, and her hair was wrapped in a scarf. All of a sudden I did a double take when I realized that it was Elaina. She wore no makeup, and she sported no jewelry. She looked very average, not at all how she had been representing herself lately. I stood back and continued to peep out at her.

She walked back inside the shop next door. When my cab pulled up, I asked him to wait for a few minutes. Sure enough, Elaina came out about fifteen minutes later, carrying a small shopping bag. Now I was curious. This was no elite place to shop, so why was she down here? I couldn't stop wondering.

When she started her engine, I instinctively said, "Follow that car."

The cabdriver looked uninterested about why. He just tapped his meter and grinned.

"I know. I know. I'll pay you. Just go," I spat out.

He whirled around the next few blocks, made a few twists and turns, careful just to stay a few cars behind Elaina's Honda, but not far enough that we'd lose her. With the midday traffic and congestion that was a challenge, yet my driver was on her tail. It was obvious that he had done this before. He was a pro.

Finally, she stopped in front of a dull-looking brick apartment building and went inside. It was tall and had six stories in all. The trash was spilling out of the trash cans, and graffiti lined the base of the building. Children played indiscriminately in the street.

I waited for a few minutes to see if she would come back out of the building, and when she didn't, I became curious.

"I'm getting out," I said, pushing my door open. "Please wait for me."

The cabdriver rolled his eyes. "Lady, please."

"Don't worry. I've got your money." I showed him two twenties. "Don't you want a bigger fare?"

He didn't answer.

"And a tip?"

"Okay, lady. Are you sure you want to do this with your legs and all?"

"Let me worry about my legs," I snapped. "You just do the driving and the waiting."

With that he got out of the cab and came over to help me onto the sidewalk. "You want me to walk you in?"

"No, it's okay," I said. "Oh, and if I'm not back in fifteen minutes, call the police."

As I walked into the building, the first thing I experienced was a putrid smell. There was no doorman or chandeliers. No elegance whatsoever. Not that I expected any. There was only one old elevator and a row of semi-rusted mailboxes. That was when I saw it. There was a mailbox with her name, Elaina Dawson, on it as big as day. So she did live here, but why would she? Why would a woman of means live here? And why did she look so wretched earlier? Why was she driving an old, banged-up car now, instead of the new ones she'd been sporting? Nothing made any sense at all. Now that I knew where she lived, however, I could start putting the pieces of the puzzle together.

I left the building as quickly as my braces could carry me, hopped into the cab, and we sped away. I tried to call Keith once again, but there was still no answer. Why didn't he pick up his phone? It was so frustrating.

When I pushed the door to my apartment open, I could smell the liquor.

"Keith, are you home?" I walked through the apartment, checking each room. There was no sign of him. This had to stop. For the past few months Keith had been throwing his life away, and now he was disrespecting our home. I wondered what was next. Tired, I plopped down on the couch and picked up the phone to call Alex.

"Hello," I said.

Alex yawned into the phone. "What's up?"

"Girl, you'll never guess what I just found out."

"No, what?"

I could hardly wait to spit it out. "That Elaina lives in a six-story tenement on Front Street."

Alex squealed in a high-pitched voice, "What?"

"I couldn't believe it, either, but I followed her," I said.

"You followed her? Keith is in on this madness too?"

"No, I took a cab," I said.

Alex smacked her lips. "Oh, that makes sense."

"I didn't start out following her, but I saw her looking sho' enough tore up down by the discount store. And you know the area so—"

Alex cut me off. "So, anyway, how do you know she lives in that building?"

"Her name is on the mailbox as big as day," I said, hardly able to control myself.

"Really?"

"Uh-huh," I said.

"Wow," Alex whispered.

"That's what I said, but now I want to know why. Why is she living there, with all the money she has been throwing around?"

"Right." Now Alex was getting the picture. "Dressing real nice, expensive jewelry, cars, and everything. Then, all of a sudden, you see her shopping for bargains and driving a hoopty. It doesn't add up," Alex said, summarizing.

"It's almost like Cinderella's spell is off," I said.

"For real," Alex agreed. "It doesn't make any sense."

"Nope." I snapped my fingers. "But I'm gonna get to the bottom of it. Believe that."

"Oh, I believe you will," Alex said.

"Then to top off my day, I come home to the whole apartment smelling like Jack Daniel's up in here," I said in my "I'm ready to kill someone" voice.

"Oh, I'm sorry."

"So am I," I said.

"What are you going to do?"

"Do? *Do?* A sista is about to snap. That's what I'm gonna do."

"No, don't do that," Alex begged.

"I'm serious, Alex. I'm gonna have a long talk with that trifling Mr. Keith Bryant, and if things don't go my way, I'm—"

"Don't you mean God's way?"

"Whatever," I said. "If things don't go right, then it's a done deal."

"You wouldn't walk out on Keith, would you?"

"Why not? It looks like he's already walked out on me." I really wasn't sure if this was true or not, but I couldn't back down now.

"Pray, Taylor," Alex whispered.

"Pray?" I paused. "I can't stay on my knees forever. I've been steadily praying, and he's been steadily drinking. You can't help somebody who doesn't want to be helped."

"That's true," Alex said.

"One more talk with Keith," I snapped, "and it's a wrap."

After I hung up the phone with Alex, I went to my bedroom to calm down. I reached for my Bible on the nightstand and held it tight. Then I opened it to Psalm 91. Keith didn't come in until after midnight. I knew when he crawled into my bed that not only had he been drinking but he had probably been with Paul. No matter what negative things I had told Keith about Paul, Keith refused to break up his friendship with him. There was no point in confronting a drunk

man, though. My last talk would just have to
wait.

Saturday morning Keith dropped me off at
Push It. Then he took off without even telling
me where he was going. We usually spent Saturday together at Push It. I had a lot on my
mind. Paul, Keith, and Elaina were all swirl-
ing around in my head. I had to get to the
bottom of this. I just had to. I didn't have any
money to pay a private detective, like Mother
Benning did when she wanted to check up on
Alex two years ago. If I wanted to find out
something, I had to do it myself.

I started texting Alex about borrowing Joshua's car and coming to pick me up. After
practically begging, with the texts going back
and forth, she finally agreed. She wasn't sure
about what caper my devious mind had imagined, but she was my sister and she was loyal.

She picked me up, and I shared my plan with
her.

"Girl, have you lost your mind? We're not detectives."

"No, we're better than detectives," I said,
placing a black cap on her head and dark shades
on her face. Then I put on a matching set, and I
directed Alex to our destination.

We were careful to park a few doors down from Elaina's apartment building so we could watch people go in and out.

"What are we doing? This is crazy," Alex said.

"Maybe, but it's the only way I'm going to find out what's going on with this Elaina chick."

"You could've told the police."

I tried to stay calm. "Told them what? Technically, she hasn't done anything to me that I can prove."

"It's their job to find proof," Alex said, so matter-of-factly that I could only stare at her.

"She'll just say I'm disgruntled about the citations she gave me," I shouted.

Alex smirked. "Well, you are disgruntled, aren't you?"

"Whose side are you on?" I shook my head. "You know this woman has been stalking me, and you know why."

"That's true." Alex moved nervously back and forth in her seat.

I put my hand on Alex's shoulder. "Calm down."

"I'm trying."

"Am I supposed to just sit back and wait for Elaina to make her next move? She's already tried to ruin my business on several occasions." I shook my head and my hands. "I've worked too hard to let that happen."

"I know."

I hit my fist against my open hand. "I've got to do something."

"I guess you're right." Alex looked out the window. "Still, we're not detectives."

"I don't have any other choices," I said.

"What about Keith?"

"What about him?" I was losing my patience. "If Keith were sober, he'd think I'm crazy."

"He'd be right. You are crazy."

"And who are you? The crazy twin?"

"I guess so." Alex laughed.

I put up my hand for a high five, and she slapped it before leaning back in her seat.

With the exception of one ten-minute restroom break, we waited for two whole hours.

Nothing unusual happened. Alex kept calling home to check up on her kids every half hour. It was sickening. If I ever got to be a mother, I hoped I wouldn't be as suffocating as my sister was.

Three hours passed. I was tired. Eventually, I had to use the restroom, so we drove slowly away from the scene for a few minutes. When we returned, my eyelids were so heavy, I decided to close my eyes for a few minutes. I instructed Alex to keep watch for me as I slumped over in the car.

Just as I was about to really fall asleep, Alex shook me and said, "Hey, isn't that what's-her-name?"

It took me a minute to realize Alex was speaking to me. I sat up in my seat and slowly opened my eyes just in time to see the back of someone turning the corner.

Still groggy, I wiped my eyes for clarity. "Who? Elaina?"

Alex leaned over me, pointing. "No, that lady who used to be your gym rival back in the day. The one who tried to outbid you for Push It."

I was confused. "You mean Shayla?"

"Yeah, that's it." Alex nodded. "Shayla."

I still wasn't convinced. "You saw Shayla McConnell around here?"

"It sure enough looked like her."

"Shayla McConnell only does the Upper East Side, boo. Why would she be around here?"

"I don't know, but it sure looked just like her."

"Which way did she come from?"

Alex hunched her shoulders. "I don't know. I just looked up, and she was right there on the sidewalk, walking that way. She turned the corner."

"Yeah, I saw someone turning the corner."

"You were asleep," Alex said in mock disgust.

"Strange." I shook my head. "Nah, maybe that wasn't her."

"Maybe not," Alex agreed.

I began to think. "But then again . . . remember when I said Elaina's Cinderella spell might be over?"

"Yeah, and?"

I nodded my head and grinned a guilty grin. "What if we've figured out who her fairy godmother is?"

"What? Are you saying that Shayla McConnell has hooked up with Elaina?"

"Wilder things have happened. If Paul has joined forces with Elaina, then why not Shayla McConnell?"

"I thought her husband had declared bankruptcy a few years back?"

"He did, but that was then. Besides he had so much money, it couldn't have broken him. Just slowed him down a little. But Shayla was a greedy one. If there was a dime left to spare, she was going to get her hands on it." I began to nod my head as pieces started to form in my head.

"And she hated me. I took the gym she wanted. I was a better physical trainer than she was. Oh yeah, she hated me."

"Maybe you're right," Alex said.

"Suddenly I know I am," I answered. "Let's follow her."

"Are you crazy?"

"No, but let's at least see where the lady that you saw went. Maybe it's not her. Let's hurry."

Alex cranked up the car, and we rolled slowly down the street, but we didn't see anybody who looked like Shayla.

"How could she have disappeared so quickly?"

"Maybe she hopped on a bus, into a cab, or had a ride waiting for her," Alex said.

"Maybe. Or maybe she went into that parking garage over there." I pointed across the street.

"Maybe." Alex drove past the garage and out of the area, going toward home. "Even if it was Shayla, how are you going to prove the connection?"

"That's easy. I'm going to look up Shayla, find out her whereabouts, and see what she's been driving lately."

A few years back, Shayla McConnell and I were competing in the same fitness circles.

With her rich husband at her side, she was convinced she could buy the title of fitness queen.

Unfortunately for her, I had already been voted the best personal trainer on this side of town, hands down. Needless to say, this infuriated Shayla because since she had married money, she had become accustomed to having things her way. Imagine my surprise when she announced one day that she'd be purchasing Push It from my boss, before I even knew it was for sale. At the very last minute her husband had some unexpected legal and financial troubles that put a hold on all their accounts just long enough for Keith and me to outbid her for the business. The rest was history, I thought, but I guess I was wrong. I should've known I hadn't heard the last of nasty-mouth Shayla McConnell.

Shayla McConnell was a Manhattan socialite who had struck gold when she married the franchise king of the East Coast. Her husband, twenty years her senior, had draped her in minks and diamonds and had squandered much of his savings by purchasing businesses for her to run. She used to take pleasure in taunting me with her wealth and prominence, knowing I wanted nothing more than to purchase the Push It Fitness Center. Humph, this whole mess had Shayla written all over it. But how would she have known about Elaina? It didn't matter.

When I got home, I began to tear through information on the Internet, Googling and reading nonstop until I had the answers I needed. Within minutes, I was able to confirm that Shayla McConnell and her husband owned several luxury vehicles that matched the descriptions of the ones I saw Elaina driving. There was a picture of them in their new Porsche and in their new Lamborghini. There was no doubt there were other cars as well. Corvettes, Ferraris, and the like. Finally, I saw an article with a photo of Shayla's husband riding in a shiny black Range Rover. Humph. It was all circumstantial evidence, but deep inside I knew it was true. I could hardly believe it, yet the pieces were all there. All I had to do was put the puzzle together.

So Elaina Dawson and Shayla McConnell had conspired against me. At some point they had brought Paul into the equation. But why Paul? He had to have done it for money, and Shayla McConnell had lots of it. Paul hadn't cared about anything else. So they had plotted and planned my destruction. But they had been caught, found out in the middle of their treacherous plan. A plan that was set in motion to rob me of my business, and my sanity. A plan to ruin my life.

Then it started to infuriate me, and I was overcome by this feeling of hatred and vengeance. I couldn't allow them to get away with this. I had to get back at all of them.

Chapter Twenty-seven

Although I woke up that morning to the sun beaming in through my Martha Stewart curtains and the colorful birds chirping about the sweet sycamore tree that stood beside my building, having a good day was the last thing on my mind. Instead, my mind was cluttered with thoughts of retribution, reprisal, retaliation, vengeance, and good old-fashioned payback. No matter how I said it, it all sounded good. It all sounded necessary. A sweet savor of strawberry pancakes wafted in from the kitchen, but even it couldn't change my mind.

I rolled over in bed after peeking through the window. Today was going to be a long day.

I grabbed hold of the side rails on my bed and pulled myself to my feet. Within minutes, I was in my chair and safely rolling to the shower. The fresh water was just what I needed, but it didn't relax me; it only empowered me. I came out, sprayed myself with Dolce & Gabbana perfume, dressed in a teal two-piece cotton pantsuit, and was ready to conquer.

I had spat out all the sordid details to Keith the night before and hadn't gotten much sleep as a result. Reluctantly, I rolled into the kitchen, where Keith was undoubtedly preparing a masterpiece.

Keith placed the two plates of pancakes on the table and poured the maple syrup. "I see that you're all dressed up and ready to go."

I spat out, "Why wouldn't I be? I've got a very important day ahead of me."

"Baby, are you sure you want to handle it this way?"

I snapped, "Are you kidding me? What other way is there?"

"I just thought that maybe—"

"Well, you thought wrong. I'm doing this," I continued. "Nothing is going to stop me."

Keith didn't say a word, but he appeared to be totally undone. He was also in no position to give me any spiritual counseling, so he left it alone. He made his usual healthy breakfast, served it to me in silence, and then said goodbye. I rolled my eyes as he walked by. Despite his strong, muscular body, he looked so weak as he exited through the front door. So much had changed in our lives in the past few months, and

I wondered if his problems had begun to affect his work yet.

As soon as he left, I called Alex and asked her to drive me downtown so I could report Elaina's misuse of her authority as a city business license inspector. Alex started making excuses and whining, but I begged. I told her how I'd been suffering all these months at the hands of these vicious people, how it was only right that I report her.

Alex finally gave in, picked me up, and drove me downtown. Ironically, I was able to watch Elaina walk into the city-owned building, practically tiptoeing in her patent leather pumps and silk skirt suit.

"Humph," I said. "Now I know where the money for her makeover came from. Now I know where the luxury vehicles came from. And now I know how truly dirty Elaina and Shayla both are. I really don't even know yet how Paul fits into all of this."

"If you report her to her supervisors, she might lose her job," Alex said.

I sucked my teeth. "So what? I want to make things as bad for her as she has made things for me."

Alex replied, "So maybe she and her son might be put out on the street if she loses her job."

"That's not my problem," I said.

"Okay. Why can't you just confront her with the truth? Now that you know what's going on, I'm sure she'll leave you alone," Alex pleaded.

"Really? I'm not so sure about that." I put my fist into the palm of my other hand. "I know what I'm doing. It's time to fight back."

"Like Mama always said, 'You were born fighting, girl.' You've been fighting all your life."

"Okay, so what? I've always had to fight." A tear ran down my cheek. "So many people have hurt me."

It was true that I'd been fighting all my life. It had come naturally to me. I fought in school. I fought at home. I fought because I wanted to be fit. I fought because I wanted to be heard. I fought because I wanted to be loved.

"Maybe it's time to be disciplined and just let it go," Alex said.

I looked at my sister, bulging from behind the steering wheel, and said, "No, you're not talking about discipline when you can't even discipline yourself enough to keep off that mid-waist bulge. What could you possibly know about discipline?"

"Hold on." Alex put her hand up. "I know you didn't just call me fat."

"Maybe I did." I opened the door and began to climb out of the car.

"There are other areas of discipline besides fitness. Okay, so eating is my weak area. But getting angry and not being able to let things go is yours."

"Let it go? Are you kidding me?" I slammed the car door shut.

"Let God fight your battles," Alex said.

If I blew Elaina's cover, Shayla would have no need for her anymore, so whatever money she had been receiving from her would stop. From the looks of things, she would be broke again.

Part of me wanted her to suffer for all of the pain she'd caused me the past few weeks, but another part of me knew that what my sister was saying was true. Something inside wouldn't let me hold it against her.

I didn't understand. What had happened to the fighting me? I clenched my teeth and my fists. I backed away from the office building slowly, climbed back into Alex's car, and told her to drive away.

I would have to settle the score another way.

Chapter Twenty-eight

Keith

Keith went to work at United Physical Therapy, one of the best physical therapy clinics in New York City. He walked through the reception area, greeted the receptionist, went to the staff area, opened his locker, and put on his lab coat. Keith was glad that he didn't work in a hospital anymore, where he had to wear scrubs. He had a few colleagues who were still in that position, but he tightened his tie and buttoned his lab coat with a sense of gratefulness.

John Anderson, a fellow physical therapist, walked up to him and patted him on the back. "Hi. How are you, Keith?"

John was blond, with a few random streaks of gray, and had a medium build. He was divorced, had two daughters, and had been working in the industry for over twenty-five years.

At fifty-four years old, he looked good for his age.

"I'm good," Keith answered with a fake smile. Nothing was real anymore. Nothing except the pain that he was feeling.

Not only was John a colleague, but Keith had once considered him a friend as well. They used to spend some lazy Saturdays playing golf together.

"You haven't been on the golf course for a while," John said.

Keith tried to avoid direct eye contact. "Yeah, I've been so busy lately." He didn't want John to notice how weary he really was. If anyone noticed, he knew they'd probably recommend a leave of absence or at least a vacation. So far he'd managed to elude his superiors, or at least as far as he could tell.

"Say no more, man. I almost forgot you two were newlyweds. And your wife's a beauty too. I don't blame you."

Keith grinned, but he wanted to tell him that it was nothing like that at all. He had been busy with business violations, looking for his brother, arguments about Paul, and Paul himself.

"An old friend of mine is actually in town, and he's needed a lot of help to get back on his feet," Keith explained.

John responded, "I can certainly understand that."

"I need to play a few rounds, but like I said, I just haven't had the time," Keith said.

"Maybe you need to make some time." John chuckled before glimpsing at his file, giving Keith a playful punch on the shoulder, and disappearing through the double doors.

Keith strode back through to the front desk, received his client's files, and headed for the treatment room. Inside the room there was a treatment table, exercise mats, a hydrotherapy area, and a range of other specialty equipment he frequently used.

His first client was Mrs. Benjamin, who was referred by her geriatric doctor after she suffered from a mild stroke six months ago. She'd come a long way since then, regaining some mobility in a once limp arm and hand. Her slurred speech had improved too.

Keith gave her a warm smile. "Hello, Mrs. Benjamin."

"Hel-lo, son," Mrs. Benjamin said with a slight speech impediment.

She was a kind older woman with silver-gray hair who lived at the nursing home in the neighborhood. Keith found it hard to understand how a woman as sweet as her could have six children and yet complain that none of them ever came to visit. He would have loved to have a mother or a grandmother like her to care about, and to care about him. He swallowed hard, remembering vaguely the day his mother left him. He was only a small boy then, and although he didn't remember anything else about her, he remembered crying and crying until his father had had enough. His dad's way of dealing with things almost always involved some kind of alcoholic beverage, and that day was no different.

Keith looked into Mrs. Benjamin's eyes and saw the loneliness, the same sense of abandonment that he himself had felt almost all of his life. At least until he found Jesus.

Keith smiled. "How have you been doing?"

"Jus-s-st fine, son. Been doing fine 'cept for this arm sometimes."

"Right." Keith assisted her with stretching out on the table. "Well, we're going to get you whipped back into shape any day now."

When he was at work, he usually felt good about himself. Not like he had felt at home lately. His daily routine included examining his patients and then making a treatment plan to help them with flexibility, strength, endurance, coordination, and/or balance. This alone kept him quite busy. Typically, Keith evaluated his patients' files and then he went about trying to reduce pain and swelling from any injury, before working on improving his patients' flexibility, strength, and endurance.

Keith engaged Mrs. Benjamin in her usual routine, one that had been personalized with considerations for her age, diet, family, relationships, and state of mind. "Hold your arm out, please, ma'am."

"Yes, sir, mighty sore this m-morning. Don't know how much we can do t-today."

"I'm sure you'll do just fine," Keith reassured her.

Trained in physical therapy with a master of science degree under his belt, he also had quite a few years of experience. His plans for many of his patients were more intense and included exercise stretching, core exercises, weight lifting, and walking, depending on the extent of the injury. Keith also used manual therapy, education, and techniques such as heat, cold, water, ultrasound, and electrical stimulation. The treatments usually caused mild soreness or swelling, but he was so good at what he did, his patients rarely complained. Keith was licensed and specialized in muscles, joints, tendons, ligaments, and bones. Some of his colleagues specialized in other areas, like nerves and related muscles, the heart and blood vessels, lung problems and breathing, skin problems, and cancer.

Mrs. Benjamin had made much progress in the few months she had been assigned to him, and Keith beamed with pride at his work.

"Thank you, son," Mrs. Benjamin said when her session was over. "You a-always know what's best."

Keith wondered if that were true. Did he really know what was best? He was brilliant in physical therapy, but in his personal life, he was spinning out of control. Taylor could be so difficult sometimes. She was beautiful, stubborn, and determined to undermine his best friend, Paul. Still, he felt guilty about not giving his wife the kind of attention he gave his patients. Despite his own problems, he knew he needed to go home and change that.

Chapter Twenty-nine

Everyone else had already gone home for the night, and we'd locked ourselves inside.

Only Keith and I remained at the gym, upon Keith's insistence.

"I don't feel up to it," I told him. "Not tonight."

But Keith didn't listen. Instead he stripped down to only a T-shirt and shorts before he began his routine.

I remembered the first time I'd seen him prepare, I was intrigued. He even had exercises that he did with his hands to prepare for physical therapy. He was so professional, intense, and yet gentle. I think I fell in love with his gentleness.

"Let's go," he said, without even a half smile.

Keith had been loud and raucous lately, which was totally out of his character. I wasn't used to this, because I was usually the loud one. Keith had always been the quiet one. Now he seemed bitter and brutal, spewing insults from his mouth. *Lord, what is happening to my husband?*

I did the flat cable fly, the flat dumbbell press, the incline bench press, the dumbbell front raise, the slant board oblique twists, and even the overhead bar extension, all with his help. My spandex tank top was drenched with sweat. I was tired and angry.

"Keith, please, I'm in pain now," I pleaded.

I found myself straddling the combo bench with leg developer. Keith stood over me, holding my legs, kneading them, pushing them.

"Push yourself." Keith held on to my legs with force. "Push past the pain."

"My legs are about to break already," I said.

"You won't break."

Keith pushed my legs back farther. I screamed as tears burst through my closed eyelids and slid down my cheeks. I tried to wrestle his arms off of me for a minute, but he pushed me back down.

"Sorry," Keith growled. "Now, work those knees."

I didn't know whether to do what he said or to slap him. I must admit slapping seemed like the better option as my body curled up in pain.

"Stretch out. Let's go."

"Okay," I grunted.

"Again. Harder." Keith's pupils were enlarged. "You can do this."

"Not if you break my legs," I yelled.

"I won't break them. I'm going to break you."

"Oh, is that what's up?" Through my tears, I could see the veins in his neck popping up, and I wondered what in the world was driving him.

"Don't worry what's up. Push that leg down."

"Ahh," I squealed. "I am pushing."

"Harder, faster." Keith's face was contorted. "You can do this."

"I'm trying," I said.

"You're not trying hard enough."

"I am," I whispered with what seemed like my last breath.

"You're weak."

Keith was never mean like this. "I'm not weak."

"Then you're pathetic."

"I am not pathetic." I pushed my leg as hard as I could against his arm. "I am strong."

He was tough, but not heartless. "Not hard enough."

"I am. I am." Sweat trickled down my brow.

"You're not." Keith let go. "Argh, this is stupid."

"Don't call me stupid, Keith."

"I didn't call you stupid. I said this was stupid." He slammed his fist down on the table, knocking over my glass of water. It shattered on the floor in front of us before Keith kicked through the debris and walked out.

Before I knew it, my thoughts had traveled back to my childhood.

I was only six years old the first time that evil little girl and her crew called me fat. When I fell over into the mud, tore my new skirt, and lost my pretty ribbon, with my twin standing by crying, I was enraged. As I crawled to my feet, whimpering, I knew that I had to get back at them. I knew I wanted revenge, and that would require that I change. I couldn't hurt them as long as I looked the way I did. I had to get beautiful and tough. In fact, in my first-grade innocence, I made up my mind about two things: number one was that I'd never be pushed around again, and number two was that I'd never be fat and ugly again.

Even then I didn't like being the underdog. I didn't like feeling helpless or boxed in. So I learned to fight for myself, for my twin, for my dignity. Day and night I'd fight even those who weren't necessarily trying to fight me, but I'd promised to hurt everyone around me before I'd let them hurt me again.

When my mind returned to the present, I prayed, "Lord, please help me to be better than the hurt little girl I used to be. Help me to be better than her. Help me to accept your way in spite of my own."

Now Keith was bringing up those same emotions. I walked with him into the locker room. "Why do you hate me so much, Keith?"

"I don't hate you." Keith took a deep breath. "I hate myself."

"Why?"

Keith dropped down onto a bench. "Because I'm horrible."

"What?"

"I realized today I may never find my brother. Or that he may already be dead in an alley somewhere." Keith buried his face in his hands. Suddenly, he didn't look brutal at all. He just looked beaten.

"You don't know that. You may still be able to find him," I reasoned.

"But either way, I can't do anything about it. I can't turn back the clock and change what I did. I can't go back and stay with him." Keith lifted his head, just in time for me to see his glossy eyes. "So I hate myself. I should be dead in his place."

"First of all, you don't know that he's dead. Secondly, there is no guarantee that you could've saved him if you stayed. He could've still gotten hooked on drugs. He could've still left home."

"Maybe he wouldn't have if I had stayed," Keith replied.

"But you don't know that. There was nothing you could've done. You two were practically the same age. Let it go." I sighed. "Let's get some help for you."

"No," Keith said.

"You're alive. Let's take care of you." I managed to get over to him and put my arm around him. I put my head on his hard chest and could feel his heart beating fast. "Okay, you're right. We may never find Robert."

Keith peeled my arm off of him and stood up. He didn't respond.

"We've tried, and we can even try again, but there is no guarantee that he's alive. But *you* are alive." I wiped my face and neck with my towel. "You can be helped. God can help you."

Keith shook his head, looking downward. "No, it's too late for me."

"It's never too late for God," I told him.

"But I've let Him down," Keith replied.

"We all have. Just let me help you. Let Him help you to get back up."

"No."

I remembered one of Mama's favorite sayings. "We serve a loving God."

"I know, but I've made it impossible for Him to love me," Keith growled.

Keith turned around and started walking toward the door.

"Wait, Keith," I said, shuffling my body between him and the door.

Keith gently moved me aside so I wasn't blocking the doorway. "What is it?"

"What about the fitness challenge tomorrow?"

"What about it?"

"We're supposed to be working on the last-minute stuff this evening," I huffed.

Keith answered with his back to me. "I'll help you when I get back."

"Promise me you won't go off drinking, Keith. Promise me. I need you back here to help."

"I promise I won't drink. I'll be back," Keith said.

Keith left me, slamming the door behind him.

My head began to spin with the mounting pressure. My marriage was out of control. My business was on the line. And I had two calculating women trying to drive me crazy.

I thought about Elaina and her probable connection to Shayla McConnell. I hadn't thought about her in years. Yes, she used to be a fitness rival, but that was then. This was now, and I wasn't in competition with anyone. All I wanted was what God had for me, and unlike Shayla, I wasn't willing to hurt anyone to get it.

It was now clear to me that I had a trio of enemies: Shayla McConnell, Elaina Dawson, and Paul Meyers, who had fooled me. Yet I was nobody's fool. I used to be bitter and violent, harsh, self-centered and jealous. Neither of these women knew the new me, the real me. Maybe if they knew me, they wouldn't be so vindictive.

Paul had gotten a glimpse of the new me but couldn't handle it. The three of them had to be trying to destroy me. I had three enemies, and if I counted the fact that my husband was loyal to Paul, instead of to me, I had four enemies. In fact, Keith was nowhere around. I felt like I had been betrayed to no end. It was almost too much to bear.

I had just hours before the fitness challenge, so I had to focus. Afterward, I would go to the police with the information I'd gathered.

Chapter Thirty

It was the day of the Push It Health Fest and Fitness Challenge. Alex had helped me organize everything, from the banner out front to the bottled water lined up on the counter. The caterers had delivered the platters of food. People from the neighborhood had started to arrive. Jasmine greeted them at the door and took them to weigh in. Where was Keith? I imagined that he was slumped over at a bar, enjoying his first love lately—alcohol. Or maybe he'd stagger in at the last minute and embarrass me with his drunkenness. Either way, I was done. I didn't understand what had come over him, but I knew I wasn't going to stick around long enough to find out. After all we'd been through together, it was over.

"Don't worry. Keith will be here soon," Alex said.

I could feel my temper rising. "No, he won't."

"What do you mean, he won't?"

"He won't be coming," I snapped.

Alex squinted her eyes and shook her head as if she didn't understand. "But this is your big day, yours and his."

"Keith's big day is in a bottle somewhere," I sneered.

"What are you talking about?"

"Keith has a real alcohol problem."

Alex opened her mouth wide. "Really?"

"Yes." I sighed. "I confronted him about it and asked him about getting help last night."

"So did he say he would go for help?"

I shook my head. "No, but I begged him to."

"Well, what happened then?"

"He told me no. He thinks he deserves to die because he let his brother down." I rolled away, turning my back to her.

"That's crazy," Alex said.

"He doesn't think so. He has given up."

"Okay, how do you know he has given up?"

"How do I know? I know because I begged him not to leave, but he told me he had to."

"Okay. I get it."

Holding back tears, I turned around to face Alex again. "Then I made him promise me not to drink again last night. I told him I needed him to come back home and help me with the final touches on everything."

"And?"

"And do you see him by my side?"

"No," Alex said.

"That's because he made his choice last night. He chose the bottle over me." I bit my lip.

"No," Alex repeated.

"Yes. He never came back last night, Alex," I said. "And it's over."

I busied myself with the weigh-ins and the measuring of waists.

Jasmine logged in the information. "Wow, it's cool how much weight people can lose if they really put their minds to it."

"I guess competition was the edge they needed," I said.

"That two-thousand-dollar reward didn't hurt, either." Jasmine slapped me a high five.

The local media had arrived and had set up in the main area.

Push It was packed with people getting weighed in and measured, participating in workshops. A line had formed in front of the two physical therapists from Keith's clinic, who were set up in a corner of the multipurpose room. A few doctors who had volunteered were checking blood pressure and sugar levels. A nutritionist friend of Keith's was giving a healthy living workshop at her table. Even a local chiropractor had volunteered his time and was busy snapping people's backs and shoulders into place.

Sharon was dressed in red and white spandex shorts with a matching tank top and was teaching a heavy-hitting aerobics class. Jacque was selling health products, such as natural vitamins and nutrition shakes at the counter. Jasmine was simply my assistant, filling in wherever she was needed. Alex stood by my side, just being my sister, advising and comforting. Joshua was giving out gospel tracts in front of the building. Other volunteers began to pour in. Everything and everyone was in place except for Keith.

"Looks like your event is a success," Jasmine said as she passed by carrying a handful of all-natural fruit smoothies.

I gave her a thumbs-up signal. "Yes!"

I snuck away from the crowd to go to my office. I rolled in, but before I could close the door behind me, I heard a voice.

"Mrs. Taylor Carter-Bryant," Elaina sneered.

I recognized her voice instantly.

"You didn't expect to see me, did you?" She came forward and backed me up into a corner.

"No, I didn't," I said, attempting to think fast.

She looked horrible. Her lips were dry, her mascara was smeared, and the tracks of her sewn-in weave were showing. She wore designer jeans with a silk blouse, but she had huge sweat stains underneath the arms. She was certainly not the poised and polished Elaina I had been accustomed to dealing with for the past few months. I could see that she was hiding something shiny behind her back.

She moved closer, and I gasped. I could feel my heart pounding rapidly in my chest as I looked around for a weapon. Before the accident, my whole body was a weapon. I thought of my old moves, but what good would they do when I was stuck in a wheelchair?

"What do you want, Elaina?"

Slowly, Elaina pulled out a shiny butcher's knife from behind her back. "I'm going to carve your legs up good so you'll definitely never be able to walk again, not even with braces."

I stuttered, "E-Elaina, I—"

"Or dance again, like you danced with my husband that night. You'll never be able to lure a man with those pretty legs again. Then your own husband will leave you, and you'll see how it feels to be alone," Elaina continued, moving toward me.

Suddenly that awful night flashed in my mind. "I already know what it feels like to be alone. The mess I used to do was because I felt lonely on the inside, because I felt I had something to prove to the world, but I'm not like that anymore."

Elaina clenched her teeth. "Yeah, right."

"Please, I'm a different person now," I begged.

"I don't care what you say," Elaina snarled. "You're lying."

I tried to lift myself up out of my chair, to summon courage from within. "No, I'm not."

I remembered Psalm 23. *Yea, though I walk through the valley of the shadow of death* . . . "Please don't do something you'll regret," I said, trying to reason with her.

I remembered Psalm 91. *I will say of the Lord, He is my refuge and my fortress: my God; in him will I trust. . . .*

"Oh, I'm not going to regret this. Just keep on begging," Elaina said, laughing.

And the next thing I knew, Elaina was lunging toward me with the knife, and I grabbed her arms with mine. We struggled for a moment, with the knife pointed uncomfortably close to my throat. I thought I was about to die. Finally, I overpowered her and knocked the knife out of her hand. She grabbed me by my legs and pulled me out of my wheelchair onto the floor. I ripped her silk blouse to shreds as I tumbled downward. We rolled around on the floor, scratching and tearing at each other. She spat at me but missed, and the saliva landed on the floor. I held her arms with all my strength until she broke free from my grip. She grabbed a lock of my hair and pulled it. I yelled, but I doubted anyone could hear me above the music and noise from the event. I loosened her grip on my hair and rolled away from her. She reached for the knife again and crawled toward me. I secretly begged the Lord to let me use my legs. *No, this battle is not yours. Call my name.*

"Jesus, Jesus, the blood of Jesus! The battle is yours, Lord." Tears poured from my eyes.

Finally, I heard noises behind me, and I noticed that Elaina's attention was diverted. My heart beat fast. I wondered if it was Shayla or Paul.

That was when I saw a muscular arm grab the knife away from Elaina. "You're not gonna cut anyone today."

It was my husband. Elaina struggled to get up as Keith restrained her with his massive body.

I was startled. "Keith?"

Keith smiled his best smile. "Who did you expect?"

I was in a daze. "You're here?"

Keith bowed his head. "Did you think I'd miss one of the most important days of our life together?"

A policeman came in right behind Keith, grabbed Elaina, and seized the knife. "You have the right to remain silent," the policeman said as he handcuffed Elaina.

Keith knelt down beside me. "Are you all right?"

"I'm fine." I looked at Keith. "How did you know?"

"I went to confront Paul about all your accusations. I should've listened to you before. Paul broke down and told me everything."

I couldn't believe that Paul had confessed. "Everything?"

"He told me that Elaina was planning to show up here today. I knew I had to call the police, even though I wasn't sure what she was planning to do."

"Paul warned you?"

"He's not the best man, but I guess he's not the worst, either. He admitted to doing it all for the money," Keith said.

"What exactly did he admit to?"

"Just to messing up the pool. He said Elaina paid him three thousand dollars just to do that, and then she promised him more if she needed more help."

"So that day I saw them together . . . ?"

"He says all they had was a money deal, nothing more."

"And Shayla McConnell?"

"He said he never met her." Keith shrugged his shoulders. "He said he thought that Elaina had her own money."

I was still shaken up. "How did you get him to come clean?"

"It was easy once I had him up by the collar," Keith said, flexing his muscles. "I'm sorry it took so long for me to come to my senses."

"Of course," I said, chuckling.

Keith held my hand. "I should've believed you, trusted your instincts."

"You thought I was paranoid."

"I thought you were letting your past street experiences get the best of you. I thought Paul was my friend." Keith sighed. "I'm sorry. I was wrong."

I pictured my strong husband holding up awkward little Paul and giggled again.

The next thing I knew, we were being questioned by the police. Then Elaina was taken away in the squad car. I told the police officers about possibly being followed on the road back from Maine. I told them about the mysterious car appearances, about the mysterious phone calls, and about the threats. Then I told them that I believed Shayla McConnell was behind all of this, that she was providing the funding for Elaina. The police took my statement and promised to look into my theory.

By the time I was done with them, my head was spinning. "How did the police get here so fast?"

"I called the police right away and told them someone was trespassing on private business property during a public event. I told them that a lot of lives were in danger. I tried to call you, but for some reason I kept getting your voice mail."

"Oh, right." I gasped. "My phone was turned off. And the lines here must've been tied up with all the calls we've been getting."

"I just knew I had to get here in time," Keith said.

My heart beat faster. "But I thought you were . . ."

Keith bowed his head. "Drunk?"

"Yes," I said.

"Not anymore," Keith said. "Not ever again."

"What do you mean, not ever again? But when you left . . . ?"

"I promised I wouldn't drink—"

I interrupted, "But you never came home. . . ."

"But I said I wouldn't drink. I didn't say I wasn't tempted," Keith continued.

I looked into his eyes. "I don't understand."

"Instead of going to the bar—and believe me, I wanted to—I went to see Pastor Martin."

"Pastor Martin?"

"Yes, I went to see him. He spent the whole night talking to me, praying with me."

I hit Keith in the arm. "Why didn't you call?"

"Oh, that was my fault," Keith said. "I should've called, but I was so messed up in my head that I thought our marriage was over. I guess I thought my life was over too. I'm sorry."

"I don't believe this." I turned away from him.

Keith came around to face me. "I wasn't ready to tell you the truth or face the truth myself."

"Tell me what truth, Keith? What haven't you told me?"

Keith let out a big breath of air. "That I'm an alcoholic, just like my dad."

"Okay, that makes sense. By the way you've been drinking and acting the past few weeks, I would've guessed you were a borderline alcoholic."

"Not the past few weeks, for years. I've been drinking heavily since high school. Not borderline. Just full-scale alcoholic."

"What are you saying?"

"I did a twelve-step program right out of college, right before I started grad school. And even though I failed, I'm going back into rehab."

"What's going to be different this time?"

"The last time I did it my way. I never tried it God's way." Keith took my hand. "Look, I know you're angry, but Pastor Martin said—"

"Pastor Martin didn't have to live with you these past few months," I whined.

"You're right, and I deserve that."

"Humph," I said.

"This time it's going to be different for me. This time I'm going to do it His way, I promise."

I glanced behind me at the crowd gathering by my office, with Alex and Joshua in the forefront. "I don't know. What about Paul?"

"Well, he asked me for a one-way ticket back to Chicago," Keith answered.

"You gave him a ticket?"

"No, I didn't, but it would've been well worth it to get rid of him." Keith sighed. "Nah, I figured the police have some business with him, anyway, so I couldn't. All he ever wanted was money, anyway."

"So he was blackmailing you?"

"Not in the usual way. It was kind of emotional blackmail. Always reminding me of my past and how weak I was, always reminding me of how he saved my life so many times before when I was drunk. Always drinking around me and inviting me out to places where they were serving drinks."

"Some kind of friend he was," I said.

Keith dropped his head. "He's no friend at all. I just couldn't see it 'til now. I guess I was so grateful for the good things he'd done in the past. Enemies come in all forms, huh?"

"I'll say. Mama always said, 'Don't trust no charming man.'"

"I guess your mama was right," Keith said.

"I guess she was." I chuckled. "As a matter of fact, I'm learning that Mama was right about almost everything."

"Yeah." Keith smiled and stood up.

"So what are you going to do?"

"I'm taking a leave of absence from the clinic so I can do this twelve-week program recommended by Pastor Martin."

I nodded my head.

"It's in North Carolina," Keith said.

"Now, that's my kind of investment," I said.

Keith smiled. "Mine too."

"I'm sorry," I said.

"Me too," Keith said. "Thanks for saving me."

"Jesus saved you." I kissed my husband as tears ran down my face. "I'm just here for the ride."

Keith grinned. "True, and what a ride it is."

"I've learned that enemies may come to steal, to kill, and to destroy, but God is so good, He won't leave us in their hands if we let joy arise. Mama was right." I lifted my hands in praise. "Then my head will be exalted above the enemies who surround me; at his tabernacle will I sacrifice with shouts of joy."

"I love my brother, and I'm still concerned for him, but I can't give up on God's promises for me because of him."

A reporter walked by and snapped a picture of us.

"Well, it looks like we'll be in the news again," I said.

Keith motioned for Alex and Joshua to come over. "Except this time we're not in trouble. We actually caught the bad guys."

Alex came over. "What a day already. Are you okay?"

Joshua approached and put up his hand for a high five. "Yes, and isn't God good?"

"All the time," Keith said, slapping Joshua five.

"As it turns out, Elaina has been perpetrating a fraud and had Paul as the eyes and ears to her whole operation," I smirked.

"It figures," Alex said as she fell into my arms.

When we got home that evening, Keith started packing for his trip to North Carolina, his journey to wholeness. As I watched him, I couldn't help but to reflect on the events of the past four months and how they'd affected me. I realized my issue was about more than the Elaina-Paul-Shayla thing. My issue was about more than just physical enemies. It was about spiritual ones as well. Not only had I wrestled with people, but I'd also wrestled with myself. I'd wrestled with my own inadequacies.

I looked at my wheelchair and knew it was time to make some decisions. I knew it was time to repent. *Lord, forgive me.* I'd struggled with trying to overcome my shortcomings long enough. It was time for real, deliberate change. I had to stop looking at my disability as the enemy. Truth be told, it was my mind-set that had been destroying me. *I can do all things through Christ, who strengthens me.*

For a long time, I had fought my disability, believing it would sure enough be the death of me. But I had found out that my issue with my legs was no different than any other issue and that I could overcome it through Christ. I had to stop fighting the injury, like I had to stop fighting my enemies. "Vengeance is mine . . . saith the Lord," and God meant what He said.

Epilogue

The Push It Health Fest and Fitness Challenge was a success. Push It took on a new identity as a leader in the fitness community, greater than it had ever been. In the process, I kind of became an unofficial spokesperson for the disabled, at least at church and in our neighborhood. By the grace of God, we'd accomplished everything we'd set out to accomplish.

Keith went through his new Christian-based alcohol recovery program, with a three-month stint in North Carolina, and came out renewed in his body and in his faith.

In the next few months, I worked out like a madwoman, regained considerable strength in my legs, and gave away my wheelchair. I donated it to someone who really needed it. I began to walk without my braces every now and then, although my gait was slow and steady with an intermittent limp.

As for the Elaina incident, I ended up testifying in three different trials over the next two years. Eventually, Elaina was charged with two counts of stalking, one count of conspiracy, and one count of aggravated assault, and was sentenced to four years in jail, with the possibility of parole. Both Paul and Shayla were charged with conspiracy and given probation.

Although Robert was seen again in Chicago, Keith never found him. We continued to pray for him, believing in his deliverance from substance abuse, and in his salvation.

As for our marriage, Keith and I became closer than ever as a couple now that there were no secrets between us, with Keith putting in more hours at Push It on a regular basis. We even added physical therapy to Push It's list of services, by appointment only, of course. God had rescued "our baby," and we were forever grateful.

Finally, and most importantly, I realized that the joy of the Lord was my strength and that that kind of joy was enough. When it came right down to it, I had to have violent faith, yet *I* didn't have to be violent. *Anyone who has suffered any injustice or injury to the body, to the spirit, or to the soul, who has lost hope, find yourself in the peace that only Jesus can bring,* I thought. *And when trouble arises, make this your mantra, "Let joy arise."*

Questions for Discussion

1. Why didn't Taylor like Paul? Do you think she should have tried harder to get along with him?
2. Do you think Taylor and Keith had a good relationship? Why or why not?
3. Why do you think Taylor was so convinced that Paul deliberately contaminated the pool?
4. Why do you think Keith never told Taylor about his family issues and/or his drinking issue?
5. What do you think Elaina's intentions were from the very beginning? Do you think her feelings became more intense?
6. Why do you think Paul betrayed his good friend for money?
7. Do you think Alex helped Taylor during her time of crisis? If so, how?
8. Why do you think Taylor kept clinging to her wheelchair when she clearly didn't have to?

9. Why do you think Taylor didn't confront Elaina at their first meeting?

10. Do you think it was a good idea for Keith to go away to the Christian-based rehabilitation center?

11. Why do you think Taylor didn't just go to the police right away?

12. Why did Taylor decide not to report Elaina at her job?

13. Why do you think Shayla McConnell linked up with Elaina to conspire against Taylor?

Bio

Ashea Goldson, originally from Brooklyn, New York, and now residing in a metro Atlanta suburb, is a graduate of Fordham University and calls herself a kingdom writer. She is a down-to-earth author, poet, educator, and entrepreneur who loves her family, her friends, and the ministry. She spends her days passing on her love of reading and language to her students at the preparatory school she co-owns and operates. She transforms herself into writer extraordinaire by evening, when she is able to fully indulge her creative passions. Her first novel is *The Lovechild,* published by Kensington. Her next three novels are *Joy Comes in the Morning,* *Count It All Joy,* and *Let Joy Arise,* which are all books in the joy series. She is currently working on her fifth Christian fiction novel, along with a nonfiction book about pursuing your purpose, which is dear to her heart. She is also at work on a number of other independent writing projects, including a screenplay. In addition to this, she hosts a BlogTalkRadio show called *WordThirst Literary Journal & Authors Showcase,* which highlights the work of like-minded authors and visionaries.

Feel free to contact her at:

 asheagold@yahoo.com

or

Log on to:

www.asheagoldson.com

UC HIS GLORY BOOK CLUB!

www.uchisglorybookclub.net

UC His Glory Book Club is the spirit-inspired brainchild of Joylynn Jossel, Author and Acquisitions Editor of Urban Christian, and Kendra Norman-Bellamy, Author for Urban Christian. This is an online book club that hosts authors of Urban Christian. We welcome as members all men and women who have a passion for reading Christian-based fiction.

UC His Glory Book Club pledges our commitment to provide support, positive feedback, encouragement, and a forum whereby members can openly discuss and review the literary works of Urban Christian authors.

There is no membership fee associated with UC His Glory Book Club; however, we do ask that you support the authors through purchasing, encouraging, providing book reviews, and of course, your prayers. We also ask that you respect our beliefs and follow the guidelines of the book club. We hope to receive your valuable input, opinions, and reviews that build up, rather than tear down our authors.

What We Believe:

—We believe that Jesus is the Christ, Son of the Living God.

—We believe the Bible is the true, living Word of God.

—We believe all Urban Christian authors should use their God-given writing abilities to honor God and share the message of the written word God has given to each of them uniquely.

—We believe in supporting Urban Christian authors in their literary endeavors by reading, purchasing and sharing their titles with our online community.

—We believe that in everything we do in our literary arena should be done in a manner that will lead to God being glorified and honored.

—We look forward to the online fellowship with you.

Please visit us often at:
www.uchisglorybookclub.net.
Many Blessing to You!
Shelia E. Lipsey,
President, UC His Glory Book Club